The Singapore School of Villainy: Inspector Singh Investigates

The Singapore School of Villainy: Inspector Singh Investigates

Shamini Flint

Minotaur Books
A THOMAS DUNNE BOOK
New York

This is a work of fiction. All of the characters, organizations, and events portrayed in this novel are either products of the author's imagination or are used fictitiously.

A THOMAS DUNNE BOOK FOR MINOTAUR BOOKS.
An imprint of St. Martin's Publishing Group.

THE SINGAPORE SCHOOL OF VILLAINY: INSPECTOR SINGH INVESTIGATES.
Copyright © 2010 by Shamini Flint. All rights reserved. Printed in the United States of America. For information, address St. Martin's Press, 175 Fifth Avenue, New York, N.Y. 10010.

www.thomasdunnebooks.com
www.minotaurbooks.com

ISBN 978-0-312-59699-6 (hardcover)
ISBN 978-1-250-01479-5 (e-book)

First published in Great Britain as a paperback original by Piatkus, an imprint of Little, Brown Book Group, an Hachette UK Company

First U.S. Edition: July 2012

10 9 8 7 6 5 4 3 2 1

For my mother

Acknowledgements

For their ongoing support: Usha Cheryan, Dominique and John Richards, Matthew and Penny Burgess, Richard and Carol Barker and Sue and Roger Barbour.

'Whoever commits murder shall be punished with death.'
Section 302, Singapore Penal Code, Chapter 224

'No man is an island, entire of itself ...
any man's death diminishes me,
because I am involved in mankind;
and therefore never send to know
for whom the bell tolls; it tolls for thee.'

John Donne

The Singapore School of Villainy: Inspector Singh Investigates

One

Inspector Singh sipped his coffee. It was instant, sweet and milky, just the way he liked it. Singh was not one for those fancy coffee machines that steamed milk, ground beans and sounded like mini-construction sites. He preferred a kettle and a teaspoon. Not that he made his own coffee in the morning. That was a task for Mrs Singh. She always had his breakfast, usually chappatis with *dahl*, a spicy lentil curry for which he had a strong partiality, and the accompanying hot drink, on the dining table by the time he had successfully completed his morning routine. This began with an aggressive teeth cleaning with a fraying toothbrush, was punctuated by the swapping of singlet and checked, faded sarong for a long-sleeved white shirt and dark pants and culminated in tying a turban around his large head. This last was not a task that could be done casually or without the full use of a mirror for fear of the point being off-centre, the turban lacking balance and symmetry or the whole thing looking like an enormous beehive.

Singh lumbered to the dining table and sat down

1

expectantly. His wife carried a fresh tray of food in from the kitchen. Mrs Singh's air of domestic subservience masked the iron will of the woman he had married by walking five times around the Sikh holy book in the *gurdwara* on Wilkie Road. He had seen her for the first time on their wedding day. As she was brought to him, doe-eyed and downcast, his uppermost feeling had been one of relief that she was not burdened with a wooden leg or squint. After all these years, he sometimes felt that his gratitude was limited to the same things – that and her cooking, of course. The smell of warm *ghee*, as the chappatis were flipped on the skillet, was making his salivary glands ooze.

He turned his attention to breakfast. Singh ate with his fingers – tearing off pieces of chappati, dipping them in the bowl of *dahl* and shovelling them into his mouth. He scanned the newspapers, seeking any snippets of news amongst the advertisements for slimming products and cheap flights and grunted when his wife addressed any remarks to him.

'I was right,' she said.

The continuation of a conversation that had been going on for several days was a key feature of their marriage. Mrs Singh would relate one of several overlapping tales, involving the scandalous doings of one of their relations, and continue it over a series of encounters with him – at breakfast, as he dressed for work and when he came home in the evenings. The inspector typically listened with half an ear, confused all the separate strands and responded only if he felt the vitriol was too unpleasant to pass without some mild reproof.

She said again, more smugly this time, 'I was right.' And then continued darkly, 'I told you what would happen.'

Another element of these stories was the regular vindication of her views by unfolding events. Inspector Singh nodded a general agreement. He did not know nor care what she was talking about but prudence dictated that he agree with her *diktat*. He chewed on his food with small tobacco-stained teeth – pleased that the food was sufficiently spicy to tickle taste buds that had lost their sensitivity after years of chain-smoking.

'They let him go to America. To New York,' she added doubtfully, unsure whether her information as to location was accurate. 'None of *our* people are there. Now he has married an American girl.' She continued, triumphant at the climax of her story, 'He didn't even need a green card. He had one *already*!'

Singh mumbled an acknowledgement.

He pulled himself to his feet, using the edge of the dining table for support. He wished that Mrs Singh did not find it necessary to cover the lace table cloth with a clear plastic sheet. No doubt it kept the cloth clean. He was a messy eater and there was always a splattering of curry on the table when he was done. But the sheet was sticky and he found the gummy sensation when he removed his elbows disproportionately unpleasant. It reminded him of the clammy hands of the dead.

Singh washed his fingers, took his mug to the easy rattan chair and collapsed into it. A gaggle of *mynah* birds with glowing orange beaks screeched and quarrelled in the garden, fighting over some hapless worm. They reminded him of his sisters-in-law. He sniffed the air. A whiff of a ripening *cempedak* from a tree in their well-tended garden tickled his nostrils. He hoped his wife would deep fry the pulpy yellow fruit in batter for his tea. The policeman leaned over, gasping for air like a fish on land as his belly and lungs compressed, and pulled on his socks and shoes. The shoes were spotless white sneakers, the laces of which he tied in a careful double knot. It was one of the many things that annoyed his superiors about Singh – his refusal to wear a sensible pair of black shoes to work every day. He remembered the last time Superintendent Chen had suggested his footwear was not in keeping with the dignity of the force.

'They're comfortable,' he had explained. 'And it means I can chase down the bad guys.'

His boss had looked down at the short fat man, puffing slightly from the physical effort of standing upright and speaking at the same time, turned smartly on the heels of his own Italian black leather pumps and marched away.

Mrs Singh spoke again. Her voice was high and sharp. Singh thought she sounded like the vocal embodiment of a murder weapon. 'I hope you haven't forgotten that Jagdesh is coming for dinner tonight.'

Inspector Singh had not only forgotten that Jagdesh was coming for dinner but also who Jagdesh was. He said, buying time, 'Of course not!'

His wife was not fooled. Her arms were folded in a bright pink *batik* caftan so that only scrawny, dry-skinned elbows were visible. 'You don't remember, *isn't it?*'

Singh was the sort of policeman who always urged suspects to take the easy way out and confess to their crimes. He realised now, facing aggressive questioning from his wife, that it was terribly bad advice. 'I'm looking forward to seeing Jagdesh again,' he said unconvincingly, feeling in a pocket for his cigarette packet.

'You haven't met him before.'

He should stay at home and cook and clean and send his wife to work, concluded the inspector. She was far too good at cross-examining witnesses. He sipped his coffee and made a face. He had left it too long and it was lukewarm.

'OK,' he confessed. 'Who is Jagdesh and why is he coming for dinner?'

'My cousin's nephew from India – I told you about him!'

Singh had given up subterfuge. He glared at his wife and shrugged fleshy shoulders to indicate his complete failure to recall the conversation.

'They're worried about him.'

'Who are?'

'His parents – he's already thirty-something and not yet married, can you believe it? They think he might find a *Chinese* girl in Singapore.'

'Are we to prevent him doing so?' asked Singh mildly. 'Perhaps we should lock him in the spare room when he arrives.'

For a moment, he was concerned that his wife had taken him seriously. Her expression was thoughtful. Her thick black eyebrows formed a straight line. He realised that she had, as was her habit, disregarded his sarcastic soundtrack to her thought processes. She was still wrestling with the knotty problem of an unmarried thirty-year-old.

'What's he doing in Singapore anyway?' asked Singh, feeling even more irritable.

'He has a job at a big law firm – he's very successful, very rich. And still no wife!'

'Lucky bastard,' muttered Singh under his breath.

This time he was not fortunate enough to be ignored. 'You're always so unhelpful. The boy is coming for dinner. I'm going to introduce him to all the nice Sikh girls in Singapore.'

'Are they coming for dinner too?'

Her eyes were like car high-beams. 'I'm sure that would make you very happy!'

Singh thought this was an unfair accusation. He was not the best of husbands by any stretch of the imagination. But, as a general rule, he did refrain from making a fool of himself

5

over pretty young things. In his line of work, he had seen too many corpses that were the products of relationships gone awry. He didn't want any of his wretched colleagues investigating his death at the hands of some angry boyfriend or husband. Singh reached for the cigarette perched on an ashtray and dragged himself to his feet. He would need a portable crane soon if he didn't lose some weight. The policeman caught a glimpse of his round belly in the tinted glass sliding front door. He had to admit that his loyalty to his wife was probably not entirely a matter of choice. Inspector Singh sucked in a deep lungful of tobacco-laden smoke and headed for the front door.

'Always you're smoking – I don't know where to hide my face!'

His wife and his doctor were of one mind when it came to his cigarette habit, thought Singh ruefully. But their motivations were completely different. He gave his doctor credit – he nagged like an old woman but he probably had Singh's best interests at heart. His wife on the other hand was just embarrassed that he was breaching one of the fundamental tenets of Sikhism – that tobacco was off limits.

His wife said warningly, 'Make sure you come home for dinner.'

Later that evening, a plane descended to a thousand metres above sea level. It flew in low over a sea that was as smooth as a plate of glass. Beautifully detailed miniature ships were dotted on its surface. The coastline was littered with high-rise office towers and homogeneous apartment blocks. Annie Nathan had her eyes fixed on the *Asian Wall Street Journal*.

There was the sudden clatter of the undercarriage descending. A few minutes later the plane touched down at

Changi Airport. Annie disembarked and hurried towards the arrival hall, ignoring the headache-inducing blend of fluorescent lights, patterned carpets and busy shop windows. She paid no attention to the mass of humanity corralled into waiting areas, watching television screens with slack mouths. She flashed her green card at the indifferent immigration officer, a middle-aged Malay woman with tired eyes, and walked to the limousine taxi rank, bypassing baggage reclaim. Climbing into a black Chrysler with ostentatious front grilles, Annie sighed with relief. She was pleased to be back in Singapore – it had been a long working day in Kuala Lumpur.

The taxi swung out onto the Pan Island Expressway and then the East Coast Parkway – a six-lane elevated highway running parallel to the coast. The concrete super-structure was draped in moss-green creepers. Turquoise waters dotted with ships – tankers, cruise ships, yachts – spread out to the left. A couple of grey warships, gun turrets and antennae protruding, looked like silver pincushions. A thin strip of muddy brown, a sliver of the Indonesian archipelago, formed part of the horizon. In the middle distance, the city of Singapore gleamed and twinkled as the setting sun reflected off the glassy skyscrapers. She could see the rows and rows of cranes at Singapore's massive port facilities, looking like long-necked metal birds peering anxiously out to sea. The same cranes and the enormous ferris wheel, the Singapore Flyer, were visible from her office windows on the sixty-eighth floor of Republic Tower.

Singapore's cityscape never failed to awaken Annie's most ambitious spirit. She enjoyed the brief sensation that she, a junior partner at the international law firm of Hutchinson & Rice, was a small but necessary cog in a massive capitalist wheel. She suppressed a quick smirk. Such thoughts were singularly out of fashion in an era of bank bailouts and erratic stock markets. Greed was no longer good but – truth be silently confessed in the back seat of a luxury limousine – it hadn't done her any harm.

Across town, Mark Thompson, senior partner at the firm of Hutchinson & Rice, sat in silence and in semi-darkness. Only his desktop monitor cast a pale blue light, throwing his angular face into sharp relief and darkening his hazel eyes. His curly mass of prematurely white hair receded from a high forehead and curled around his ears. A shaggy moustache, still a youthful brown, encroached on his upper lip like an untrimmed hedge. Australian by birth and Singaporean by residence, he looked like the popular image of a successful attorney in the American South. He would have appeared natural in cream linen and a bow tie, holding forth under whirring ceiling fans to a sweaty, overweight jury of his inferiors. Instead, he wore a dark suit and a heavily embroidered cream silk necktie. His hand reached for the telephone and hesitated. He pulled open the bottom drawer of his desk and took out a silver hip flask. A long swig settled his nerves. Mark Thompson squared his shoulders, bracing himself for the ordeal ahead. He picked up the telephone.

Two

Annie walked up her driveway through a green tunnel, the branches of the trees entwined overhead. The white walls of her single-storey bungalow glowed pink, reflecting the dying embers of the sun. A single oriole, its yellow plumage looking like a sliver of sunlight, followed a crazy elliptical flight path across her garden. There was a warm moist smell in the air, the scent of freshly cut grass, mingled with frangipani blossoms and impending rain. Her gardener from India had been dismayed to find that she had a frangipani tree, covered in glossy ivory five-petalled flowers, in the garden. 'A ver-ry bad tree, *tangachee*. Only for graveyards.' Annie had no patience with what she considered superstitious nonsense. She was more impressed that the gardener had spotted her South Indian paternal roots and addressed her as "little sister" in Tamil.

She kicked off her shoes and headed barefoot for the kitchen, sauntering through the living and dining rooms that were crowded with seasoned wood furniture. She could smell the musky, spicy odour of old teak – an aroma as invigorating as fresh coffee. The kitchen was bright, modern and filled with the latest gadgetry. Annie was unable to cook and unwilling to clean, but her kitchen was a shrine to the latest in expensive kitchen technology. She mixed herself a stiff gin and tonic, took the drink out to the veranda and collapsed into the solitary cushioned easy chair.

The strident note of a telephone penetrated her doze. She fished her mobile out of her bag, flipped it open reluctantly and held it to an unadorned ear.

'Hello.'

A gruff voice said, 'Annie, is that you?'

Her reply, 'Yes, Pa,' was drowned out by a paroxysm of coughing. Her father had been a three-packet-a-day man for forty years and there were moments when he was too hoarse to speak. But he would still light up.

'Pa, can you hear me? How are you?'

'Good, good. How about you?'

'Fine – tough day at work.'

'You work too hard. When are they going to make you a partner?'

'They did. Six months ago. I called and told you.'

'Well done!'

She waited for the inevitable.

'Annie, I need a small favour.'

'I'm *not* giving you any more money.'

'I just need a few thousand. You know I hate to ask!'

'Hate to ask? Since when?'

'I'll pay you back. This is my big chance.' Her father sounded husky with nervous expectation. He continued, his voice hesitant, 'Or we could use some of the other money?'

Annie was adamant. 'Absolutely not!'

She couldn't believe he had even suggested such a thing. Her grip on the phone was so tight that her palm was moist with sweat. How could her father do it? Come to her time and again for money. Always convinced it was for the last time. His eternal optimism was too hard for her to fathom. She sighed. She was tired. Her back ached. She gave in.

'How much do you need?'

'Fourteen thousand ...'

'I'll send it tomorrow.'

'Thank you. I'll pay you back this time, I promise.'

Annie snapped the phone shut. Her father did not call back. She had not expected him to – he had what he wanted. She settled back in the easy chair, trying to rediscover the state of blissful peace that had been so rudely interrupted. It was impossible. Memories of her father washed over her; him wagering the family income on his latest big idea; her mother begging him to stop – to think of his daughter; the bailiffs at the door to repossess their furniture, the car – they had even taken her mother's wedding ring once. She, Annie, had learnt to value money – to earn it and hoard it – but her father was still a gambler, thirty years on. She tried to calm down, to remember that she was a successful woman who had fought for and won her financial independence, but it was difficult. Every time she had a conversation with her father, her childhood insecurities resurfaced and she felt again like a small child cowering from the bailiffs behind her mother's long skirts.

Her mobile rang again and she groaned at the phone number flashing on the screen. It was the office. She remembered her conviction in the taxi that this high-flying corporate lifestyle suited her down to the ground – she was not so sure any more. She earned money only to hand it to her father like sweets to a spoilt child. And now someone was looking for her late on a Friday evening. She was really not in the mood for some imaginary crisis from a client who thought her charge-out rates meant that she was part-lawyer and part-nanny. Annie picked up the phone.

'Yes?' she said curtly.

'Annie, is that you?'

This time her groan was heartfelt but silent.

'Yes, it is.' She injected a measure of politeness into her voice. Mark Thompson was her boss, after all.

'Are you back in Singapore?' he asked.

'Just got in,' she replied, and then mentally kicked herself for wasting a gilt-edged opportunity to pretend she was out of town.

'Come into the office for a meeting at half past eight,' Mark continued, unconscious of her reluctance or ignoring it.

'What's it about, Mark?'

There was no answer. He had hung up.

Annie stared at her phone. Mark, for all his faults, was unfailingly polite. Something must have annoyed or upset him considerably. She really hoped it had nothing to do with her. She wondered whether to call him back – her hand hovered uncertainly over the dial.

Inspector Singh glanced covertly at his watch, the leather strap of which was embedded uncomfortably into his plump wrist. It did not keep time particularly well but it was sufficiently accurate for him to be quite certain that he was toast as far as his wife was concerned. It was late evening already. She had been adamant that he be on time to play Cupid to this unfortunate young man that she had invited for dinner at the behest of his interfering relations.

'Are you listening to me?'

Singh glanced up, straightened his back – realised that this was a mistake as it only drew attention to his beer gut –

and slumped back down. He said, 'Of course, sir,' hoping he hadn't missed anything important. It was unlikely. This was his monthly "you're a disgrace to the Force" lecture – it was just unlucky that his superintendent had found a spare moment when he, Singh, had a dinner engagement.

'You're a disgrace to the Force,' shouted his superior. His face, ordinarily the smooth calm mask of a career politician, was mottled with anger.

'Yessir!' said Singh, who knew the routine.

The fact of the matter was that they couldn't get rid of him because of his success rate. Even in Singapore, where there was limited accountability for those at the high end of the food chain, there would be questions asked. The press, cowed as they were, liked him. He was splash of colour that was visible even in newsprint. He would have to screw up big time to give the Force an excuse to sack him. Being over-weight, wearing white sneakers, smelling faintly of curry, beer and old-fashioned cologne – Old Spice in the bottle with the sailing ship – just wasn't enough.

He said again, 'Yessir,' in case he had merely imagined the response rather than uttered it. He was finding that, as he grew older, the thought was not so much the father of the deed as in lieu of it.

'Look at you!'

Singh refrained from pointing out that this was not possible without a mirror. Besides, the parts that offended his superiors – the excess weight, the white sneakers and the outline of a packet of cigarettes in his pocket – *were* visible to him.

'I'd put you back in uniform – but we couldn't find one to fit you!'

Singh bit off a smile. This was a new line and actually quite a good one. The old man had probably thought of it in

13

the shower. That would explain why he had been called in this particular evening. He knew Superintendent Chen all too well. His boss wouldn't want to waste such a pithy insult.

Music played quietly in the background, the soundtrack from Shah Rukh Khan's latest movie. A platter of vegetable samosas, smelling faintly of cardamom and cloves, sat on the front table. Mrs Singh intended them as a starter to whet the young man's appetite. She wandered into the kitchen and sniffed at the dishes she had painstakingly cooked for dinner that evening. She was quite sure that Jagdesh Singh, a young man far from his home in Delhi, would be missing his mother's cooking. A feast of curries and chutneys was hidden under food covers, ready to be served when Jagdesh arrived. She was convinced that the way to a man's heart was through his stomach. If she reminded him of the importance of good authentic home cooking, he was bound to see the value of a pretty Sikh girl. Certainly, he was that much less likely to hook up with some slip of a Chinese thing who would stuff him with greasy fried noodles every evening from the nearest hawker stall.

It was eight in the evening and her husband had not put in an appearance yet. At this rate, he would arrive *after* her guest – the height of bad manners. She would not put it past him to be intentionally tardy just because she had specifically asked him to turn up on time. He had a peculiar sense of humour and a complete disdain for the family and community obligations she took so seriously.

Besides, he seemed to think that the entire police force would collapse without his efforts – or at the very least that half a dozen murderers would elude justice for every hour he was not at work. She shuddered. When she had married Singh, he had been a junior policeman with a bright future.

He had been smart, fit and ambitious. She had imagined him as the commissioner of police, attending functions at the *Istana*, the palace residence of the President – wife by his side, of course. Instead, Singh had been assigned to his first murder case and never looked back. He had abandoned his bright future to devote his life to the business of hunting down killers. It was all so sordid. People didn't get killed without good reason. She, Mrs Singh, didn't condone murder, of course. But there was no doubt in her mind that the victims were at least partly to blame. One just didn't see that sort of excessive behaviour in good families. As far as she was aware, there had never been a murder in the Sikh community in Singapore – unless you counted that time when Balwant Singh reversed over his wife in their driveway. But he had been eighty and as blind as a bat. She had to assume that he hadn't meant to do it.

She gripped the table edge with work-roughened knuckles. She could not understand her husband's fascination for death. It was very peculiar, and quite unhealthy. It meant that he fraternised with some very odd people and his chances of progress within the force had been hamstrung. Murder was not a path to promotion, that much had been evident as her husband slowly crawled his way to the rank of inspector.

She thought of this young unmarried man, Jagdesh Singh, who was coming for dinner: young, handsome – if his probably prejudiced mother was to be believed – with a lucrative career. She devoutly hoped that he would not disappoint the Sikh wife she would eventually find for him.

The phone rang, its shrill tone penetrating her melancholy contemplation of the untouched dinner spread, and she answered it with a curt "hello".

'Aunty, I'm very sorry but something has come up at work. I can't make it tonight.'

'Who is this?' She knew full well but the young man was being presumptuous.

'It's me, Jagdesh – Jagdesh Singh. I was supposed to come for dinner but now I've been called back to the office.'

She liked his voice. It was rich and deep with the lilting cadences of a North Indian – so much more pleasing to her ears than the rolling "r"s of the South Indian. She liked that he called her "Aunty". She wasn't his aunt, of course. They were distant relatives by marriage. But she couldn't stand these modern manners where men and women young enough to be her children addressed her by her first name. It was so rude – it felt like a slap in the face every single time.

She said, 'OK. Another time then.'

'Thank you, Aunty. I'm really sorry.'

Mrs Singh replaced the receiver. There was no need for further chit-chat. She didn't like spending time on the phone unless it was to gossip to one of her three sisters about the shortcomings of her husband.

Mrs Singh spooned some long-grained *basmati* rice onto a plate. She added tiny helpings of each dish – there was a reason she was stick thin – but she did want to sample her cooking and make certain she hadn't lost the skill for which she was justly famed. She sat down at the table and, unfazed by the plastic table cloth that so bothered her husband, tucked in.

Quentin Holbrooke pulled into his reserved parking lot in the brightly-lit basement of Republic Tower in a black four-wheel-drive vehicle. He was a youngish man of medium height, with grey-speckled hair and protuberant pale blue eyes in a thin face. He smelt strongly of expensive men's aftershave. He noticed his colleague, Annie Nathan, pull into the adjoining lot in her convertible BMW.

'What are you doing here?' Annie asked. Quentin hardly ever allowed work to interfere with his Friday night pub-crawls along the old warehouses-turned-trendy-nightspots of Clarke Quay.

'I got a call from Mark. Do you know what it's about?'

'Haven't the foggiest.'

'Not my idea of the way to spend a Friday evening!'

Annie nodded her agreement, her bangs escaping a plain black hairclip and falling over her eyes.

He noticed that his colleague looked tired – her eyes were buried deep in dark hollows and her golden skin was sallow. Her hair, usually worn loose and curling past her shoulders, was drawn back in a tight, damp bun. She must have hurried to get to the meeting on time.

They made their way to the lift lobby together. She walked with long, even, mannish strides. He matched her pace but had a curious rolling gait, feet splayed and legs slightly bowed, that seemed more appropriate for a ship deck. In the lobby, Quentin hunted for his swipe card amongst the array of gold and platinum credit cards in his wallet.

'Damn, can't find my card. Do you have yours?' Quentin asked.

Annie rummaged in her handbag and found it. They started up to the sixty-eighth floor. Beating her to the main entrance, Quentin typed in his four-digit personal code and they walked into the reception area. Annie fumbled for the light switches just inside the door and a few discreet lights in the ceiling and a lamp behind the reception desk came on.

The décor in the reception area was designed to suggest both tradition and discretion. Leather-bound law reports lined one wall, although none of the lawyers who worked at the firm consulted them, not in an era of online statutes and case law. Three Oriental paintings, fine brush strokes depicting songbirds, adorned the opposite wall. The air smelt faintly of lilies. A vase of fresh white flowers, yellow stamens trimmed, stood tall on the receptionist's table. So late on a Friday evening, the office was silent and deserted. A few rooms had their lights on. It didn't indicate that anyone was at work. The junior lawyers did not switch off their lights in the evenings. It was a practice developed to suggest to inquisitive partners that work was still being done long after the lawyer had left for the day.

At the end of the corridor was the office of Mark Thompson, Senior Partner. His door was closed.

'You go ahead,' said Annie, disappearing into her own office.

Quentin nodded absently and carried on towards Mark's room. A quick tap on the door was met with silence. He knocked again, this time louder, and received no response. Quentin shrugged and tried the handle. The door opened easily. He poked his head into the room apologetically and said, 'Mark? Annie and I are here for the meeting.'

Three

Annie heard Quentin scream for help, the sound muffled by the heavy doors. She stood stock still, the hairs on her arms standing to attention like soldiers on parade, left her office at a run and burst into the room at the far end of the corridor. Quentin was standing by Mark's desk, his hands cupped firmly around his mouth and his protuberant eyes popping with shock.

Mark was sitting in his chair apparently oblivious to the presence of the two lawyers. His head was resting against the table, his cheek flat against the surface. There was complete silence except for a regular muffled tone. It sounded familiar but she couldn't pinpoint its origin. As she sidled up to Quentin, Annie realised with a horrid sinking feeling – as if she was in an aeroplane that had just hit a nasty patch of turbulence – that the background noise which had puzzled her was the telephone receiver lying on its side, a few inches away from Mark Thompson's outstretched hand.

And then she saw what Quentin had seen – a dark rivulet of blood matting Mark's hair, turning it almost black, running from a gash on his head down the side of his face. Annie gagged, and swallowed the taste of her early dinner. She could smell the cold rusty iron scent of blood.

Quentin edged forward, every small step betraying his reluctance to approach the body. He gingerly put his hand to Mark's wrist.

Annie guessed he could not bring himself to feel for a pulse on the neck – it was too close to the blood.

He shook his head at Annie.

Annie was as pale as the corpse. She gulped, 'Is he dead?'

'I think so.' Quentin's voice cracked, like a boy on the cusp of adolescence. 'I can't find a pulse,' he continued, rubbing his hands on his trousers, unconsciously trying to erase the lingering feel of death.

'I'll call an ambulance and the police,' she said weakly, reaching into her pocket for her mobile phone. She dialled 999, realising as she did so that it was the first time in her life that she had resorted to the emergency services. She explained quickly that they had found a body, ignoring the sceptical tone of the officer.

Quentin was shuffling from foot to foot, unable to stand still in the presence of the dead.

Annie, hanging up at last, noticed how wan he was. 'Maybe we should wait outside. The police won't want us in here.'

She left unspoken that it was the last place she wanted to be, closeted in a room with a dead man whose blood dripped from his head to the floor like water from a leaky faucet.

Quentin led the way out with alacrity but having made their escape, inspiration left them and they stood outside the door like undisciplined sentries, watching the minutes tick by on the office wall clock.

'Good evening, you two. Am I late for the meeting?' A

cheerful voice that betrayed its Indian origins struck a discordant note. A tall, broad-shouldered man with jet-black hair swept away from a high forehead and soulful brown eyes wandered towards them.

'What's going on? You two look like you've seen a ghost!'

Quentin winced at his choice of words and, to her embarrassment, hot tears rolled down Annie's cheeks.

'What is it?' Jagdesh sounded worried now. He came towards them and patted Annie awkwardly on the shoulder.

'Mark's in there – we think he's dead,' Quentin answered.

'You're pulling my leg, right? That's just not funny, chaps!' Jagdesh's Delhi accent, more pronounced in times of stress, contrasted oddly with his public school idioms.

He continued, taking in their expressions and Annie's tears, 'Heart attack? Just goes to show, doesn't it?'

What exactly Jagdesh thought it showed was never to become clear. Annie said, her voice high-pitched with anxiety, 'He's been murdered!'

The prolonged sound of a buzzer held down by an impatient finger interrupted Jagdesh's response.

At the entrance, Annie and Quentin found a short, rotund Sikh man who flashed a badge at them. The policeman marched in like an irate client who had just received the firm's bill for services rendered. A number of uniformed policemen trailed in his wake.

Jagdesh had answered a ringing telephone on the way to the door.

'Who's this?' asked the Sikh policeman tersely.

'One of our colleagues, Jagdesh Singh,' answered Annie promptly.

Inspector Singh's brow wrinkled. He said, 'Mr Singh, do not communicate the situation here to anyone,' and then, assuming compliance, he asked Quentin, 'Where's the victim?'

The young lawyer silently indicated Mark's closed door, and the turbaned man, using a handkerchief, pushed the door open and went in.

Jagdesh, who had fallen silent during this exchange, now spoke into the phone again. 'Ai Leen? I think you'd better come in with Reggie. Come as soon as you can.' Then, 'Who's the towel-head?' he demanded, hanging up.

Annie thought this was a bit rich coming from Jagdesh. He too was a Sikh like the policeman. He shared the same surname, Singh – which meant "lion" – as the inspector and all other men of Sikh origin. Jagdesh merely eschewed the other overt trappings of Sikhism, like the turban he was ridiculing.

Quentin silently handed over a card.

Jagdesh read it out loud, 'Inspector Singh, Central Police Division. No wonder they got here so quick – the station's just down the road. I wonder ...'

He was not given a chance to finish as the policeman stepped out of Mark's room. Annie wondered if he had heard Jagdesh mock his headdress; he gave no sign of having done so although he did shoot a glance at the Indian lawyer. His thickset face remained expressionless but his dark eyes were alive with interest. Annie guessed he wasn't often called in for murders in one of the high-rise offices in Singapore. Murder in Singapore was exceedingly rare. And when it did occur, it tended to be an ill-fated lovers' quarrel or a foreign maid driven by desperation to kill an abusive employer. However experienced this policeman was, this present situation – a murdered expatriate – would be something new.

She stared at the inspector, unable to hide her curiosity. His turban added at least two inches to his height. It was neatly tied and a dark colour. A triangle of white formed a contrast just above the middle of his broad forehead. He had a salt-and-pepper moustache and a beard that hedged a wide mouth. A full pink lower lip suggested a pout. A sagging breast pocket on the inspector's white shirt contained more pens than could reasonably be required of one person, however prolific a writer. The policeman's dark trousers, worn over rather than under his stomach, were held in place with an old leather belt that was marked with the creases of his slimmer days.

The policeman ignored Annie's scrutiny, beckoned to his men and issued a few quick instructions. Two of them set off down the corridor and started peering into individual rooms. A third took up position outside Mark's door.

'Is there anywhere these men can wait?' Inspector Singh asked Annie, gesturing at the two men in white. 'Ambulance personnel. We won't need them for a while.'

Annie led them to a conference room and, as an afterthought, invited them to sit down. Jagdesh and Quentin trailed after her, unsure of what to do and glad of a temporary purpose.

'Wait here, all of you.' Inspector Singh issued commands with the calm certainty of one accustomed to being obeyed.

'Where are you going now?' asked Jagdesh as the inspector headed for the door.

'None of your business,' was the inspector's offhand response.

'What about his family? Should we notify them?' This time it was Quentin with the question.

'You haven't called them yet?' asked the inspector.

'No,' said Annie, wondering why they had not done so. That should have been their first instinct after phoning 999. What had held them back? The reluctance to be the bearers of bad news?

'We haven't had time – we were waiting for you,' Quentin clarified.

It was a plausible explanation, thought Annie, but not accurate. There had been time if they had wished. But individually and collectively, consciously or unconsciously, they had chosen to ignore the immediately bereaved.

Inspector Singh did not cavil at their explanation. He merely inclined his head briefly in agreement. A man of few words apparently. 'I will see to it. There's a wife?'

'And two kids, both in school in England. His address is #15-04, Tanglin Vista Apartments,' explained Jagdesh and gave him the telephone number from memory. Jagdesh had phenomenal recall that assisted his performance as an outstanding commercial lawyer and was the envy of his less gifted colleagues.

'She's his second wife,' blurted out Annie.

The inspector gave no sign of having heard. He did not inquire further and left the room.

'Why'd you tell him that?' asked Jagdesh, frown lines chasing his hairline across a broad forehead.

'Prepare him for the surprise, I guess.'

The next few hours took on the unreal quality of a waking nightmare for Annie; one of those dreams where the circumstances are too unlikely to be real and there is a measure of subconscious scepticism. But here there was to be no relief upon awakening. Men in white bubble suits wandered up and down the corridor. Blue-uniformed personnel stood around. There were sharp barks of command. Light bulbs flashed as photos were taken. Voices were heard on the telephones. Strips of yellow tape were used to cordon off parts of the office. Annie felt as if she was a bit-part actress in a television crime series.

A turban appeared around the door and a crooked finger

summoned the lawyers. They glanced nervously at each other and traipsed out of the room obediently. As Singh led the way down the corridor, Annie noted again his peculiar shape – pointy head and small feet in white sneakers with a massive girth in between. He looked like a character from a children's cartoon – one of the Teletubbies. She suppressed a slightly hysterical giggle.

She noted that Jagdesh, his fellow Sikh, towered over the inspector, but it was the shorter man who was the band leader. Jagdesh trailed in his wake like a ten-year-old being led to the headmaster's office. Quentin might as well have been invisible. His shoulders were hunched and his gaze lowered. His aftershave failed to mask a faint smell of dried sweat.

Singh waved them into chairs and Annie's two colleagues sat down on either side of her. Her index finger went to her mouth and she chewed on the end vigorously. When it came away, a red droplet of blood oozed out of the tip. Her mind replayed the picture of Mark Thompson lying dead in his office. She gritted her teeth – the nausea was almost over-whelming.

Inspector Singh looked at them in turn, his expression enig-matic. At last, he asked, 'So, any guesses who killed your boss?'

He noted the young female lawyer, Annie Nathan, steal a quick glance at the other two and filed away her reaction.

'He had no enemies that we were aware of, sir,' Jagdesh answered calmly. His physical stature gave his words a convincing air of credibility.

'Business rivalries?'

Quentin spoke up. 'Sure – we all have those! It was just professional. No one *hated* Mark. Not enough to kill him.'

Singh eyed the lawyer who spoke with certainty but whose voice was shaking with doubt. What he had said was patently absurd. Mark's body was a tangible contradiction of Quentin's insistence that he had no enemies.

Jagdesh said aggressively, 'If he had any enemies, we certainly didn't know of them.'

The other two lawyers maintained a determined silence. Singh deduced that this was the unspoken consensus. No one wanted to be the first to break ranks and start naming suspects. They knew full well that any omissions would hinder the policeman in forming an accurate picture of the dead man. But for now they were keeping their secrets.

Jagdesh wondered aloud, 'Reggie and Ai Leen haven't turned up. That's strange – they said they were on their way.'

'And what about the others?' asked Quentin. 'Presumably all the partners were invited to this mysterious meeting.'

'Some of them are here, in another room,' was Inspector Singh's deadpan response.

He was pleased with the widening eyes and sudden inhalation of breath that this remark produced. The lawyers were smart – short of clapping them in irons, he could not have emphasised his authority over them more clearly. He was the policeman. Information was in his gift, to be distributed or withheld at his discretion. And now they knew it.

'Why are you keeping them away from us?' asked Quentin, his tone betraying a fear that the murder was going to embroil them in an experience going well beyond the immediate horror of sudden death.

He did not receive a response from the taciturn policeman.

Jagdesh's well-shaped lips were pursed with displeasure. 'I don't understand why you're hassling us anyway. It must have been some stranger who killed Mark!'

'That's your honest opinion – that some *stranger* killed your boss?' asked Singh.

Jagdesh and Quentin both nodded immediately. Again, the policeman noted that Annie was not so quick to assert a position. She opened her mouth to protest, then shut it again.

Inspector Singh pounced like an overweight cat on a rubber ball. 'What do you know?'

She bit her lip.

'I'm bound to find out – you don't want me to think that I don't have your full cooperation.' His manner was quietly authoritative – more effective than mere insistence.

Singh noted out of the corner of his eye that Quentin's Adam's apple was bobbing like a rubber duck in a bath.

The silence grew until it filled the room. Singh had been in the same position many times before. His witnesses were hiding something – within each of the three lawyers an internal debate raged. It was visible in their eyes; each one of them wore a slightly fixed stare, desperately trying to keep their features from hinting at any unpleasant truths.

It was Jagdesh who spoke first, his voice at a higher and more penetrating pitch than normal. The policeman concluded that he had made a conscious decision that Singh was certain to find out whatever it was they were keeping from him – and obfuscation would just reflect badly on all of them. 'After eight in the evening, the lifts can't be operated except with a swipe card or by filling in a visitors' book and being escorted by a security guard to the correct floor.'

'Who has a card to this floor?' asked Singh immediately, not slow to see the implications of what he was saying.

'Only the partners,' confessed Quentin reluctantly.

The other two looked as if they wished they could contradict him but it was the simple truth.

'Where is the visitors' book kept?' demanded the inspector, ignoring the undercurrents of tension and dismay.

'In the lobby, with the security guards.'

Singh beckoned a uniformed policeman who scurried off to do the inspector's bidding. He needed to retrieve the visitors' book and question the security guards. He looked at the lawyers. He guessed they were all desperately hoping that some suspect would emerge – it would suit them down to the ground if some stranger had left his name and address with security downstairs. Singh shook his great head. The survival instinct was always quick to show itself, he thought, leaving the dead ignored and unmourned when the living felt threatened.

Jagdesh interrupted his train of thought to ask sheepishly, 'Excuse me, sir – I hope you don't mind me asking – but I was supposed to have dinner with an Inspector Singh and his wife this evening. My mother arranged it – it wasn't you by any chance, was it?'

Singh slapped his palm on the table. 'I knew your name sounded familiar – you're the thirty-something in need of a wife!'

Jagdesh laughed out loud, exposing large, even white teeth. 'That's what my mother believes, sir. I think she's asked Mrs Singh to introduce me to all the unmarried Sikh girls in Singapore!'

Singh could understand his amusement. If his fellow Sikh, an imposing hulk of a man, with liquid eyes and an attractive, slightly melancholy manner, was unable to find a wife without the help of Mrs Singh, their race would soon be extinct.

Singh groaned suddenly and the trio around the table gazed at him in surprise. 'I forgot to tell my wife I'd been called out for a case,' he explained.

There were murmurs of feigned sympathy around the table.

The Sikh policeman said, 'I'll need your passports. Bring them into the station by lunchtime tomorrow. The address is on my card.'

There was an audible gasp from Quentin. His eyes were bloodshot and red-rimmed from the tension of the last few hours and he repeatedly blew his nose on a handkerchief. Every few moments he would shut his eyes, in an action somewhere between a blink and a conscious action. It came across as a nervous tic. But what was he nervous about?

Jagdesh was the first to acquiesce. The big Sikh was bearing up well, at least physically, appearing no more bemused and tired than if he had stayed up an extra couple of hours watching television. The whites of his eyes were still as clear as Singh's starched white shirt. He said, 'Yessir!' in a theatrically cooperative tone. Singh wondered whether Jagdesh thought he'd have an easy ride because he was a family acquaintance. If he did, he was in for a disappointment.

Maria Thompson sat half upright, half lying on a red velvet couch. A figure with less poise would have been described as slouching. She wore a silk kimono dressing gown with a dragon embroidered on the sleeves and back. Smooth unblemished legs with child-like bare arched feet were hooked over a sofa arm and her almond-shaped eyes were fixed on a widescreen plasma television, the sound turned down to the point of inaudibility. Maria Thompson's oval face, with its smooth flat planes of cheek, was expressionless. She appeared mesmerised by the silent figures on the screen.

On the mantelpiece, a few silver-framed photographs of Maria and a smiling white-haired man with a shaggy dark

29

moustache, at least thirty years older than her, were neatly arranged. In one, the couple stood side by side formally, not touching. In another, he was smiling down at her in a close-up of their faces. The photos were in black and white and had all been taken on the same occasion. The clothes, an elegant body-hugging white satin gown and a black tuxedo, were the same in each. A stranger might have assumed from the artificiality of the teeth-exposing smiles that the pictures had come with the frames.

Someone pressed the doorbell and she heard the chiming of electronic bells. Maria Thompson stirred instinctively, then remembered herself and lay back. The clicking heels of sensible shoes marked the progress of the Filipina maid as she walked down the hallway to the main door. She returned a minute later and stood respectfully at one end of the room, an older woman with wiry grey hair. Maria Thompson had no intention of employing young attractive domestic help – after all, who knew better than her, her husband's predilections? The maid's uniform, a black dress with a frilly white bib and apron – a pastiche of the costumes in a Victorian period drama – was carefully starched and ironed.

'Ma'am, there is a visitor to see you.'

'Who is it?'

The maid paused for a moment, her elderly face aging ten years in an instant. 'He come from the police, ma'am.'

Maria Thompson sat up a little straighter although her face remained bored.

'Why is he come here, ma'am? I have done nothing wrong, I swear it!'

The Filipina maid found the courage to voice her fears, although her papers were in order and she had never supplemented her income in Singapore by working in more than one home or moonlighting as a prostitute.

The mistress of the house, who had done both before marrying Mark Thompson, senior partner at Hutchinson & Rice and her erstwhile employer, went out to meet the police.

Jagdesh Singh lay in bed staring at the corniced ceiling. He had his hands folded behind his head and was resting on a soft pillow. The bedclothes were rumpled and his quilt was bunched up over his legs. He rubbed his feet together. They felt cold – as if his heart had become bored with pumping blood through his large body and decided to abandon the task before reaching the extremities. It was past midnight but he couldn't sleep. He was as wide awake as if he had an intravenous caffeine drip.

He wished he had gone to that dinner with the Singh family and ignored Mark's urgent summons. None of the problems he was facing would have come to a head if he had just done that. It seemed that this was yet another fork in the road where he had taken the wrong path. He paused to wonder how the Sikh inspector felt about having a distant relative involved in one of his cases. He had not seemed bothered – treating him with the same casual rudeness as he had the other lawyers. Family, or not, he was a suspect in a murder investigation. The chubby policeman did not look like someone who played favourites.

His mother had told him, when insisting that he accept an invitation to the Singh home for dinner, that the Sikh policeman was famous throughout Singapore for his incredible knack for solving murders.

'He is very high up in the police force,' she had said. 'They cannot manage without him.'

He picked up Singh's calling card from a side table and examined it in the dim light of a bedside lamp. He was only an inspector, the fat man with the traditional headgear, hardly "very high up". It didn't surprise him that his mother had exaggerated – it was a common Sikh pastime to puff up the importance of relatives. His parents were delighted to bask in the reflected glow of their Sikh family – and happy to claim as close relatives the most distant connections by blood or marriage if they thought it would add to the family pride.

It was one of the reasons they were so anxious to get him a wife. His mother was keen to parade her son, the successful lawyer working for an international law firm in Singapore, before the Sikh community in New Delhi. It would be her crowning glory. His younger sister was getting married in a couple of weeks but that did not provide the oldies with the same satisfaction. In their traditional society, only the marriage of a son could do that. Jagdesh arched his head so that it pushed against the downy pillow. The back of his neck was sore – the tension of the last few hours, he supposed. It felt as if his head was too heavy a burden for it. He touched his throat – his glands were swollen. He was coming down with something. He felt tired – more than tired, completely drained of energy. Quentin had been sniffling too – he'd probably caught something from him. Jagdesh closed his dark lids and felt a few unexpected pinpricks of self-pity. He wondered whether he should just bite the bullet and let his interfering relatives arrange a marriage for him to some nice Sikh girl. It was the most practical solution to his difficulties.

'I am Inspector Singh from the Singapore police. Are you Mrs Mark Thompson?'

Maria gave a brief, suspicious nod.

'I'm afraid I have some bad news, Mrs Thompson.'

32

A simple form of words that was generally understood to be a herald of death. Maria Thompson was no exception.

She whispered, 'My family?'

Her voice was trembling, emotion-charged, the face starting to crumble. It was like a mannequin coming to life, thought Singh.

He nodded, somehow conveying both firmness and sympathy in the simple gesture.

'What has happened to them? Tell me, please. Oh God! Tell me!'

'It's your husband, Mrs Thompson. I'm sorry to have to tell you that he's dead.'

'My *husband*?' she repeated after him blankly.

Inspector Singh put out a hand, an involuntary gesture of comfort.

The second wife of the dead man fell to her knees, as if in prayer.

The police officer could not make out the words she was saying over and over as she rocked back and forth. Then he heard her. The words were indeed in the manner of a prayer. She was on her knees repeating, 'Thank God!'

The usually impassive face of the inspector betrayed his complete surprise.

Ten minutes later, Mrs Mark Thompson was again on the velvet couch, this time sitting bolt upright, kimono folded decorously over both knees. She clutched a mug of hot chocolate close to her chest. For comfort or to give her hands something to do, wondered the policeman. He sat across from her, stiff-backed in a stiff-backed chair, at a slight angle so that the woman had to turn to gaze at him directly. For a while they did not speak. His eyes took in the genuine antique Chinese rosewood furniture, buffed to gleaming, and the brushstroke paintings of mountains, fields and blossoms. A highly polished grand piano stood in the corner, lid down. Two vases filled with green bamboo shoots stood on either side of a gilt-framed mirror. The room had all the passion of a shop display.

Maria, her face blotchy with crying, was defensive. She said, 'I think maybe you bring me bad news of my children. I have one boy and one girl, eight years old and six years old ... from a ... another marriage. They are in the Philippines. For a long time I have not seen them.'

Singh did not miss the heartbeat of hesitation before the word "marriage".

She continued, her voice growing louder, her Filipina accent more pronounced, 'Of course, I am very upset that my husband has died. But a mother always thinks of her children first!'

Her explanation was defiant but threadbare, decided Singh.

His gaze strayed to the photos on the various surfaces – all of her and Mark – none of these children that she valued so highly.

'Mark said that I would be happier without reminders of my past in the house.'

'And were you happier?' Inspector Singh was not afraid to ask the unexpected.

'I miss my children!' she snapped.

He did not respond to her sudden anger but instead sipped the tea that the maid had brought him, blowing gently on the surface to cool it down.

Her flash of spirit died as suddenly as it had appeared. She asked, 'What happened to my husband? Was it a car accident? Mark is very careless to drive sometimes.'

Watching her face – each feature as delicate as fine china and framed with long straight black hair – the inspector said,

'He was murdered. He was beaten repeatedly on the head with the paperweight he kept on his desk.'

She dropped her steaming mug, both hands going to cover her mouth. They both watched the cocoa stain spread dark across the cream carpet like blood from a wound.

'Who did it?' A whispered question – she was either a brilliant actress or a woman who was almost prostrate with shock. Not even a policeman of his experience could be sure, thought Singh. He realised that the unexpectedly young, exceptionally beautiful second Mrs Thompson should not be underestimated.

'At present, we do not know. We are launching an investigation, of course.' He was prepared to take her question at face value, setting aside his suspicions for a moment to answer her query honestly.

'It was *her*. I know it! She hates ... hated him. And me also.'

Each word was said with rising hysteria, her open mouth revealing small uneven teeth, a small flaw in her otherwise perfect features.

'Who do you think killed your husband?'

'His wife!'

Singh allowed his eyebrows to creep towards each other, a sign of growing impatience. 'I thought *you* were his wife,' he said.

'His first wife ... his ex-wife – Sarah Thompson! He left her to come to me. I tell you, she killed him. She will come for me next. You must stop her. Oh God! What will happen to my children?'

Four

His team looked nervous but excited. They stared at the inspector like children at a magician's performance – watching every detail, expecting the unexpected, prepared to be awed. So far, the only thing unexpected or awe-inspiring for Inspector Singh was the size of the team with which he had been provided that morning. This was not going to be one of his lonely investigations into the death of a foreign worker at the hands of his *mandur*. The whole paraphernalia of police work was to be at his disposal. The top echelons wanted the case solved – but they also wanted the process to look like something out of a cop drama. There was to be no stinting on expenses or personnel – not while the foreign press was camped outside his station and Singapore's reputation as a safe and desirable place to work was at stake.

He counted four rows of corporals and sergeants – notebooks open in front of them, pens at the ready. He wondered who remained to police the streets. Not that it was necessary. He recalled a recent case where he had been seconded to Kuala Lumpur with its dusty, grimy streets. In orderly

Singapore, the population hardly ever jaywalked, always waited for the little green man before crossing roads, and never littered. All things considered, the higher-ups could spare him a few good men.

The room they were gathered in was brightly lit and pleasantly cool. Whiteboards covered the walls. Information notices with the crest of the Singapore police on the top left hand corner were neatly taped to bare spaces. The inspector cleared his throat to elicit the attention of his subordinates. He needn't have bothered. Their eyes were fixed on him anyway.

Just as Singh opened his mouth to speak, he was interrupted by the door opening. Superintendent Chen walked in briskly.

'Good morning, Inspector. Good, good – I see you have assembled the team,' the superintendent said, and received a curt nod in return.

Surely, it was a bit early in the investigation for the boss to start poking his nose into things?

'I just came in to remind everyone that this is a very important investigation. The victim, Mark Thompson, was a well-known and respected member of the expatriate community in Singapore. We must do all we can to hunt down the murderer. This case *must* be solved.'

Singh's bottom lip – always in a slight pink pout – was thrust out more aggressively. Apparently, it *wasn't* too soon for the higher-ups to start trampling over his turf.

His superior officer glanced down at him. 'Did you have anything to add, Inspector?'

'I believe all murderers should be hunted down, sir. Not just the killers of "a respected member of the expatriate community".' Singh could not keep the snide tone out of his voice.

'Of course, of course – but this killing has consequences for the economy of Singapore. We don't want our foreign talent to feel threatened.'

Singh took a deep breath and held his tongue with difficulty. It was the cold hard reality that even in murder there was a pecking order. He might not like it that Mark Thompson was to receive priority treatment because he was "foreign talent", as wealthy expatriates were referred to in Singapore. On the other hand, he deserved to have his killer brought to justice as much as the next person.

'We're all keen to get to the bottom of this, sir,' said the inspector, unexpectedly diplomatic for a man of his reputation.

Superintendent Chen looked surprised but pleased that his most difficult subordinate was toeing the line. 'Carry on, carry on – I don't want to interfere.'

Like hell you don't, thought Singh. Out loud, he said, 'Mark Thompson was murdered at his desk. The number of viable suspects is limited.' He ran through what he had learnt about the keycard system at Republic Tower.

Superintendent Chen interrupted, his thin face a picture of disappointment. 'Are you sure it wasn't some outsider – a foreign labourer – maybe from Indonesia or Bangladesh?'

Singh's response was squeezed out from between gritted teeth – 'I'm not sure of *anything* yet, sir. But it does seem likely that the killer was one of the *partners* called in to attend the meeting that evening. I don't believe in coincidences of that magnitude any more than I believe in God.'

Chen folded his arms tight, a pained look on his face – he had a reputation for fervent religiosity – but he nodded his willingness for Singh to continue.

'Sergeants Fuad and Lim, you look at the phone records of all those called in for the meeting. I want to know when they were called in by Mark – it will help us narrow the time of death.'

The fat policeman continued, 'Corporal Dass, check the CCTV tapes – if big brother was watching, I want to know.' Dass looked puzzled at the reference but nodded his head at once. 'You two,' said Singh, pointing a grubby finger at a couple of uniforms – he had no idea what their names were – 'start trawling through bank accounts and computers. If this was a matter connected to Hutchinson & Rice, the law firm – money is most likely at its root.'

'We need to look into who benefited from his death,' interjected the superintendent. He had obviously been brushing up on his investigative techniques, thought Singh dismissively, in all likelihood by re-reading his Agatha Christie collection.

'Check his finances – ask his lawyers if he left a will,' said Singh to the only female officer in the room, a pretty Malay woman with heavy make-up to cover what he suspected was an attack of acne.

He continued, addressing the room at large this time, 'Do we have the preliminary scene of crime report yet?'

A middle-aged man with thick, black-framed glasses handed over a bulging file. Singh raised an eyebrow and the forensics man interjected hurriedly, 'To summarise – no fingerprints on the murder weapon – it was wiped. Prints of the deceased and a number of lawyers and staff were found in the room.'

'There's nothing particularly sinister about that,' remarked Singh.

The man nodded in agreement. 'The blood in the room matches the blood type of the deceased *only*.'

'Anything else?'

'The swabs of the sinks on the premises found the deceased's blood in the pantry sink.'

'So the killer washed his or her hands ...'

'That is the most likely conclusion, sir,' agreed the forensics specialist.

'A shame that they didn't use the bathrooms instead,' muttered Singh.

A front row sergeant looked puzzled but it was only Superintendent Chen who dared put the question into words: 'Why does that matter?'

'Male and female toilets, sir. Our perpetrator was in a hurry to clean up and get out. I'm sure he or she would have used the appropriate facilities.' He continued, 'We had better search the residence of each of the partners as well as the wife and ex-wife. We might get lucky and find a rolled-up, blood-stained T-shirt at the back of the clothes cupboard.'

'What about witness statements?' asked Chen.

Inspector Singh looked around the room at his bright-eyed, bushy-tailed subordinates. His glance fell on Corporal Fong, his latest right-hand man, leaning forward in his chair so earnestly that Singh feared he might tip over and end up on the floor. 'I'll do the interviews myself,' he said, his voice at its most gravelly.

He realised that he had assigned tasks to no more than half the enthusiastic youngsters in the room. What in the world was he going to do with the rest of them? He glanced at the superintendent – the lines on his brow were like a child's drawing of waves in the sea. The boss wanted more tangible progress; muddy footprints and half-smoked cigarette butts soaked in DNA-ridden saliva. Very well, thought Singh, he would investigate, but he would also play the pantomime investigator. 'The rest of you,' he said, 'divide yourselves into teams of two and follow every single one of those partners. I want to know *everything*; where they go, what they eat, how many times a day they take a leak – got it?'

There were enthusiastic nods around the room.

Superintendent Chen looked pleased.

All the partners of the Singapore office of Hutchinson & Rice, bar one, were gathered together at the penthouse club of their office tower block. The absent partner lay in a chilled steel drawer at the morgue of a Singapore hospital, naked except for the small plastic identification tag tied to his left big toe. Their offices were still out of bounds. Cheerful yellow bands which the television age had taught everyone to identify as a police barricade were taped across the entrances. Two blue-uniformed policemen, each equipped with a gun, a knife and a truncheon, had politely ushered the lawyers away as unwanted visitors to the scene of a crime.

Jagdesh decided that the session functioned as a combination of group therapy and council of war. The partners sat around the gleaming polished table, ignoring or oblivious to the panoramic view of sapphire seas and cloudless skies visible through the ceiling-to-floor reinforced glass windows. Annie and Quentin had arrived promptly at nine. Quentin did not look great. His nostrils were inflamed and he dabbed at a constant trickle of mucus. His face was gaunt, as if he had lost weight overnight. Annie was not her usual self either; there were dark rings under her eyes and thin lines running from nose to mouth. Jagdesh, glancing in the mirror while shaving that morning, did not think he was showing any overt signs of strain. Not yet, anyway, he thought grimly. He still felt as if he was coming down with a cold but he was holding up well compared to his peers.

It did not take long for each of them to run through their story – the constant questioning by Inspector Singh the previous evening had perfected their tales. The other part-

41

ners listened in silence as Quentin described finding the body.

Stephen Thwaites, the most senior partner after Mark Thompson, took charge of the meeting with a reassuring air of calm authority. 'Who else came in last night?'

'We did,' said Reggie Peters reluctantly, nodding at Ai Leen to indicate whom he meant by "we". 'Mark called me in for some sort of meeting – I picked up Ai Leen on the way. By the time we arrived the police had taken over.'

He continued angrily, 'That policeman refused to tell us anything except that Mark had been murdered.'

Reggie was sweating despite the cool of the room, droplets of moisture on his forehead and upper lip. His remaining strands of hair clung damply to his flushed scalp and there was a frothy speck of saliva in the corner of his mouth.

'He was extremely rude. How dare he treat us like that? As if we were common criminals.'

Jagdesh wondered what an uncommon criminal was. Was it the nature of the crime or the criminal that attracted the sobriquet?

'We weren't even allowed to make phone calls ... and we were in *my* office!'

Reggie had reached a new pitch of self-righteous anger. It was bad enough to be subjected to the authority of some local policeman. But to have that happen in his own domain – that was adding insult to injury. A red-faced man at the best of times, he was crimson with annoyance. Jagdesh knew that Reggie was very conscious of his own dignity. He lost his temper with subordinates over imaginary slights. His condescension towards the locals was neo-colonial. Jagdesh, an Indian from Delhi, usually found him offensive. Today he felt sorry for him. It was perfectly apparent that Reggie's contempt for Singapore officialdom had not been on display the previous evening.

'I thought he was competent enough,' he intervened.

Quentin shot a quick glance at him – no doubt wondering whether he was defending the inspector because he was a fellow Sikh and a family acquaintance to boot.

Ai Leen had hardly uttered a word, although she had been with Reggie the previous evening, leaving him to describe his version of events.

Now she said in her quiet firm tone, 'Inspector Singh did not appear rude to me.'

Reggie, who had been on the verge of disagreeing heatedly with Jagdesh, subsided at this contradiction. Ai Leen, her contribution to the conversation over, reverted to stony-faced silence. Unlike the rest of the partners who were dressed casually, Ai Leen had arrived for their meeting dressed for a day at the office. She wore a powder-blue twin-set with a double string of freshwater pearls around her neck. Her face was carefully made up, eyebrows plucked into a fine inquiring line. She looked as if she was about to meet an important client, rather than discuss the murder of Mark Thompson.

Stephen was the next one to speak. He said briskly in the plummy baritone that would have ensured him a successful career as a barrister, 'We'll let the police worry about who did it ...'

'You haven't presented us with your alibi yet,' interrupted Reggie.

Stephen ignored the jibe. 'I was home in bed with a headache and did not pick up any messages from Mark until this morning,' he continued. 'It must have been some stranger, possibly someone mentally unbalanced. The police will track him down soon enough.'

'But how can we know that?' Quentin asked, rubbing his

eyes with his palms like a tired child. 'What about the card keys?'

Stephen shrugged off the question. '*Our* first priority must be to avoid a scandal – for the sake of his family and the firm.'

'It's what Mark would have wanted,' murmured Reggie, belatedly cooperating when the issues were spelt out in terms of his own self-interest.

'Listen to yourself, you sanctimonious bastard,' growled Jagdesh, getting to his feet and looming over his seated colleague. 'Mark doesn't deserve to be the subject of a damage limitation exercise!'

'Well, that's what he was in life. Why should his death change anything?' asked Reggie angrily. 'Drinking, pissing off clients, screwing the help – his death is only the final scandal!'

'Let's take a step back here,' said Stephen calmly. 'We need to stick together. I think we ought to issue a press statement … and close the office for a few days. We should get in touch with the widow, help arrange the funeral. God knows what Maria will do if we leave it to her.'

There were nods of agreement around the table. The business of living must go on, thought Jagdesh, resuming his seat and frowning at his fellow partners. The dead become a dead weight and are left behind.

'Someone should contact Sarah Thompson,' said Quentin.

'Joan will handle that,' muttered Stephen, looking embarrassed.

Jagdesh nodded his agreement. Joan, Stephen's wife, had been a close friend of the ex-Mrs Thompson before she had fled back to the relative anonymity of the United Kingdom after the collapse of her marriage to Mark.

'I suppose someone *would* have told Maria?' asked Quentin doubtfully.

'Yes,' said Jagdesh. 'The inspector mentioned he was going to stop by last night and tell her.'

'It might be a good idea to draft a statement now. Make certain when the story does break, we have a response,' suggested Annie, ever practical.

Stephen retrieved a writing pad from his briefcase and a carefully sharpened pencil. Jagdesh wondered whether the pencil was an affectation, a step up from quill and ink. Perhaps it indicated that, despite a job whose stock was words, he distrusted the permanency of the written word. He was an interesting man, Stephen – overweight and jowly, with a spidery scrawl of broken veins on a prominent nose. His bushy, tufted eyebrows overshadowed dark observant eyes. Bluff and hearty in manner, he had a sensitive streak that was not far from the surface.

Now he said, 'The partners of Hutchinson & Rice regret to announce the sudden death ...' He glanced round enquiringly, seeking input into his macabre task.

A waiter sidled into the room with the late edition morning papers. He laid them gently on the table and then scurried out of the room.

'EXPAT MURDERED!' screamed the headline, and in only slightly smaller print below, 'MAID (NOW SECOND WIFE) ACCUSES EX-WIFE OF MURDER!'

Quentin's voice reflected his bewilderment. 'But Sarah Thompson isn't even in the country.'

'I'm afraid she is,' confessed Stephen. 'Sarah's been staying with us. I didn't mention it before because it might have embarrassed Mark.'

'But we have to tell Inspector Singh!' exclaimed Annie.

'Not now, we don't,' said Jagdesh wryly, gesturing at the paper.

Inspector Singh sat at a round Formica-topped table on the verandah of the old civil service club on Dempsey Road.

45

His buttocks sank into the cushioned green *faux* leather seat. The day was picture perfect in the way that was possible only on a Saturday afternoon in the tropics – dappled sunshine, blue skies with streaks of wispy white clouds and snatches of birdsong. Only the low rumble of traffic from Holland Road suggested to the observant that they were in the middle of a metropolis.

Inspector Singh had just tucked into a massive South Indian meal. A banana leaf, neatly folded in two, disguised the remnants of the senior policeman's lunch. His young colleague did not appear to know that banana-leaf etiquette required that leaves be folded after meals.

Singh noticed Corporal Fong glance at his watch and scan the restaurant quickly. He probably feared being spotted by someone senior in the force. Inspector Singh did not see an unsolved murder as a reason not to partake of an early and comprehensive lunch. Fragrant biryani rice, three varieties of vegetables – aubergine, sliced ladies fingers and spinach – a rich lentil gravy, deep-fried slices of the muscular *tenggiri* fish, mango pickle and crisp poppadums had been accompanied by a large bottle of icy cold beer. This would normally have left the older man with a feeling of languid contentment. But watching the young policeman pick at his food nervously had impaired his enjoyment considerably.

The inspector knew that none of these sources of aggravation justified his dispensing with the services of the constable. The young man had come highly recommended, straight out of the police academy where he had topped his class. More often than not, he, Singh, had to make do with the dregs of the force – the smart graduates were too valuable to waste on murder investigations. They were needed for securities fraud, criminal breach of trust and other wrongdoings that made Inspector Singh sleepy just think-

46

ing about them. But, just for once, his bosses didn't want him to fail. The murder of an expatriate in Singapore was a terrible blow to the carefully cultivated reputation of the island state. Singh remembered the dead man, sprawled across his desk, with a gaping head wound the size and shape of which had matched the paperweight on the desk. A paperweight that had blood, fragments of bone and hair stuck to its surface. It was an ugly case – the murderer had been angry and determined. Unfortunately the suspects were canny, wealthy lawyers who knew their rights all too well.

Singh belched. This was no time for post-lunch self doubt. He made his way to the long sinks, washed his hands, rinsed his mouth and lumbered back to the table. His fingers were stained a faint yellow – traces of the turmeric that had coloured the curries. The policeman sat down heavily and ordered a glass of *teh tarik*.

Corporal Fong, perhaps unaware that he had already incurred the displeasure of the other man, leaned forward earnestly and asked, 'What do you think about this case, sir?'

'What do I think about this case?' Singh grinned complacently at the other man. 'I think it is going to make or break careers ... but more likely break them.'

The remaining partners paid the necessary but awkward visit to the widow, opting to go together rather than have to deal with Maria individually. Even Reggie had decided to come along although Quentin was certain that he was motivated more by curiosity than by sympathy. He couldn't imagine that there was a fragment of genuine feeling in Reggie Peters for the deceased or his family.

Maria Thompson was wearing unrelieved black, which contrasted dramatically with the paleness of her skin. She received their condolences with a hint of disbelief, a shrug of her shoulders conveying her thoughts more accurately than her formal words of acceptance. The uniformed maid brought them tea and they sipped it in the lounge, struggling to make any sort of small talk. Quentin wondered, wiping his streaming nose with a serviette, why the Thompsons felt the need to dress their help like an extra in a period television drama. Had Maria been trying to distinguish herself from her previous role? Or had she too worn a frilly apron and served tea with quiet decorum while the previous Mrs Thompson presided over the table? He cast a sidelong glance at Annie, his closest friend in the office, to see if she had noticed the incongruity. She was staring at the widow with a wooden expression.

Maria Thompson was willing for Stephen to organise the funeral, once the coroner released the body, as long as it was held in Singapore. However, she was adamant that "the murderer" not be present.

'She's not the murderer, she's the mother of his children, for God's sake,' said Stephen, his patience tried to breaking point. His personal friendship with Sarah Thompson was making the widow's intransigence even harder to deal with.

'She will try to kill me too, I know it. I have asked the police to watch her,' was the uncompromising response.

'We can hardly expect her to be grateful for our sympathy or advice. She knows how shocked everyone was at the marriage,' pointed out Jagdesh when they had escaped the premises as soon as was decent and were standing outside, squinting in the bright sunshine on Tanglin Road.

Annie slipped the sunglasses perched on her head onto her nose, waving away a curious butterfly with satiny black and green wings. 'None of us were very supportive when she married Mark.'

'What did she expect?' snapped Ai Leen. 'That we welcome a gold-digging slut with open arms?' Her question was aggressive in both content and tone. Her hands were on her hips, her head thrust forward angrily on a slender neck. The designer emblem on her outsized sunglasses caught the light and twinkled like a miniature star.

'I'll bet she killed Mark,' commented Reggie. 'That woman would stop at nothing.'

As usual, thought Quentin, Reggie had to have the last word. He had to admit, though, that the putty-faced, over-weight banking partner had a point – pinning the murder on the widow would be the best solution for all the lawyers.

Corporal Fong was an interesting shade of pale green. Perhaps, thought Singh, he should have warned the young man that the first thing on the agenda after lunch was the post-mortem at the Singapore General Hospital. On the other hand, this was probably the most effective introduction to a murder investigation for a corporal who was still wet behind the ears. After all, it was his opportunity to meet the victim.

The unfortunate victim, Mark Thompson, lay naked on a steel table. There was a Y-shaped incision across his chest running down towards his abdomen. The initial external investigation had not revealed much except for the wound at the back of his head which the pathologist, Dr Maniam, had looked at with some awe and growled that he would leave for last.

Singh looked at the pale white body of the senior partner. He seemed almost bloodless, the flesh flaccid and fatty. There was a sprinkling of grey hair on his chest and nether regions. The pathologist, with the help of his assistant, pulled back the skin, muscle and soft tissues and cut through each side of the rib cage with an electric saw that buzzed like a dentist's drill. It caused Singh to run his tongue over his teeth nervously. He didn't mind autopsies, but he was afraid of dentists. Singh peered at the heart and lungs and then stepped back as Dr Maniam, with some heaving and panting, started dragging organs out of the body. He cut through connecting tissue with an instrument that looked like a long sharp bread knife. The pathologist muttered his observations out loud for the benefit of the tape recorder that was recording his findings. His assistant started weighing organs on a kitchen scale that reminded Singh of the ones used in wet markets by the chicken sellers. The inspector wrinkled his nose – the sweet cloying smell of raw meat put him in mind of the butcher where his wife bought mutton on the bone for her rich curries. Still, it was nothing compared to the stench that would be forthcoming when the stomach cavity and intestines were sliced open. Singh noted that the corporal had prudently retired to a far wall. He had escaped the sights, but the sounds and smells would pursue him to his safe haven.

Singh's foot began to tap impatiently as the assistant, wrapped in green scrubs and a face mask, sliced organs thinly for a histology examination. He knew that it was necessary and a part of the standard autopsy procedure but he wasn't particularly interested in the results. The cause of Mark Thompson's death was evident to the naked eye – microscopic examinations of the bits and bobs Dr Maniam was extracting with such enthusiasm were superfluous. The head wound looked like a bloody open mouth screaming for attention – and perhaps justice.

Dr Maniam glanced at Singh's tapping foot and glared at the fat policeman. His eyebrows looked like two furry caterpillars facing off. His attention was drawn back to the body cavity as he extricated the liver. It was large and a pale orange colour. The pathologist hefted it up with one hand and held it out for Singh who wrinkled his nose but obediently took a step forward.

'A bit of a drinker, I see!' exclaimed the doctor proudly.

Singh scowled. 'So? Mark Thompson didn't exactly die of alcohol poisoning, did he?'

Dr Maniam's annoyance was written on his face, but he turned to Mark Thompson's head wound. 'All right, I see you're not going to be satisfied until I start looking at this mess.' He used tweezers to extract fragments of bone from the wound, dropping each piece into a steel bowl.

Singh held out a plastic evidence bag with the pewter tiger paperweight in it.

'Fingerprints?'

'Wiped,' said Singh tersely.

Dr Maniam took out the pewter statue with its marble base admiringly. 'It's really beautifully weighted to beat someone's head in.' He measured the base with a ruler and did the same for the head wound. He pointed at an indentation in the skull and held the makeshift weapon against it. It was a perfect fit.

'I think I can confirm your murder weapon.'

Singh nodded. 'The bits of bone and hair on it are a bit of a giveaway too.'

Dr Maniam's nose hairs quivered but he opted to be amused rather than annoyed at this sarcasm. His guffaw caused Corporal Fong, still standing as far away as he could from proceedings, to look up and then turn away quickly. Singh supposed that the blood-splattered floor, overalls and table were a bit off-putting. It brought back memories of a crime drama on television where the pathologist had conducted the autopsy in a spotless dinner jacket before

51

proceeding to a black tie dinner. Dr Maniam looked like he might have been on a killing spree himself.

Singh snapped, 'Is there anything you can tell me that I *don't* already know?'

'Well, any findings at this stage are preliminary . . .'

'Give me something!'

Dr Maniam sighed. 'Well, the first blow would have knocked him unconscious if it didn't kill him outright. He didn't see it coming.' The pathologist picked up one of Mark's hands. 'No defensive markings anywhere.'

Singh was listening intently, his eyes focused on the doctor.

'The murderer then delivered a series of frenzied blows – far in excess of what was needed to kill him.'

'Hatred?'

'Or panic,' remarked Dr Maniam.

'Blood?'

The pathologist looked thoughtful. 'Certainly on the hand holding the weapon, some on clothing perhaps. The back of the head doesn't splatter that much. The first or second blow would have killed him so most of the damage was inflicted after death. Post-mortem injuries don't bleed much either.'

'He or she?'

'Either – with a weapon like this. The blows could have been struck by a woman just as easily as a man.' He held the paperweight to the wound, shifting it from hand to hand. 'I would guess – but it's no more than a best guess – that the killer was right-handed.'

'Well, that narrows it down to about ninety per cent of the population,' said Singh sarcastically.

Dr Maniam chortled. 'I don't want to make your job too easy for you.'

Five

Singh sat down in the armchair reserved for his use in the living room. It creaked silently and enfolded him in its familiar embrace, contours snug to his ample frame. It was a relief to be home. It had been a long day and it was far from over – he had told young Fong to follow him back and brief him on any developments as policemen spread out across Singapore searching homes and examining hard drives. But he had felt an uncontrollable desire to escape from the precinct. It was the continual presence of Superintendent Chen that had driven him away. His boss had popped into his office every quarter hour to demand updates, and then looked disappointed that no firm leads had developed in the previous fifteen minutes. He, Inspector Singh, was not accustomed to being closely supervised as he went about his police business – and he didn't like it.

His wife darted into the room, her hair drawn severely back from her face. It gave her face the tautness of a facelift. She placed a mug of sweet, milky tea at her husband's elbow. He grunted an acknowledgement but paid her no heed beyond that. However, ignoring his wife had never been an effective method of shutting her up and it wasn't this evening either. She was still harping on a single subject. 'I cooked *five* dishes – I can't believe you didn't tell me you weren't coming home!'

Had he fled one nagging creature only to run into the orbit of another, wondered Singh. 'I was called out for a murder. I completely forgot about dinner – I told you that,' he replied, with an air of great patience.

'I wouldn't be surprised if you murder these people yourself – just so you can be late to come home!'

Singh guffawed loudly, his belly vibrating with humour.

Mrs Singh had the grace to look sheepish. 'I've been reading about your case in the newspapers – some expat got killed!'

He nodded his large head thoughtfully and said, the closest he had ever come to confiding in his wife, 'It might be a difficult one to solve. Too many lawyers involved.'

'It's in the *Straits Times* that you're in charge. I won't know where to hide my face if you don't find the killer.' Once again, his wife's priority was the possibility of personal embarrassment. If Singh was seeking sympathy, he had obviously come to the wrong place.

The fat man stretched and felt a pain between his shoulder blades as his muscles did his bidding reluctantly.

'Anyway, everyone knows who did it.'

Singh raised an eyebrow.

Mrs Singh's long nose was wrinkled with disapproval. 'It was the maid!'

'The second wife, you mean?'

'Of course – who else?'

Singh dragged himself into an upright position. He ran his tongue over the front of his teeth, feeling the plaque build-up. He was aggravated by his wife's – and the press's and the public's – willingness to immediately pin the murder on the widow, purely, as far he could see, on the grounds that she had previously been the domestic help.

'There's no evidence that she murdered him!'

'She stole a husband, right? I'm sure she could kill one also.'

Singh eyed his wife, almost admiring her ability to draw conclusions from unrelated facts. He knew he was going to regret what he was about to say but he couldn't resist the temptation. 'I have a few *other* suspects.'

She shrugged her bony soldiers and her caftan fluttered like a sail in a mild sea breeze.

'Including Jagdesh Singh!' the policeman continued.

'Who?'

'You know – your no-show dinner guest who needs a wife. I met him at the crime scene. He's a partner at that law firm – and they're *all* suspects!'

'You're being silly. He would never be mixed up in something like this!'

'You've never met him. How could you possibly know that?'

'He's a good boy from a good family – *our* people would never kill anyone.'

Give me time, thought the inspector, glaring at his wife.

He gulped his tea in order to avoid escalating the argument and was pleased to hear the doorbell ring, its tone that of an old-fashioned telephone.

Mrs Singh peeped out from behind a curtain and said, 'For you.'

'How do you know?' he asked, moved by curiosity.

She answered disdainfully, 'Chinese,' and left the room.

The inspector was forced to acknowledge yet again that

his wife would make an excellent detective. Perhaps he should take her conviction that Maria Thompson was the killer seriously. It was true that, despite living in multi-racial Singapore, for someone of his generation, a Chinese visitor would almost definitely have to be a work connection.

It was Corporal Fong, diligently following the inspector home to report on his various assignments. Inspector Singh listened as he delivered a summary of his report in an admirably brief manner. There was nothing in it to surprise the inspector but he had to go through the motions and cover the angles. 'To sum up, nothing in the register at the front desk, no cards issued for that floor except to the partners ... so one of them killed him ... or Mr Thompson escorted his killer up.'

'I agree, sir.'

'That's a relief,' remarked Inspector Singh.

Fong continued to nod enthusiastically and his senior was left to rue his inability to detect sarcasm and to wonder whether, despite his top marks in the academy, the policeman should be allowed out of the police station.

'CCTV tapes?' Singh asked curtly.

'Corporal Dass requested them, sir. But the cameras were being serviced so no tapes were running.'

Inspector Singh was impressed by this industry, but his response gave no sign of it. 'The murderer is a lucky man – or woman ... we will have to change that.'

'Yessir!'

'Check the CCTV tapes from the *surrounding* buildings.'

Fong nodded, his expression rueful. Singh guessed he was annoyed that he had not thought to do that himself. At least this solemn Chinaman was setting himself high standards.

'Anything else?'

'There's this, sir.'

Inspector Singh stared at the sheet of paper Fong had handed to him. It consisted of a list of numbers that had been called from Mark Thompson's desk phone on the evening of his death. Corporal Fong had carefully cross-referenced the list to the telephone numbers of the partners and jotted down each name next to the relevant number. As Singh had suspected, Mark Thompson had put in a call to every single one of his partners that evening, commencing with Stephen Thwaites. A few had been called twice, even thrice. Clearly he had found it difficult to get through to some of them but Mark Thompson had been determined to summon every single one of them.

Singh placed the list on the table, leaned forward and continued to stare at it, his bearded chin resting on his clasped hands. He noticed that he had left faint fingerprints on the document. He would really have to wear gloves, he concluded, if he ever decided to commit a crime – either that or resort to cutlery to enjoy his wife's curries. He puffed up his cheeks and exhaled slowly.

'Is something the matter, sir?' Corporal Fong asked tentatively.

Singh's frown was so deep that it narrowed his forehead, moving him, in appearance at least, a couple of evolutionary cycles backwards. He tapped the document with an index finger. 'Human nature!' he said, his tone revealing his aggravation.

'I beg your pardon?'

'I'm a student of human nature, young man – *that* is how I solve murders.'

Singh noted that his assistant appeared bemused but attentive, as if he expected the senior man to embellish his answer.

Instead, the inspector snapped, 'So what does human

nature tell you about Mark Thompson and this list?'

Fong opened his mouth and shut it again. Singh noticed for the first time that he had a small rosebud-shaped mouth that was slightly incongruous on a man's face.

Singh drummed his stubby fingers impatiently on the table like a schoolgirl practising her scales on the piano.

The constable stared at the list as hard as he could – upside down as he was across the table. 'I don't quite understand, sir,' he murmured eventually.

'Neither do I!'

'What do you mean, Inspector?'

'Looking at this list, I am pretty sure I *know* who the murderer is – based entirely on my intimate understanding of people's behaviour ...'

Fong stared at the sheet of paper as if he expected the word "murderer" to be scribbled next to one of the names.

Singh cracked his knuckles together. 'But unfortunately, human nature and the facts we have at our disposal are pointing in different directions!'

Singh continued to peruse the list. Should he tell his young sidekick what he thought? So far, there wasn't a single strand of evidence to hang his theory on. He sighed. He might be a student of human nature but it was only incontrovertible evidence that interested bad-tempered judges at murder trials. He would keep his suspicions to himself. It was entirely possible he was being too clever for his own good.

He noticed that Fong was looking at him sceptically. The young man had not yet achieved the confidence necessary to tell the boss that he was chasing windmills with his theories on human nature but he wasn't buying the older man's hypothesis either.

Fong asked tentatively, 'So *who* do you think did it, sir?'

The inspector's lips were pulled back in a parody of a smile. 'That's for me to know and for you to find out! I would hate to colour your judgement with my suspicions.' He continued, 'You can go now, unless there's anything else?' He used the tone of weary resignation that he reserved for subordinates.

Corporal Fong looked embarrassed. 'A partner from Hutchinson & Rice has been trying to contact you, sir. But you had left the office and your mobile was off. He was very *kiasu*, so they put him through to me ...' He trailed off, unknowingly having annoyed the inspector again by using street slang to explain the inquisitiveness of the caller.

Inspector Singh, his interest piqued, asked, 'Who was it? What did he want? Did he confess?'

'No, sir. This partner is from the London office.'

Maria Thompson was on the phone. She was angry. Her voice sounded like shattering glass.

'What do you mean, I must wait? I need the money. It's *my* money!' She paused for breath. 'What does it matter to me if he is killed? *I* did not do it.'

The response at the other end was not to her satisfaction. Her long red nails – expensive acrylic extensions – gripped the phone like the talons of a bird of prey. Her large swollen knuckles – six months of luxury could not easily erase the marks of fifteen years labouring in other people's kitchens – were white with tension. Previously invisible lines appeared around her mouth and fanned out from her eyes.

'I cannot wait!'

She slammed down the phone and glanced at the slim diamond-encrusted wristwatch that Mark had bought her. He had been generous with possessions and keepsakes but not with the cash she needed so badly. And he had watched

59

her like a hawk to ensure that she did not pawn her gifts. She paused to hurl an abusive thought into the ether, wishing it had been possible to direct her insults at Mark while he was still alive. But she had been too dependent on his goodwill and largesse to reveal what she really thought of her wealthy older husband.

It was almost time to set out. Further argument with the insurance people would have to wait. She was not going to risk being late – not for this moment that she had thought of, dreamt of, longed for all the years she had been toiling in Singapore.

She rifled through her clothes in the walk-in wardrobe. Bright-coloured designer labels predominated. Mark Thompson, in the early days of his infatuation with her, had said that she turned his life from a dull black and white film into one of glorious colour. She had immediately adjusted her wardrobe accordingly. If he wanted an iridescent butterfly, she would be that creature and anything else he desired. Maria Thompson had known that another opportunity to escape the general fate of the Filipina diaspora was unlikely to come her way.

She chose a hot-pink pantsuit with wide lapels and a broad belt and spent twenty minutes on her face, erasing every sign of age and care with the help of a cosmetic set bristling with jars, potions and brushes. She peered into a mirror, seeking the woman she had been once, the woman who had left her village outside Manila so many years ago. Finally, she slipped on a pair of high-heeled Jimmy Choo's and climbed into the back seat of a limousine. She barked her command at the driver: 'Changi Airport!'

The young lawyer with the prematurely grey hair sitting across from Singh exuded confidence – the evidence was there in the firm set of an otherwise mobile mouth and the distinctive chin that was thrust forward slightly. He would have been a handsome fellow – almost too good looking if there was such a thing – if it were not for a dent across the bridge of his nose that made him look like a prizefighter who had been in one bout too many. Singh wondered whether it indicated a man who was not afraid of a little violence and then shook his head. David Sheringham had probably walked into a table when he was a toddler – a broken nose was hardly conclusive evidence of an aggressive disposition. Besides, this man had just turned up from London so he wasn't even a suspect. Despite this, the lawyer's insistence that he speak to Singh had stirred his curiosity enough for him to arrange a meeting that evening. Already the policeman was regretting the decision – his home-cooked dinner was growing cold. He dragged his thoughts away from the hollow feeling in his stomach to the matter at hand.

'So you're a partner from London. What are you doing down here, then?'

The lawyer did not seem put out by the question. 'Keeping the firm's reputation intact if possible; helping out with the manpower shortage.'

Singh chuckled suddenly – he had never heard a murder referred to as a manpower shortage before. 'Keep the reputation of the firm intact, eh? Might be difficult as it looks like one of your lawyers bumped off the senior partner!'

The young man grimaced, the expression emphasising the bump on his nose. Perhaps he was like Pinocchio, thought Singh, and it was possible to tell when he was lying.

'I'm still hoping there's some explanation for this key thing.'

'No harm hoping – but I'm relying on the evidence,' said

Singh cheerfully, 'and so far the most likely killer is one of your lot.'

Sheringham nodded pensively.

Singh was pleased that he was not naïve – or bloody minded – enough to deny the obvious. 'In fact, based on the partners' meeting Mark Thompson called just before he was killed, I think this murder had something to do with the firm of Hutchinson & Rice.'

'What do you mean?'

'Maybe one of your lawyers was misbehaving and Mark Thompson found out?'

'Highly unlikely,' insisted Sheringham.

'More unlikely than your senior partner being bludgeoned to death at his desk?'

David Sheringham touched the side of his nose with a long finger to indicate that the inspector had made his point.

'What sort of things was Mark Thompson working on?'

'Not an awful lot ...'

'More queen bee than worker ant, eh?'

Sheringham shrugged.

'Any smoking guns?'

There was a quick shake of the head. 'Not very much would make its way to London anyway.'

The portly inspector was quick to spot the implications of his carefully chosen words. 'Not very much? But something did!'

'It's irrelevant.'

Singh didn't bother to point out that the only thing that was irrelevant was the opinion of the young lawyer. He merely bided his time, chewing on his lower lip as he watched David Sheringham wrestle with the issue.

As he suspected, the partner from London had a practical streak. There was no point denying anything that could be obtained, albeit with more leg work, from another source.

'Mark believed that one of the directors of a Malaysian client company, Trans-Malaya Bhd., an infrastructure development outfit, was insider dealing. He wanted to withdraw from the transaction.' He continued, his voice taking on a pedantic tone, 'Insider dealing is where a party uses information not in the public domain to trade shares and make an illegal personal profit.'

Singh growled, 'I know what insider dealing is – I don't understand why it concerned London.'

'Not all the partners believed that Hutchinson & Rice should withdraw on principle.' David Sheringham ducked his head, his expression sheepish. 'The transaction was a bit of a cash cow.'

'Why didn't you just tell the Malaysian company about the director?'

'You know as well as I do that insider dealing is difficult to prove – perpetrators use third party brokers and numbered accounts to squirrel away the profits ...'

The inspector pondered the new information for a moment. It was difficult to see yet how it could have led to the death of Mark Thompson. Still, it was the first hint of dissent within the ranks of the legal firm. He would have plenty of opportunity to rattle a few cages and see if the lawyers could be persuaded to reveal more secrets.

As if reading his mind, David Sheringham said, 'We would appreciate it if the police conducted their inquiries in the most discreet fashion possible.'

Singh eyed him curiously. 'What's that supposed to mean?'

'It would be better if the interviews were conducted in our offices rather than at the police station. It gives us a chance to avoid those reporters in the foyer.' He gesticulated with his head to indicate the gauntlet he had run trying to get in to see the inspector.

'You must be bloody joking if you think I'm traipsing across to Republic Tower every day just to save your firm some embarrassment.'

'Superintendent Chen has already agreed to my suggestion.' David Sheringham's tone was mild and polite. Singh had to appreciate the fact that he refrained from sounding triumphant despite having lined up the big guns on his side.

The policeman's stomach growled angrily and for once it was an echo of his mood.

Maria Thompson had her face pressed up against the glass wall at the arrival hall of Changi Airport. She scanned the passengers with anxious eyes. She spotted them – two slim, dark-haired children, a boy and a girl, holding hands and looking worried. An airline employee loaded their small suitcase onto a trolley from the revolving baggage carousel and then escorted them towards the green lane exit. Maria moved forward slowly and then with a rush, enfolding them in a fierce embrace. They stood stiffly in her arms for a moment and then found the confidence to return her tight hugs. Tears smeared her make-up but nature stepped in to erase some of the lines of care that had developed in the years since she last saw them.

Six

Singh decided immediately that he disliked the first Mrs Thompson. He knew the type all too well. A middle-aged white woman, spray-on tan, arms and legs toned by personal coaching sessions with wiry male yoga instructors, full lips – Botox probably. He noted the short skirt that exposed the blue ink tracings of varicose veins behind her knees. Her large feet were crammed into a slim pair of sandals, toenails painted a bright red peeping out the ends.

He had insisted that Sarah Thompson come to the police station first thing that Sunday morning. She was still a guest with the Thwaites family and he had no intention of interviewing a suspect while other suspects eavesdropped enthusiastically. His instructions to interview suspects at the law offices presumably only applied to the lawyers. Now, they sat across from each other on the plastic folding chairs that Fong had carried in. Singh did not want to be seated behind his desk when he talked to the woman. He had found over the years that witnesses and suspects found it easier to be economical with the truth to someone behind a big desk.

He glanced up and noticed Fong standing rigidly to attention by the door. The corporal looked poised for action and Singh wondered whether he expected Sarah Thompson to make a dash for freedom in her uncomfortable shoes. He turned his attention back to the woman, noting the faint lines running from her eyes down to her puckered mouth. The tracks of tears – like in that old Smokey Robinson song? This was after all the scorned woman – the question was whether she had lashed out in anger and killed her philandering husband.

'How did you feel about your ex-husband's death?' asked Singh.

'I couldn't be happier that the bastard's dead!'

Singh eyed her thoughtfully. This was strong, intolerant language from a murder suspect. Did her anger run so deep that she could not hide it even in the fraught circumstances of a police interview? Or was she confident that, whatever her feelings, this was not a crime that could be pinned on her? Singh noted that her pale eyebrows were almost invisible, in stark contrast to Maria Thompson's carefully plucked and re-drawn dark eyebrows. So much for the eyes being windows to the soul, thought Singh sourly. He couldn't even get past the eye*brows* of the many wives of Mark Thompson.

'Did you kill him?' The question was blunt and to the point and he saw her jaw clench.

She crossed and uncrossed her legs and Singh caught a glimpse of red panties. He really, really hoped that it hadn't been a misplaced effort at a flirtatious gesture.

Sarah Thompson denied culpability with a quick shake of the head and added pointedly, 'How would I have got into the office?'

Singh scowled. Details of the limited access to the office

66

had leaked into the morning newspapers. And now this woman was using it as an excuse.

'Mark Thompson might have escorted you upstairs.' It sounded lame, even to his own ears.

Sarah guffawed – her tonsils were the same colour as her underwear and toenails. 'Mark was a pathetic excuse for a human being but he wasn't a fool!' Her gaze, as she looked across at him, was calculating and it reminded him of the old moneylenders sitting under trees in his youth, able to determine the credit-worthiness of a client with one glance. She continued, 'And anyway, I have an alibi.'

'Where were you?'

'On a casino ship – far from these sunny shores – with Joan Thwaites.'

Singh wagged an officious finger at his young corporal; that would be easy enough to check. And if it was true, this vengeful, unhappy woman was off the hook.

'Who do *you* think did it then?' he asked, and sensed rather than saw her relief that he appeared to take her alibi at face value.

'Surely that's obvious?'

Singh raised his bushy eyebrows, inviting her to carry on. It was an unnecessary gesture. This woman had been waiting for an opportunity to point the finger of blame and she needed no second invitation.

'That slut! She married him for his money, and she killed him to get her hands on it.'

'I assume you're referring to Maria Thompson?'

'Of course! Who else?' This was her last word on the subject because her red lips closed tight – intensifying the creases around her mouth that gave away her age despite the highlighted blonde hair and expensive face lifts.

Singh escorted Sarah Thompson to the door with all

politeness and then sat down in his cushioned chair. He spun around a couple of times, enjoying the sensation of mild dizziness it prompted until he noted Fong looking at him askance.

Planting his large feet in their spotless white sneakers firmly on the floor, he stopped mid-spin, leaned back comfortably and clasped his fingers over his large belly. 'Hmmm – the ex-Mrs Thompson claims to have an alibi. Pity! Ex-wives always make such good suspects.' He brightened up. 'Unless she's lying, of course.'

'Why would she have waited this long to murder her ex-husband?' asked Fong. 'It's been more than six months since Mark Thompson ran off with Maria.'

Singh pondered the woman who had just left. She was not the first middle-aged woman whose husband had left her for a nubile young Asian beauty. Many men were drawn to the gentle air of submission that characterised so many of these pretty young things. He remembered that his own wife had been quietly domestic for the first few months of their marriage before her natural assertiveness had emerged. The majority of relationships between older white men and young local women ended in tears – the critical question was whether the one between Mark Thompson and his Filipina bride had also ended in death.

'What next, sir?' asked Corporal Fong timidly when Singh didn't respond to his remarks.

'I'm going to go and see that good-looking young woman, Annie Nathan.'

'Would you like me to come along?'

Singh grinned. 'Don't worry – I don't need a chaperon!'

Annie noticed a dark sedan draw up at the front gate. The short yet dignified figure of Inspector Singh emerged from the front passenger seat. He was dressed, as always, in black trousers and a long-sleeved white shirt that was starting to wilt after a long day. He wore his trademark snowy sneakers and had, as before, a breast pocket full of pens. The weight had caused the pocket to sag and a blue stain had developed where a pen had leaked.

The inspector walked over at a leisurely pace, glancing about him at the two-door convertible in the driveway, the black and white colonial-era bungalow and the glint of blue from the pool. Annie felt a stab of guilt at the luxury that her life as an expatriate in Singapore allowed her. She noticed that Singh's trousers were faintly shiny on the thighs and around his ample posterior – it was obviously a well-worn pair. Perhaps Singaporean policemen were poorly paid. Certainly they were unlikely to earn as much as a junior partner at an international law firm. However, Inspector Singh showed no reaction to her home, either of envy or enthusiasm, although Annie did detect evidence of a mild pleasure in the curvature of the plump pinkish lower lip when he accepted her offer of a beer. Apparently he was willing to drink on duty. She got an icy Carlsberg from the fridge and a glass of water for herself. He took a healthy swig, draining a third of the glass immediately.

'I'd like to ask you a few questions,' he said, wiping the froth off his beard with the back of his hand.

'Of course,' said Annie. 'Although I'm not sure how I can help you.'

'An investigation is a process of elimination. All information is useful,' he said ponderously.

'Well, if you eliminate me as a suspect, I'd be delighted.'

He did not respond to this attempt at light-heartedness and it was her turn to have a quick gulp of her drink.

'Tell me about the office.'

'What sort of thing do you want to know?' she asked.

'Anything – the organisational structure, the people.'

'It would be better to get that sort of detail from Stephen Thwaites. He's the most senior person in Singapore, after Mark.'

'I'd like to hear it from you.'

Acquiescing, Annie told him what she could, trying to stick to the facts and keep her opinions to herself. 'There are seven partners – including Mark, that is – twenty-five associates and about thirty staff including all the secretaries and accountants – and the tea lady.'

'And only the partners have keycards that allow access after hours?'

'We felt it was necessary to protect client confidentiality. Others need to be escorted up to the office by the security guards.'

Singh steepled his fingers thoughtfully but made no comment.

'Did anyone sign the visitors' book that evening?' Annie asked.

'No.'

'But you can't think that one of the partners killed Mark. I mean, why would any of us do that?'

'That's what we're trying to find out,' the inspector said.

'What about Mark's key? Did he have it on him?'

'Yes.'

Annie's hope that an outsider might be a viable suspect flared.

'Although Mark wouldn't have let just anyone in, especially if he had just called a meeting of the partnership,' Singh continued.

Annie's crestfallen face reflected her disappointment.

The policeman added, 'The wife and the ex-wife are possibilities, I suppose.'

Annie remembered the last time she had seen Sarah Thompson. Mark Thompson's wife had stormed into the office, crying and shouting – hysterical. Stephen had gone to Sarah, tried to calm her down and, more importantly, quieten her down. Annie, in a meeting with clients, had apologised hurriedly and slipped out of the conference room.

When Mark had finally appeared at the door of his office, Sarah Thompson had attacked her husband, swinging and kicking at him, screaming incoherently. It had taken a few moments for Annie to discern individual words in the abuse. 'You're sleeping with her – my God, you're having an affair with *Maria*.'

Mark had managed to get a grip on his wife's arms, preventing her from hitting him again. The lawyers and staff had been standing around, uncertain what to do, desperately conscious of the clients littering the office.

Annie waited for Mark to deny having an affair. She had no idea whether he was or not but it seemed the prudent thing to do. Instead, Mark had asked, his voice breathless from the physical task of holding his wife at arm's length, 'How did you find out?'

Annie had seen her own dismay reflected on the face of the other lawyers – the office foyer was no place for confessions of adultery.

'How did I find out? How did I find out? She told me! My *maid's* just told me that she's been sleeping with my husband.'

There was a collective gasp as the identity of the mysterious Maria became known. Mark had broken the ultimate taboo of the Singapore expatriate community.

Sarah was sobbing, her shoulders heaving, like a child lost in a supermarket – anger giving way to despair. Mark dragged her into his office and shut the door but snatches of

71

conversation had still been audible. Annie had never liked Sarah, a large-boned, sunbed-tanned woman with a braying laugh and a condescending attitude. But an alcoholic, philandering husband was a high price to pay for an expatriate entitlement complex.

'You should tell me.'

Annie stared at the inspector leaning comfortably back in his chair, hands entwined on his belly. She had a sudden premonition that it was a pose she would see often in the coming weeks.

'I beg your pardon?' she asked.

'You should tell me what you were thinking. From your expression I would deduce that it has a significant bearing on the investigation.'

Annie pressed two hands to her hot cheeks. She was blushing like some character out of a Jane Austen novel. She decided immediately that there was no way she was going to get into the blame game. Let the inspector find out about Mark's infidelities from one of the other partners. She, Annie, would keep her nose clean. In any event, Mark was unlikely to have escorted Sarah up to the office so she was not a credible suspect despite her cast-iron motive.

'Mark *must* have escorted his killer upstairs,' she insisted. 'Nothing else makes sense!'

'It's possible,' agreed Singh. His tone, however, was sceptical.

'What about Quentin's key?' asked Annie, casting around for anything that might distract the policeman from his focus on the partnership.

'What about it?'

'He didn't have it that day. He must have lost it.'

'Mr Holbrooke hasn't mentioned this to me. I'll raise it with him.'

72

'Yes, do ask him,' said Annie insistently. 'That must be the explanation.'

'Why would a stranger coming across a lost key use it to murder your senior partner?'

Annie's optimism that Quentin's lost key would provide a convenient solution evaporated like a rainwater puddle on a sunny Singapore afternoon.

The inspector drained his glass. He stood up, a short figure with a gimlet eye, nodded to Annie and made his way up the driveway. Annie watched him go, noticing how carefully he placed his feet to avoid soiling his pristine sneakers in muddy patches on the gravel. She was uncertain what the visit had been about. She felt rattled. Why had he come? He had asked her for information that he could easily have obtained from any one of the more senior partners. She shook her head and ran a hand through her glossy dark hair. She could not avoid the sensation that his visit had been some sort of test. Had she passed? Or failed?

Annie watched the police car reverse out of her driveway, going over her conversation with the inspector in her head. Then she fetched her mobile phone and rang Quentin.

He picked up at once. 'Hello?' he said, in a tentative voice.

'It's me, Annie.' She automatically tried to sound reassuring.

'Oh! I was expecting the good inspector,' he replied, the relief audible. 'He called me and the line got cut.'

It was Annie's turn to be surprised. 'He rang you? But he's just been here.'

'Why? What did you tell him, what's going on?' Quentin's voice moved up an octave as he barked questions at her.

'Nothing important,' she said, trying to calm her friend. 'I just mentioned that you didn't have your keycard that evening.'

'Jesus Christ, Annie!' Quentin exclaimed. 'I didn't tell him about the key. Now he's going to think I've been lying to him.'

'But why didn't you tell him?'

'Because he would assume that the only reason I would claim to have lost my key would be to create some doubt ... there's no way that some stranger picked up the key and killed Mark. Why the hell would they?'

'You're reading too much into this, Quentin.'

'Don't be so damned naïve!' he snapped and hung up.

Corporal Fong waited patiently in the lift lobby of his apartment tower block. A couple of small children were playing in a corner, kneeling down to roll their marbles. Loud whoops of laughter punctuated their game. Fong glanced up uneasily – flowerpots had been known to fall off balcony ledges, killing unwary people below.

The lift door slid open and he stepped in. A plastic bag of garbage in the corner emitted the rancid smell of garlic and rotting seafood. One of the residents had obviously been too lazy to ride down to dump the rubbish in the skip under the building and had left it neatly in the corner of the lift, hoping someone else would take it out. Fong usually did. Today he couldn't be bothered. He had already spent the whole day dancing to the inspector's tune. He would be damned if he did anyone else's dirty work.

He ran a frustrated hand through his neatly cut black hair, feeling the rigidity of the gelled strands. This was his first assignment and it was a complex case full of political undertones as the privileged expatriate class found itself under investigation. There was plenty of room to shine. Unfortunately, the inspector appeared to believe he was good to shine shoes and not much else.

He had not been near a witness or a crime scene all day. Fong slammed his fist into his palm, an unexpectedly overt display of temper. When he was ordered to join the team investigating the murder of Mark Thompson, his head had been filled with dreams of glory. He had pictured himself nabbing a suspect as he made a desperate attempt to escape. The renowned Inspector Singh would have gripped his hand and pumped it up and down, almost teary with relief that Corporal Fong had saved the day – and his reputation. The reality had been far different. The senior policeman had hardly uttered two words to him. It was not an auspicious start to his career. He almost wished that he had been sent to the airports as a glorified security guard. At least there was less room for humiliation. And now the lard-bucket claimed that he knew who the murderer was, based on "human nature". That was a likely story. He, Fong, would continue to rely on good old-fashioned evidence like fingerprints and CCTV tape, not on a fat man's unreliable understanding of the behaviour of murderers. Not that there was any hard evidence so far; the fingerprints at the scene of the crime were susceptible to a hundred innocent explanations, the searches of the lawyers' residences had turned up squat – no sign of the blood-stained, rolled-up T-shirt of Inspector Singh's fantasies – and they were still waiting for bank statements.

Fong let himself into his home, unlocking the iron grille and the wooden door irritably. It was not as if they had any possessions worth stealing. Home was a tiny two-bedroom subsidised Housing Development Board flat that he shared with his parents. His mother was watching a Cantonese serial on cable television. She guffawed loudly, her carefully primped and curled grey hair askew. She barely acknowledged his entrance.

75

His father lay on a thin mattress on the living room floor. He had been hurt in an industrial accident a couple of years before retirement and was paralysed from the neck down. Corporal Fong saw that the old man had not been moved that day. He went over to him and, smiling reassuringly, turned his father on his side. If he was too long in one position, he developed bed sores. His mother hardly bothered to care for his father these days. Any love she had borne for her husband had long since been destroyed by the enforced intimacy of that living room, where she stared at the television and he stared at the ceiling. She still spoon-fed the old man a thin soup twice a day but from the stains on his mouth and down his chin, even this was done impatiently. Fong sighed and wished once more that he had the money to hire a nurse and move them all into a larger place. As it stood, his small constabulary salary was barely enough to cover the essentials.

Quietly, he sat down next to his father. The old man blinked at him. His head reminded Fong of a newly hatched bird, bald and crinkled, big wet eyes staring at him in quiet misery. He wiped the old man's face with a wet towel and fluffed up his pillows.

Singh gently closed the file that had been waiting for him on his desk when he returned from his interview with Annie. He very much feared that this was not going to be one of those murders solved through the convenient discovery of some incontrovertible piece of evidence. So far, searches of the lawyers' homes had been disappointing. The office computers had yielded nothing of interest, not even the usual downloads of sport and porn – the firm's firewalls were the most effective money could buy and the lawyers had been well protected from their own unsavoury proclivities. It had always been a long shot, but Superintendent Chen would be disappointed.

There was a cursory knock on the door and the superintendent marched in as if summoned telepathically by his thoughts. Singh decided immediately that he would buy himself a steel helmet to replace his turban if that was indeed the case.

'Any developments yet?'

Singh scowled. He ignored the question and instead asked, his tone sharp, 'Why did you agree to hold the interviews at the law offices?'

'To keep the lawyers happy.'

'We're looking for a murderer, not running a babysitting service!'

'And when you find your murderer you can drag him or her back here with my blessing – in the meantime, I want those expats treated with kid gloves.'

Singh's lips formed a thin, stubborn line – he didn't like where this was going.

Superintendent Chen leaned forward, two hands splayed on Singh's desk. 'Let me be crystal clear – I don't want complaints about police tactics circulating in the expat community. There's no point solving this murder if we drive these people away. Do you understand me, Singh?'

The inspector hesitated for a long moment and then nodded, a curt dip of his turban. If he wanted to stay on the case he would have to humour the higher-ups. And he most definitely wanted to stay on the case, not to preserve Singapore's reputation as a safe haven for wealthy foreigners but to find some justice for an unsuspecting old man who had been beaten to death at his desk.

Chen was prepared to appease his subordinate now that he sensed a victory. 'Keep up the good work,' he said in ringing tones, as if he was addressing a parade ground filled with enthusiastic rookies instead of a solitary bad-tempered policeman, and hurried out of the room.

Seven

Annie arrived at the office early; she had lain awake half the night dreading the moment when she would have to step onto the premises again. She was out of bed before the sun had cast its light tendrils into her lush garden, sending the nightjars winging their way to bed and signalling to her cat that it was time to come home after a long night marauding through the neighbourhood.

She was the first to get in. Perhaps the rest had not suffered from her sense of nervous disquiet, she thought, although the last time she had seen the partners – when visiting the widow – they had all been exhibiting various degrees of tension.

Annie felt uneasy in the semi-darkness. She flicked on as many light switches as she could, bathing the office in fluorescent light. She was determined that no corner should remain shadowy and fearsome. After putting her briefcase in her own room, she went to the pantry to get a cup of coffee, and saw Mark's room at the end of the corridor. Memories of Mark washed over her; laughing, officious, dogmatic, drunk. Then – sprawled over his table, red blood staining his white hair like a cheap dye.

She made her way along the corridor. It was as deserted as it had been on the evening of the murder. She wondered whether Mark's office had been cleaned. She doubted that the police cleared up when they were done with their forensic analysis although they had informed the partners that their offices were no longer off-limits despite it having been three short days since the events of Friday. Like everything else in Singapore, efficiency was the paramount consideration. Presumably, however, this speedy approach did not extend to the actual murder inquiry. Inspector Singh, at least, seemed to have a painstaking approach to the investigation.

Annie felt her steps slowing as she approached the door. There was a terrible feeling of déjà vu in her every action. The doorknob to Mark's room was cool to the touch. The hairs on her arm jumped to attention. Annie stood stock still and took a full deep breath. She had to check, convince herself that the events of Friday night had been real.

Mark's room had been cleaned out. The original furniture was still there, but the books and files and other paraphernalia of practice had been cleared away. The contents that had made the office his own – the pictures of his two children building sandcastles on the beach, the still-life paintings that she had always disliked so heartily, even the stationery, including that blood-stained paperweight on his desk – were gone. The carpet bore no trace of blood. She could make out the faint outline where fresh squares of new carpet had replaced the old. Only a hint of disinfectant in the air suggested that the changes to the room were recent, that something as prosaic as hard scrubbing had gone into the transformation.

Her absorption in her surroundings kept her from hearing a firm light tread along the corridor. Someone came up silently behind her and grabbed her arm. Annie gave a convulsive shudder and swung round, lashing out with a closed fist.

Her wrist was caught in a firm grip. 'Who are you?' the man asked sternly. 'What are you doing in here?'

Not answering, Annie stared at the tall stranger, her eyes wide with sudden fright. She tried to pull free and was intimidated by the strength she sensed in the long thin fingers of her captor.

He released her abruptly, leaving Annie rubbing her wrist absently. His fingers had gripped her hard enough to bruise.

He spoke again, more gently this time, as he took in her pale face and expensive, conservative suit. 'This room is off limits. Are you Mark's secretary?'

At this question, Annie recovered some of her equilibrium. She frowned at the man, parallel lines of irritation running along her forehead.

'I think the proper question is, who the hell are you and what are you doing in this office?' She shot out the questions like a machine gun firing on automatic.

'I'm sorry. I should have introduced myself – David Sheringham.' His reply was measured and she noted that his voice was an even tenor, fluid and soothing.

Although she gave no hint of it, Annie recognised his name. David Sheringham was the law firm's troubleshooter. Based in London, he was a partner with a thriving banking practice. He was also always first on the scene if there was trouble in the offing within Hutchinson & Rice. Angry clients, potential litigation, misbehaving partners, any hint of fraud or impropriety – if it affected the firm's interests, David was sent out to solve the problem.

'I didn't know *murder* was within your remit,' Annie said pointedly.

'Only where the suspects include the entire partnership of an office,' he replied. Only a slight curl of thin lips gave away his surprise that she knew who he was.

'So London is concerned that one of us will turn out to be a murderer and has sent you to investigate,' said Annie matter-of-factly.

David shrugged.

Annie was not sure whether he was shrugging off the accusation or acknowledging its accuracy. It was an elegant gesture, and perfectly obfuscatory. A memory of the policeman in charge of the investigation hopped, fully-formed and fat, into her mind. She wondered what the two men would make of each other. Both of them were, in their completely different ways, thoroughly intimidating.

Ching, Annie's excruciatingly cheerful secretary, called out, 'Phone, line two for you.'

Annie picked up the phone as a welcome distraction from her unnerving encounter with David Sheringham. 'Hello, Hutchinson & Rice, Annie Nathan speaking.'

'Annie! I am glad to reach you. I was wondering why I got no feedback from Mr Thompson. Maybe you can tell me?'

The voice was familiar but she couldn't place it. 'I'm afraid I don't know who this is,' she said apologetically.

'Tan Sri. Tan Sri Ibrahim,' the man at the other end replied in his heavy Malay accent.

Tan Sri was an honorary title bestowed in Malaysia. It was a rare honour and indicated that the bearer was a senior figure in political or business circles. Annie recognised the name immediately. It was the Managing Director of

82

Trans-Malaya, the target company in her Malaysian takeover deal.

'Tan Sri! Of course. I'm so sorry – I should have realised it was you.'

The response was cheerful. 'No problem. I'm calling because I haven't heard anything from Mark. I spoke to him last Friday to explain my concerns.'

He paused for a moment while Annie tried to make sense of his rambling tale. 'I wasn't making any accusations, but, you know, certain quarters drew my attention to the problem.' He continued, 'I have been calling his mobile phone. I just got back from Redang. My family and I were away for the weekend. My son is a very keen diver.' The Tan Sri, met with silence from Annie, was becoming garrulous.

Annie found her voice. 'Tan Sri, I'm sorry to have to inform you that Mr Thompson is no longer with us.'

'He's gone back to London?'

'No, I mean Mark's dead!'

'Dead! *Ya' Allah!* When did this happen?'

'Last Friday.'

The old man's voice was filled with genuine regret. 'I didn't mean to cause him stress – although it is a serious matter.'

'I'm afraid that Mark did not have a chance to discuss the issues you raised with me, Tan Sri. Perhaps you could fill me in?'

The Tan Sri hesitated. 'I called him because I thought it would be better to discuss it with a *senior* person at your firm. Is there anyone else who has taken over?'

'I am the most senior person on the file now, Tan Sri,' Annie answered resolutely.

The Tan Sri did not take much convincing. 'You see, my analysts have told me that the share price of Trans-Malaya has been spiking from time to time in the last few months. It has always coincided with some important disclosure about the takeover. Someone has been insider dealing – you know, using his insider knowledge to trade the shares of the company. This is illegal in Malaysia.'

'And most places, Tan Sri,' said Annie automatically, her mind racing.

The Tan Sri had not finished with his revelations. 'Obviously, I was concerned by this,' he said. 'Insider dealing is not unheard of in Malaysia, but I will not have it in my company.'

Annie pictured the Tan Sri – a soft-spoken, elderly man with snowy white hair and a wrinkled brown face – one of "nature's gentlemen". Her first impression that he was an honest man had been correct.

'What did you do, Tan Sri?' asked Annie politely, still unsure where he was going with this lengthy explanation.

'Well, I had my senior staff carefully investigated. There was no sign that they were involved.'

'What are you trying to say, Tan Sri?' A cold fist had wrapped itself around her heart.

'The only other people with the necessary information about the takeover are from Hutchinson & Rice. I think – and I told Mr Thompson – that one of your lawyers is insider dealing, and must have made a lot of money doing so.'

Annie stared at her phone as if it was a hooded cobra poised to strike. The police would be quick to deduce that the insider would have had a cast-iron reason to kill Mark. Annie's mind played over the various possibilities. Each time her thoughts led to the same inevitable conclusion. Inspector Singh would soon discover that there were only two people on the file, aside from Mark, who had access to the information at the root of the insider dealing. Quentin Holbrooke was one of them. She was the other.

Singh sat in a generously proportioned chair at the head of a polished table. An intern in a short skirt walked in with a cup of coffee and a couple of cookies. He decided he liked the quiet, respectful tone the law firm had adopted. He understood now why most of his colleagues preferred dealing with white collar crime. He would wager they were always treated like royalty by suspects. He, Singh, was more accustomed to standing knee deep in a monsoon drain peering at a bloated corpse or looking at the broken body of some domestic worker who had fallen to her death cleaning the external windows of an apartment block.

A door opened and Quentin and Jagdesh walked in. It was clear that they had not expected the policeman to be ensconced in the room. The blood drained from Quentin's face – it reminded Singh of the way he drained the dregs from the bottom of a beer glass. Jagdesh nodded a greeting, a concession to family ties perhaps.

Annie was the next lawyer to make her way into the room. She was pale and her movements were jerky. Singh rested his chin in his palm and gazed at her curiously. This was a different woman from the confident creature who had welcomed him to her house the previous day. Quentin made his way around the table to where Annie was standing and gave her a tight hug which she returned. Singh perked up – was there something between them? Understanding the relationships between suspects was always crucial to a murder investigation. He noticed that David Sheringham, who had slipped into the room while he was staring at Annie, was watching them too, his expression thoughtful.

Reggie and Ai Leen marched in next, breaking off their low conversation as they discovered the other occupants. Ai Leen was dressed in her favourite pastel. Today her shade of choice was a delicate pink. Despite her air of quiet reserve, there was something about the Chinese Singaporean female partner that suggested a tenuous control over her emotions. The veins in her neck were taut and prominent. She clasped and unclasped her hands in her lap as if debating an appeal for relief from some deity.

People took seats round the conference table. Jagdesh and Quentin flanked Annie on one side and Reggie and Ai Leen were on the other. Singh wondered if these were battle lines. He could understand the younger lawyers sticking together. But he was puzzled by the apparent closeness of Ai Leen and Reggie – from what little he had seen of them they did not appear to have anything in common. Singh wrinkled his nose. He had a tendency to read too much into innocuous circumstances at the beginning of an investigation.

Stephen strode into the room with the confidence of a senior partner. The desultory conversation between the lawyers petered out.

'This meeting has been called to discuss the assistance we can provide to the police.' Stephen's deep voice managed to sound threatening.

'We've done all we can. What else do they want?' It was Reggie, quick to anger at the idea of further interaction with the police.

Stephen ignored him. 'Inspector Singh is here to outline what he requires of us. Inspector?'

Singh saw Reggie run his finger around his collar. He suppressed a smirk. It served him right. The lawyer's attitude was appalling, varying as it did between hostility and servility. He knew the type all too well; the expatriate who had become accustomed to being treated with groveling respect by natives of every stripe in Singapore – whether shopkeepers, bank tellers or waiters – and now expected it as his due. Well, Reggie Peters was in for a nasty surprise if he expected

Inspector Singh of the Singapore police to *kowtow* to him.

'As you know, my team and I are currently investigating the murder of Mark Thompson,' began the inspector. 'Death was the result of several blows to the head on Friday between seven and nine p.m. The actual cause of death was either an extensive skull fracture pushing fragments of bone into the brain or internal bleeding between the skull and the dura mater, the membrane covering the brain.'

The inspector paused to let the import of his words sink in. The lawyers were pale – the details of death were too much for them.

'Suspects ...,' Singh rotated his big head a hundred and eighty degrees to take in the full complement of partners, '... would ordinarily be required to present themselves at the police station for questioning.'

Reggie's brow was gleaming with a thin sheen of perspiration despite the cool of the air-conditioned room.

'However, I have been instructed—' the inspector paused. 'I have been asked to conduct this investigation—' again he paused, biting on his plump lower lip, apparently at a loss for the best form of words '—in a more "user-friendly" way. There are a number of reasons for this, one of them being that this case has attracted a great deal of media interest, including the foreign press.'

'Meaning you can't determine the content,' remarked Quentin rudely, referring to the widely held perception that the authorities controlled the Singapore press.

The inspector ignored him and continued. 'So, I am going to hold interviews with the partners at *these* offices.'

'Inspector Singh and his team will commence their interviews this morning,' added Stephen hurriedly, no doubt to discourage his lawyers from making a beeline for the exits.

The inspector rose to his feet by dint of pushing against

the arms of his chair and using the momentum to propel him out of the seat. He looked around the table at the partners, all staring at him with expressions that ranged from sullen fear to anger. He pointed a stubby finger at Annie Nathan and said, 'You're first!'

In his office, Quentin Holbrooke took off his glasses and wiped them carefully with the piece of satin cloth he kept in his desk drawer – he hated it when his vision was clouded with fingerprints or bits of lint. He pulled a tissue from the box on his desk, blew his nose hard and glanced at the mucus – the green slime was streaked with blood. He wiped his nose gingerly. It really hurt.

Stretching his hands out in front of him, Quentin was not surprised to see that both hands were shaking. He really did not feel good this morning – he was out of breath and had a pounding headache. It felt as if some creature had crawled into his ear in the night and was now trying to escape by excavating through his forehead using power tools. What was worse, Stephen Thwaites had just announced that the fat inspector would be arriving shortly to interview them all. He explained the offices had been chosen rather than the police station in a bid to stem the tide of gossip in the tabloids. But it was a move hardly calculated to calm the nerves of the already rattled partners.

Quentin thought about his conversation with Annie about the missing keycard. Panic-stricken about drawing attention to himself for any reason, he had felt a raw surge of pure anger when she mentioned telling the fat policeman about it. In retrospect, it was not a big deal. That policeman, Singh, was not naïve enough to think that he had used such a clumsy method to create the possibility of more suspects. Quentin knew that he had to try and get a grip on his emotions. The one sure way to present himself as a more likely suspect than the others was to behave erratically.

Quentin stretched out a hand to his phone, noticing how slim his wrist had become. He was definitely losing weight – that morning he had buckled his belt a notch further in than before. He picked up the receiver and made a quick call to a mobile number – he knew the number by heart.

'Ya?'

'I need more.'

'How much?'

'As much as you have.'

There was a chuckle on the line. '*Wah*, you really know how to party, man!'

Quentin was not interested in small talk. 'Can you do it?' he snapped.

The Chinaman on the other end was all business. 'No problem, boss. Usual place. Tomorrow – eleven a.m. – make sure you bring cash.'

'You are Anikka Nathan, associate partner at Hutchinson & Rice?'

Annie nodded.

'Please speak your answers for the record,' snapped Singh. The clicking sound of Corporal Fong commencing to type punctuated his remarks.

'I am,' said Annie clearly.

'We are investigating the murder of Mr Mark Thompson. Would you please recount the events leading up to the discovery of the body?'

'But I've told you all that already,' protested Annie.

'We might discover something that was missed previously,' said Singh optimistically. He knew there was no point trying to catch Annie out in a contradiction. She would have fine-tuned her tale in the preliminary interviews on the night of the murder. But Singh never hesitated to make witnesses repeat themselves. Even the overly practised delivery of information might constitute a clue to his sensitive ear. He didn't want his witnesses to recite the facts, he wanted them to paint him a picture – and he was prepared to ask the same questions over and over again until every brushstroke was complete.

'I was in Kuala Lumpur for the day and got back to Singapore that evening.'

'What time did you get home?' he asked.

'About six,' she replied.

'Your flight, SQ 118, landed at 5.15 that evening. That was a fairly quick trip,' the inspector remarked.

He could see from the way that she bit her bottom lip that she was dismayed he had been checking on her movements with such diligence but all she said was, 'I travelled first class and without any check-in luggage.'

'What did you do between the time you got home and when you took the call from Mr Thompson?'

'I had a drink and fell asleep in the easy chair on the verandah.'

'Your phone records show that you received a call from the office at exactly seven in the evening. Between that time and nine p.m. when Quentin Holbrooke found the body, Mark Thompson was murdered. What did you do after you received his call?'

This is it, thought Singh, the moment to produce the alibi. Unsurprisingly, none was forthcoming.

'I drove to the office,' she replied.

'That took an *hour*?'

'Well, I had a shower and watched the eight o'clock news before setting out,' Annie responded, a hint of sarcasm in her voice.

'It is best to be precise in a murder investigation,' said the inspector heavily, ignoring her fit of pique. 'What happened once you got to the office?'

'I bumped into Quentin in the car park.'

'When did he first mention that he had lost his swipe card?'

'He was rummaging in his wallet in the lobby ...'

'Did his actions seem contrived?'

'No,' snapped Annie.

Singh remembered the embrace she had exchanged with Quentin that morning. He wondered whether she was in some sort of relationship with him and that was at the root of her defensiveness. In his experience, protecting lovers was one of the main reasons that witness testimony became unreliable.

'What happened next?' asked Singh, filing away his suspicions for later consideration.

'We went upstairs. Everything seemed normal. I stopped by my office while Quentin went ahead to Mark's room.'

'Wasn't that odd?' demanded Singh.

'What do you mean?'

'You said that it was unusual for a meeting to be called late on a Friday evening, demanding the presence of the partners. Isn't it a bit strange that you, having rushed to the office, should take your time about actually going in to *see* Mr Thompson?'

'What are you suggesting?' asked Annie truculently. A wall of hair fell across her face and she pushed it away. She slipped a scrunchie off her wrist and tied her long dark hair away from her face.

Singh was impressed. This was a witness who did not fear exposing her face, and every expression, to scrutiny. If she was a liar, she was confident that she was an expert.

'I'm asking you why you decided to go to your office instead of going directly to see Mark Thompson?' growled the inspector. His voice had taken on an aggressive tone, a prosecutor now rather than an investigator.

'Hindsight is a wonderful thing,' said Annie angrily.

Singh was pleased to have provoked her.

She continued, 'It seemed a perfectly natural thing to do at the time. I had been out of the office all day in KL.' She shrugged. 'I just wanted to see whether anything had come up during the day – that's all!'

The inspector did not press her. He was satisfied that she was rattled.

'When did *you* realise he was dead?'

'I thought Mark was sleeping – I wondered how he'd slept through Quentin's yells. Then I saw the blood in his hair ... and down the side of his face. His eyes were sort of open and staring.' Annie shuddered.

'Then what happened?'

'Quentin checked for a pulse and confirmed that he was dead.'

'Very cool behaviour,' remarked Singh.

Annie scowled but did not leap to Quentin's defence. Perhaps they weren't in a relationship after all.

'Mr Jagdesh Singh joined you at this point?'

'Yes,' replied Annie. 'We had come out of Mark's room and were trying to decide what to do when he turned up.'

'Was there anything odd in Mr Singh's reaction?'

'No, not really,' Annie said. 'Jagdesh only seems to get worked up over cricket.'

Inspector Singh smiled happily. 'I myself watch cricket. In fact, I used to open the batting for my school in my younger days.'

The inspector noted Annie staring at his portly figure

from across the desk. He supposed it was difficult to imagine him as having once been a sportsman.

He dragged himself back to the present with difficulty. 'Why do you think that Mark Thompson called a meeting of the partners just before someone beat him to death?'

Annie winced at his choice of words but Singh had no qualms about being graphic in his descriptions. He had noticed in the past that even murderers preferred not to be reminded of the colourful details of their crime. It always struck him as oxymoronic that a human being could take the life of another and then feel queasy about a description of death.

'I have no idea,' she insisted.

Singh looked disbelieving. 'Doesn't it seem likely that Mark Thompson discovered something about one of the partners, called a meeting to discuss it, and was killed to keep a secret?'

Annie remained silent. Apparently, she was not going to be provoked into agreeing with a hypothesis that placed any of the lawyers in the firing line.

Singh altered his strategy to take her caginess into account.

'I believe that you are currently working on a Malaysian takeover?'

'Yes.'

'I noticed the deceased was the designated senior partner on the Malaysian deal?'

'Yes, he was,' said Annie. 'That's just a cosmetic exercise, to reassure clients that someone senior is involved. I sometimes find that useful. Being young, a woman and Asian, it's like three strikes and you're out. I have to prove myself to doubtful clients.'

'And to some of your colleagues, I'm sure,' said Singh.

'*You* must know what it's like ...'

'Tell me anyway.'

'I turn up for a meeting and the clients look past me for the "real" lawyers. They never actually say so but for four hundred dollars an hour, they expect a *white* face at least.'

Singh nodded. As a Sikh in Singapore, he had battled the same prejudice against minorities – only his error was not to have been born Chinese. This girl had a chip on her shoulder; she had not been able to keep the bitter edge out of her voice.

'But the firm promoted you to partner anyway?'

'It was an uphill battle!'

Singh was not surprised. In many ways, they were in the same boat – good at their jobs but otherwise square pegs in professions that only valued uniformity.

'Did Mark Thompson play any role at all in this transaction?' the inspector continued. He drummed his fingers on top of the thick file to indicate his subject.

'He attended the kick-off meeting. The senior people at the company, Trans-Malaya, were present as well as a few Government bigwigs. It seemed a good idea to have him along.'

'And was it?'

'Yes. Mark was very good with people.'

'So a client may have approached him directly – gone over your head?'

'I guess so,' she conceded grudgingly.

'*Were* there any issues?'

'Like what?'

'You tell me.'

'No!'

Singh, looking down at the files in front of him, glanced up at this vehemence.

Forewarned and forearmed by David Sheringham he asked, 'What about the insider dealing?'

Her face was bloodless. For a brief moment she looked like the cadaver of Mark Thompson. Her next words were confident, aggressive even, but the slightly unsteady voice reinforced Singh's opinion that she had just received a fright. 'What about it?' she asked.

He said nothing, curious to see what she would say next.

His witness made a quick recovery – she muttered, sounding petulant now, 'I don't see what relevance insider dealing by a Malaysian director has to Mark's death.'

'My dear child, every little bit of information helps us form a picture of the victim. *I* will decide what is important.'

He ignored her grimace at his choice of address and looked at his notes again – were there any loose ends to tie up?

'I see you received a call just before Mark's from an Indonesian number?'

'My Dad rang. He lives in Bali.'

The policeman nodded approvingly. 'You are close?'

'He's all the family I have left.'

'And you called Mark back that evening?'

'Yes, just to find out what the meeting was about. He refused to tell me.'

Singh leaned back in his chair, folded his arms neatly over his belly like an undertaker arranging the limbs of the dead, and barked, 'Fong, I like my coffee milky and sweet!'

Fong returned and placed the mug of coffee at the senior man's elbow. He noted that the inspector had a cigarette clamped between his teeth. He wondered whether he was obliged to remind him that smoking indoors was illegal in Singapore.

Singh took the fag out of his mouth, exhaled a cloud of

white smoke through his nostrils and smiled broadly – a man without a care in the world. 'We can begin the next interview now.'

Cigarettes apparently had a calming effect on the policeman. In the circumstances, Fong decided, it was best to allow him his bad habits.

'Perhaps you would be so good as to fetch Mr Thwaites.'

The corporal, correctly interpreting this as a command despite the polite form of words, leapt to his feet and knocked a sheaf of papers to the floor. He hesitated painfully, unable to decide whether to clear up first or hurry out in search of Stephen Thwaites.

The inspector raised an eyebrow – he might as well have cracked a whip. It certainly had the same effect on the nervous young man, who scurried out of the room.

Fong returned alone a few minutes later.

'Well, where is he?' demanded the inspector.

'He said he would be here in a short while, sir. He was just finishing something.'

'Listen carefully, corporal – we are conducting a murder investigation. No one, I repeat, *no* one keeps me waiting!'

This last shout was still resonating when there was a firm knock on the door and Stephen Thwaites walked in. Although the inspector must have been perfectly audible outside the door, Stephen gave no sign of having heard anything amiss. He ignored the corporal – no surprise there, thought Fong grimly – and stuck his hand out to the inspector. They shook hands briefly.

Stephen apologised for keeping them waiting.

The inspector responded with an elaborate shake of the head – his turban emphasised the gesture by increasing the size of the arc. 'No problem, no problem at all. We understand that you're a busy man. Please sit, sit.'

Singh patted his brow with a large white handkerchief, stubbed out his cigarette on the Malaysian file and carefully placed the half-smoked cigarette back in its carton. He bent over with some difficulty to retie the shoelace on his left white trainer which had come undone. Apparently, he had no qualms about keeping his witnesses waiting while he attended to trivial matters, thought Fong, mildly amused by this petty revenge.

Singh sat up again slowly, his breathing an asthmatic wheeze.

'Fong!' he barked in a peremptory voice and the corporal leapt to his feet again, almost overturning his table as he did so.

'Fetch Mr Thwaites a drink. What will you have? Coffee, tea?' he asked.

'A glass of water would be good.'

'Very well, you heard him,' he said sharply to the corporal, who bolted from the room. Fong wondered whether he should have asked to work at the canteen in the police academy; it would have been more useful training for his current role than anything else he had learnt so painstakingly.

'Our job is similar in many ways,' he heard the inspector say as he headed out of the office. 'We both have to nurture and guide the young.'

'True, true,' said Stephen, who appeared determined to match the inspector's theatrical bonhomie.

Fong gritted his teeth and almost slammed the door but managed to desist at the last moment. His was the lowest rank in the force but his stout superior would probably find a way to demote him if he showed any attitude. He came back in with a glass of water that he placed carefully in front of Stephen. He had professionally wrapped the glass in a serviette so that the condensing moisture would not bother the drinker.

'We can begin whenever you're ready,' Stephen said.

'No particular hurry,' said the inspector. 'No one is going to run away, eh? Not while I have your passports, anyway.'

His hearty guffaw was met with a weak smile from Stephen Thwaites.

The inspector waved the corporal to his seat and turned to Stephen. 'I understand that your wife and the first Mrs Thompson are good friends?'

Taken aback by the line of questioning, Stephen could not help fidgeting in his chair. His authority dissipated and he became an errant schoolboy across the table from a head-master.

'I'm not sure how that's relevant,' he murmured.

'We'll let me be the judge of that, shall we?' insisted the inspector, still all smiling politeness and visible teeth, but now predatory.

'Yes, they're good friends.'

'I imagine both of you had a lot of sympathy for Sarah Thompson, the wronged wife. Hell hath no fury, eh?' Singh chuckled and his belly vibrated an accompaniment.

Stephen remained silent.

'In fact, you were a good friend of Mark's?'

Fong could almost see the wheels turning as Stephen wondered whether he should deny a close relationship. The lawyer did not see any particular trap, or perhaps an innate loyalty and honesty made him say, 'Well, yes. We were the two senior people in the office and had a lot in common, plus our wives – well, my wife and his ex-wife – got along.'

'But you did not always have your wives along, eh, when you were together?' said the inspector, winking elaborately at Stephen, who appeared bemused and a little worried.

The lawyer twisted a bulky gold signet ring on his little finger and asked, 'What's that supposed to mean?'

'I believe,' Singh made a show of consulting his notes, 'you were picked up with Mr Thompson two months ago at a Balestier Road *brothel*?'

Eight

Balestier Road – a seedy street of mostly dilapidated old shophouses selling chicken rice and *bah kut teh*, a medicinal-tasting pork belly soup – was notorious for its hotels that charged by the hour. There was no reason Singh could think of for either Mark or Stephen to be at one, except for the obvious.

Stephen opted for blank denial. 'It's not true,' he said, folding his arms to convey certainty.

'Come, come, Mr Thwaites. We are both men of the world. There is no doubt at all that you and Mr Thompson were arrested and subsequently released without charge. Your positions in the expat community and the fact that you were not caught, how shall I put it, *in flagrante delicto*, kept you out of prison. But the Singapore police maintain very good records,' he continued and grinned meaningfully at the lawyer.

Stephen's gaze found its way to the floor, unable to meet the accusing eyes of the inspector.

'You must agree that your presence there requires

explanation.' The inspector leaned back in his chair, completely relaxed and confident that he had the upper hand.

Singh knew very well that visiting businessmen of a certain type thought a stopover at an Orchard Towers bar or club followed by an assignation in Joo Chiat Road or Balestier Road a must in Singapore. After-hours trips to sordid joints peddling sex were an integral part of business in South East Asia, whether it was the notorious bars in Pat Phong in Bangkok with its sex shows and brothels or the equally unpleasant but less well known strips in Kuala Lumpur or Jakarta.

'Mr Thompson had been married again for just a few months. He seems to have strayed very soon. And what about you? How many years of marriage has it been?' asked Singh.

'Thirty-five!'

'Domestic troubles?'

'It's really none of your business, Inspector,' grumbled Stephen.

Singh slammed his fist down on the table and everyone in the room jumped. 'That's where you're wrong, Mr Thwaites. In a murder investigation, *everything* is my business, whether in the boardroom *or* the bedroom.'

'But how could this have a bearing on Mark's murder?' asked Stephen, his tone almost pleading.

'I don't know yet,' confessed the inspector. 'Maybe he was blackmailing you over this incident and you decided to kill him?'

'That didn't happen!' cried Stephen. Damp patches were showing through his blue shirt now, crescents of sweat at his armpits. Singh smiled. Only experienced crooks knew not to wear blue shirts to a police interview.

101

'I'm inclined to believe you,' said the inspector unexpectedly. 'But you need to tell me the truth. Otherwise, I'll have to question your wife about the state of your marriage.'

Stephen's expression was one of disbelief. 'You wouldn't do that, would you?'

Singh raised an eloquent eyebrow.

Stephen sat upright in his chair and his hand went to his throat to straighten his tie. His gravelly voice steadied. 'I'd hoped to protect Mark but you leave me no choice,' he said. 'Mark invited me out. I could tell from his voice that he'd been drinking heavily. If you don't know yet, Inspector, Mark was an alcoholic. I decided to join him and try to get him home. I didn't want any scenes in public which would embarrass the law firm. Besides, he was my friend.' Stephen sighed. 'I was frankly surprised to receive the call from him. My wife refused to acknowledge Maria, which curtailed my association with Mark.' He continued, 'When I met him that evening, he said he'd been receiving anonymous letters saying Maria was moonlighting as a prostitute.'

Inspector Singh's ears pricked up at the mention of letters. 'Did he show them to you?'

'No, I'm not even certain they *existed* in the first place. It could just have been an excuse for his suspicions.'

'Why would he suspect her of something like that?'

'I'm sure I don't have to tell you, Inspector, it's not unknown for foreign workers in Singapore to get involved in that racket. They're mostly here for the money with large families back home to support.'

'But why would she continue after marriage to a wealthy man?'

'That was one of the arguments I put to Mark. He seemed to think she might still need money, I don't know why.'

'Hmmm,' said the inspector. 'It should be possible to find

out.' He turned to Corporal Fong. 'Make a note of that,' he urged.

Stephen continued his narrative, his voice steady and low. 'Mark dragged me to a bar in Orchard Towers ...'

Singh listened intently as a senior partner of a reputable law firm tried to explain how he had found himself hunting for Mark's wife in a place notorious for its sleazy bars and discos.

He could almost picture them as they weaved their way between tables and onto the dance floor. The strobe lighting, bodies gyrating and the smell of cheap perfume must have been overwhelming.

'I tried to keep up with Mark. He was swaying on his feet. He kept grabbing young women by the arm, forcing them to look at him, trying to identify Maria.'

There was a silence in the room. Stephen cleared his throat and continued, 'A group of Filipino men became aggressive. I had to drag Mark away. I begged him to go home. But he took it into his head that he was going to Balestier Road to hunt for Maria in those cheap rent-by-the-hour motels. I did my best to persuade him not to. I had these horrible mental pictures of him bursting in on half our clients and accusing them of using his wife as a prostitute!'

Singh felt a sudden desire to laugh. The tale would be farcical if it did not contain the roots of tragedy.

Stephen rubbed his eyes tiredly with a thumb and forefinger. 'In the end I went with him. I thought I might be able to stop him getting hurt.'

'What happened?' asked the inspector.

'Mark could barely walk in a straight line. I suggested to him that he wait while I had a look around. He refused. We were still in the middle of an argument when the police raided the place and arrested us. I think you know the rest.'

'So you never did find out if she was there?'

'Of course she wasn't,' said Stephen. 'It was just a fit of drunken jealousy.'

'A pretty extreme case,' remarked the inspector.

'That would only be relevant if the corpse was Maria's!'

The inspector collapsed in his chair as if the revelations were too heavy a burden for his burly shoulders. The break-up of Mark's marriage must have appalled everyone. Conventional wisdom – as articulated by Sarah Thompson and his own wife – was that Maria had married Mark for his money and the marriage would not see the year out. The reality was even more sordid. However unacceptable Mark's behaviour had been, having an affair with his domestic help, getting caught by his wife and then marrying Maria – it was this last point which had really electrified audiences – Singh felt sorry for the way things had turned out. He shook his head. He must be getting soft in the head, feeling pity for a wealthy, successful man who had married a beautiful woman.

'Let's turn to the murder, Mr Thwaites,' said the inspector. 'Where were you on the evening of Mr Thompson's death?'

'I am afraid I don't have a very convincing alibi.'

The inspector waited placidly for him to continue, making no comment.

'I popped into the office briefly in the morning but then went over to Bintan—' Stephen mentioned a popular Indonesian island resort not far from Singapore '—for a round of golf with a client. We played nine holes and were rained off. I had a couple of beers with him and took the ferry back. The crossing was choppy and I'm not a great sailor. I switched off my mobile phone, climbed into bed and slept soundly. The next morning, I found a message from Mark ordering me to the meeting. I had missed it. A short while later, Jagdesh Singh called me with the news.'

'So you were *asleep* during the murder?' asked Inspector Singh, a disbelieving note creeping into his voice.

'That's my story, I'm afraid.'

'Can anyone vouch for you being home?' asked the Inspector impatiently. 'Wife, children, maid? *Someone* must have seen you.'

'My wife was away that evening on one of those overnight casino cruise ships, with Sarah Thompson, if you must know. The help had the day off and the children are away at university,' explained Stephen.

'Pity you're not having an affair with the maid, eh?' remarked Inspector Singh.

Singh was pleased to have a second interview under his belt – figuratively speaking. He ran a thumb along the band of his trousers, trying to make himself more comfortable – there was certainly no space under his belt literally. He turned to Fong. 'Well, there's no time to waste. Let's see the Indian. And tell David Sheringham I want to see him next,' he added, as Fong reached the door.

Corporal Fong hurried out to summon Jagdesh Singh and in a few moments the tall Sikh was in the room greeting them in his distinct musical accent. 'My turn for the third degree? That's all right ... I haven't got anything to hide. So you're welcome to trot out the thumbscrews – it won't make any difference.'

There was no response to his jovial remarks. Singh stared at his relative with genuine interest. He noted that the teeth of his witness were shiny and even. The policeman ran his tongue over his own teeth – they were not in such pristine condition. He doubted that corrective dental work was that advanced in Delhi. The inspector had heard of medical

105

tourism. Apparently, this young fellow had the financial clout to be a dental tourist. He wondered once more why his wife had been assigned to find Jagdesh Singh a bride. He would bet his beer money that the combination of good looks and deep pockets that the fates had bestowed on Jagdesh Singh would have had the women flocking around.

'I guess this is no joking matter. Ignore me ... I just get like this when I'm nervous!' Jagdesh spoke again, unnerved by Singh's thoughtful contemplation.

'There is nothing for you to be nervous about, Mr Singh, unless you killed Mark Thompson.'

Here the inspector stopped and looked at Jagdesh inquiringly as if to give him an opportunity to confess. Unsurprisingly, his young relative by marriage eschewed the opportunity to put his head in a noose. Just as well, thought Singh. He certainly hoped this young fellow was not the killer. He shuddered to think what his home life would be like if he was forced to arrest the Sikh partner. Domestic bliss it would *not* be, thought Singh, wincing at the mental image of his wife and her sisters on the warpath. He dragged himself back to the matter at hand with difficulty and noticed that his countryman was looking at him quizzically. That would never do – he did not want rumours of incompetence to seep through the gossipy Sikh community in Singapore. It was time to focus on the nuts and bolts of the investigation. He hurriedly ran through his list of questions and received the stock answers.

Jagdesh did not have a relationship of any sort with Mark Thompson that extended beyond the workplace. Unlike Stephen Thwaites, he would not characterise Mark as a friend. 'More of a colleague,' he explained.

He did not have an alibi for the couple of hours before the meeting. He had been on the verge of leaving for dinner at the Singh residence when he had received Mark's call, hence his belated telephoned apologies and no-show.

'A pity you didn't visit as planned,' was Singh's wry comment. 'My wife would have been an unimpeachable alibi.'

'I certainly wish I had come along for dinner, sir. I hear that Mrs Singh is a magnificent cook.'

Singh glared at the lawyer to indicate that he was not going to embark on some family-style gossip with him. If Jagdesh was trying to form a bond based on their tenuous family links, he, Singh, was not having any of it. It was bad enough that he was already hoping to exonerate this man purely on the grounds that he feared his wife's ire at any other conclusion.

It was time to cut to the chase. 'So who killed your boss?'

Jagdesh pinched the bridge of his nose between two fingers, the action of a man who could feel a headache coming on. Singh noted that there were food spots on his tie. They might only be related by marriage and have nothing in common physically but they did seem to share a common genetic heritage when it came to being messy eaters.

'I can't believe it was one of the partners,' said Jagdesh. His tone was quiet and reasonable. It reminded Singh that this man was a highly successful lawyer – it would not do to underestimate him or treat him as a mildly comic figure just because Mrs Singh had been tasked with finding him a wife. After all, he himself was regularly underestimated on the grounds solely of his beer belly and fancy headgear.

The inspector's response to Jagdesh's doubt was aggressive. 'Really? I have no difficulty at all believing that one of you lawyers is a murderer. The only question in my mind is *which* one of you did it!'

Jagdesh stared at the policeman. Singh noticed for the

first time that the whites around his dark brown pupils were now shot through with faint red veins. Dusky shadows formed crescents under his eyes.

Despite his calm tone, this was a man who was feeling the pressure. But was it the understandable pressure of a man unwittingly and innocently caught up in a murder investigation or was there a more sinister reason?

'Mark Thompson called a meeting of the partners. Before it could be held, he was killed. Difficult to avoid the conclusion that he was murdered to avoid revealing something, a secret that one of you lawyers was prepared to go to any lengths to hide.'

Jagdesh's hand went to his throat, and then, as if he belatedly realised it was a telling gesture, he dropped it back onto the arm of the chair.

'Well, do you agree?' demanded Singh argumentatively.

'I have nothing to hide!' insisted Jagdesh. But his gaze found his lap as he said it and he would not meet the policeman's eyes.

If it bothered David Sheringham that he was using Mark Thompson's old office, he gave no sign of it. Singh wandered around the room, sniffing the air like a curious dog. He could smell disinfectant but not even his broad nose, trained over the years to recognise the scent of blood, could pick up any hint of the murder.

'So, Mark Thompson was an alcoholic?'

David smiled thinly. 'I see that none of our secrets are safe from you, Inspector.'

'Keeping secrets is tantamount to obstructing me in the course of my investigations. I'm sure I don't have to tell you that's a crime.'

David raised an elegant shoulder. The gesture was rueful.

'I didn't want to blacken Mark's name unnecessarily.'

He sounded as if he meant it, thought Singh. Was it possible that this partner who had flown in from London was actually quite a decent chap? The fat man's thoughts turned to Ai Leen and Reggie – it seemed unlikely if Sheringham's colleagues were anything to go by.

'He was lying right there – sprawled across the desk. Blood everywhere!' Singh pointed at the desk where David sat leaning on his elbows.

The younger man's face blanched white under his tan. He was not as immune to his surroundings as he would like to pretend. 'Must you remind me?' He removed his arms from the desk as if he expected them to be stained with another man's blood.

Singh's retort was sharp and to the point. 'You need to know that protecting a dead man's reputation is *exactly* the same thing as protecting that man's killer.'

David Sheringham nodded slowly.

His close-cropped grey hair made him look older, thought Singh, but he was probably in his mid-thirties. He was nobody's fool if he was a trusted senior partner at an international legal firm at such a young age. The question was whether he was going to use his talents to assist or impede the investigation. So far Sheringham had been reasonably helpful – revealing the insider dealing on the Malaysian file even if he had waited to be prompted before doing so. On the other hand, his machinations – with the collusion of Superintendent Chen – were the reason that he, Singh, had to conduct large chunks of the investigation in the suspects' lair instead of the more intimidating surroundings of a police station.

'What do you want to know?' asked Sheringham.

'Why did you keep Mark around? He must have been more of a liability than anything else.'

'These old firms have a very traditional partnership structure. It's actually quite difficult to get rid of someone who doesn't want to leave.'

'And Mark Thompson didn't want to leave?'

'Who would? The money, the status ... it's a lot to give up. I don't think Mark was even ready to admit that he had a drink problem.'

'Was he standing in anyone's way?'

Two vertical frown lines appeared in the middle of David's forehead. 'What do you mean?'

'The next most senior partner is Stephen Thwaites, right?'

'You're asking me if Stephen might have killed Mark?'

'"*Vaulting ambition, which o'erleaps itself?*"' declaimed Singh theatrically.

David shook his head emphatically. 'No way. He was Mark's friend, and one of his last supporters amongst the senior partnership.'

Corporal Fong had been sent to fetch the car because Inspector Singh did not deign to make the trip to the basement car park. It did not surprise him. The fat man – he reminded Fong of those many-layered Russian dolls – did not look like someone who opted for long, or even short, walks.

Apart from being used as tea boy, Fong had found it an interesting day so far, although he really didn't know what to make of Inspector Singh's methods. There had been nothing in the police academy about his style of questioning. Fong had been taught to work through the evidence methodically whereas Singh flitted about like a butterfly in a meadow of flowers. Still, he had the lawyers off balance. Producing the brothel visit had been a masterpiece. Stephen Thwaites' face had been a picture. He, Fong, had not even known about the incident. At this thought, he frowned. Whatever his view of the boss might be, the boss had far too low an opinion of him to share vital information. Fong was the bag carrier, driver and coffee maker, nothing more.

A few moments later, he drew up in front of the gleaming building in the unmarked police car. Singh was waiting for him, a squat, brooding figure. Even from a distance it was possible to discern his impatience. The evidence was there in the tapping foot and the folded arms.

However, when the boss clambered into the car, he seemed in a delighted mood. 'Well, well, well,' he said to his sidekick. 'That was very interesting, eh? We make progress!'

He rubbed his pudgy hands together like a cartoon villain.

Fong had to remind himself that Inspector Singh was one of the good guys.

'What's the plan now, sir?'

'We follow up some leads. And I need to interview Maria Thompson.'

Fong's curiosity overcame his reluctance to expose himself to one of the inspector's biting put-downs. 'What sort of leads, sir?'

Inspector Singh hesitated, chewing on his plump bottom lip as if debating whether to share his thoughts with the young policeman. At last he said, 'You tell me – what do you think we should do next?'

Fong wondered whether the undertone of impatience he detected was merely his paranoia working overtime. Either way, this was a chance to actually contribute to the investigation. 'We need to find out why Mark Thompson thought his second wife needed money and search for the anonymous letter – if it really existed …'

If Singh was impressed, he did not show it. He stared out of the window pensively, elbow on the door ledge, chin in his hand.

'So Mark Thompson was an alcoholic ...' he said thoughtfully, 'who thought that his trophy bride was still working the night shift. Stephen Thwaites did *not* want Thompson's job and was trying to be his friend. Anikka Nathan did not mention the insider dealing until I brought it up and Jagdesh Singh becomes very nervous indeed on the subject of lawyers with secrets. Curiouser and curiouser!'

Above them, the sky was almost black, even though it was still early in the day. The storm that had been gathering announced its arrival with a thunderous clap. A moment later, the rain was sheeting down. Fong switched the wipers on at maximum speed. He would be better off with a pair of oars, he thought, as the tyres skidded gently on the running water.

Singh slapped a hand against his thigh triumphantly.

'What is it, sir?'

'I'll ask my wife to find out what Jagdesh Singh is hiding! If she can't ferret out the information, no one can.'

Fong refrained from commenting on the inspector's plan to draft his wife into action. He already had one sidekick whose primary duty seemed to be to wait on him hand and foot – did he really need another?

Determined to contribute to the discussion, he said, 'There's the widow as well, sir.'

'Do *you* think Maria Thompson did it?'

'She's definitely the most likely person so far,' he responded carefully. 'She had motive *and* opportunity.'

Singh scowled. He rubbed the window with his shirt sleeve – the rain outside and the air-conditioning inside had caused the glass to fog over.

'Well, I certainly hope she isn't our murderer ...'

'Why is that, sir?'

'It would make those partners far too happy.' He

112

snorted loudly. 'Firm of lawyers, eh? More like a school of villainy ...'

Fong ignored this unexpected diatribe. He asked, 'Back to the station, sir?'

Singh glanced at the corporal. Fong adopted an expression of artificial determination to mask his nervousness.

'Yes, take me to the station,' he said. And to Fong's delight, he added, 'And then go and see Mrs Stephen Thwaites. Check on the ex-Mrs Thompson's alibi.'

Annie strode down the corridor towards her office, replenished coffee mug in hand. She massaged the back of her neck with strong fingers as she walked. The strain of the earlier interview had left her head and neck aching with tension. The secretaries, whose desks lined the walls, turned in unison to stare at her and then hastily busied themselves. A brief lull in the wild speculation going on in the passageway, she suspected. 'Is there any news? Do they know who did it?' The strident whisper was from a senior secretary, Yoke Lin, a buxom woman in heavy make-up and a tight-fitting floral dress. Everyone within earshot gave up the pretence of work to listen.

Annie shook her head. 'No, no developments yet.' She gave them a quick smile to show that she was not evading the question but telling the simple truth.

The dark clouds that had been gathering so ominously on the horizon unleashed their full might over Republic Tower. Rain lashed against the reinforced glass. It appeared as if someone was chucking buckets of water at the window; individual drops were all but indistinguishable. From time to time, the sky was lit up with sheets of lightning. It was so dark outside, night might have fallen. Annie stopped to admire the ferocity of the storm.

'It's amazing, the sheer power of storms in this part of the world. In England, we get so used to icy pinpricks of rain all day. It won't be fun trying to get a taxi in this weather!'

David Sheringham was standing at Annie's elbow – he appeared to have a knack of creeping up on her unawares. She nodded at him, acknowledging the friendly overture but still cautious. This was the spy from head office. Everyone in the office was kowtowing to him already, but she was not so easily convinced of his good intentions. Having made up her mind resolutely on these points, Annie heard herself asking, 'Where are you staying? I can give you a lift if you like.'

'That would be wonderful,' he replied enthusiastically. Light and shadow played across his face as another multi-pronged jagged fork of lightning cleaved the air. 'I'm at the Raffles. Is that on your way?'

Annie raised an eyebrow at him. There was no stinting on the expense account if he was staying at Singapore's luxurious Raffles Hotel.

He correctly interpreted the look and grinned. 'There must be some perks in a job that involves going round offices accusing your colleagues of murder.'

Annie shrugged. He was right. Hutchinson & Rice could afford it anyway. 'I'll meet you in ten minutes in the lobby.'

She ran a further gauntlet of secretarial stares and collapsed into her chair. Her workplace was clean and bare and functional, the only personal belongings a green-leafed potted plant and a small photo of her mother, a bubbly Caucasian woman, smiling broadly for the camera. Her mother had died when she was eleven – leaving Annie alone in the world except for her father. It seemed so long ago that he'd asked her for more money – money that she'd transferred to him just that morning. She knew that he would have no more need of her until his next financial crisis. Annie shook herself like a dog after a rain shower; this was not the time to be brooding about her father's iniquities. She gave herself a stern mental warning to avoid letting self-pity overthrow her judgement altogether. She had to believe she would put this episode behind her. And to ensure such an outcome she needed all her wits about her.

Looking at the time, she realised that she was late to meet David. She turned off her computer, grabbed her things and headed down to reception.

'Sorry,' she said breathlessly as she reached the lobby and found him waiting patiently.

'No problem.'

'Let's go! Before we get stuck in traffic.'

'There speaks someone who's forgotten how lucky they are to work in Singapore,' said David as they stepped into the lift lobby.

'What do you mean?' asked Annie.

'That there's hardly any traffic, not even during rush hour.'

'Quite true, although rain and rush hour combined do cause a few hiccups.'

The lift arrived and the doors slid open silently. Ai Leen stepped out. There was a tension about her that was reflected in her tired face and dour expression. She walked past them without a word or a backward glance.

David put a hand out and the sensors stopped the elevator doors despite the occupants jabbing aggressively at the "close" buttons. As he ushered Annie in before him, they both ignored the scowls of the people inside. The occupants of Republic Tower did not appreciate waiting.

Annie could see, gazing at their reflection in the lift doors, that she barely reached up to David's shoulder. She was pleased at an opportunity to study him discreetly. He was just over six feet tall, loose-limbed and clean-shaven. His eyes were very dark, probably grey, under winged brows that were delicate enough to be feminine. His hair was liberally sprinkled with premature grey, and cut aggressively close to a well-shaped head. He was a distinguished-looking man, except for the prize-fighter's nose.

As Annie pulled out of the car park, the heavy rain drummed down on the soft roof of the convertible. It was impossible to speak above the rain and the intermittent claps of thunder, so she concentrated hard on driving, trying to make out the other cars on the road, their rear lights barely discernible. Minutes later, Annie turned into the gravel drive of the Raffles Hotel, a beautiful white structure with long bay windows, surrounded by palms and flowering plants.

'Why don't you come in for a coffee at the Tiffin Room?' asked David, as she pulled up in front of the building.

'Sounds too good to refuse,' said Annie, making up her mind quickly.

At the entrance, a massive Punjabi man, resplendent in a gold-braided white uniform with shiny buttons and a turban, unfurled a massive golf umbrella and held it over Annie's door. She got out and handed the keys to him as he escorted her to the terrace. David, not waiting for similar treatment, joined her, brushing the drops of rain off his jacket and running his fingers through his glistening wet hair.

In the lobby, Annie stopped as she always did to admire the polished old wood, thick carpets and gleaming chandeliers. A sparrow flew a circuit around the hall, chirping merrily at the visitors. A couple of backpackers behind her were turned away because they were dressed in shorts and sandals. David, who was either inured to the splendour or hungry, was already at the entrance to the Tiffin Room. They were shown to a quiet table by a window.

Immediately, David's eyes turned towards the food on display. 'I was planning a trip to the gym but I think I'm going to have a late lunch instead. Join me?'

'I might just have a cup of tea and some dessert,' said Annie.

David ordered a pot of tea while Annie loitered around the buffet table, raising covers one by one. She walked back to the table, a heaped plate in one hand, sat down and accepted a cup of tea from the waiter, adding a generous dollop of milk and sugar.

David peered at her plate. 'Good God!' he exclaimed. 'What *is* that?'

Annie smiled warmly at him, dimples showing.

'I'm all Asian when it comes to food!'

Her plate was heaped with brightly coloured desserts, pink and white stripes, green slices, a bright orange sliver, yellow bits, in all shapes and sizes – squares, rolls, triangles and balls.

'What is that stuff made with?' he asked. 'Some of the colours look toxic!'

'To be frank, I'm not sure,' she said. 'Coconut, *pandan*, *durian*, water chestnuts, corn and who knows what else.'

'*Durian!* A fruit that proves the non-existence of God.'

'The *durian* is the King of Fruit!' exclaimed Annie, defending the watermelon-sized fruit with the dangerous spiky exterior, rich yellow flesh and extraordinary odour.

'I've heard it's like eating apple pie on a bog.'

Annie laughed. 'Are you aware that gravity was discovered by a Malay farmer long before Newton? Unfortunately, he was sitting under a durian tree.'

She stopped mid-sentence and stared over her companion's shoulder. Curious, he turned to follow her gaze. A sleek, distinctive woman with long straight hair to her waist, heavy make-up, conspicuously expensive clothes and chunky jewellery was standing at the entrance holding two children by the hand.

'The second Mrs Mark Thompson,' Annie whispered.

Mrs Thwaites had agreed to see Corporal Fong after lunch, at the Thwaites' residence on the tree-lined avenue that was Nassim Road. It was an amazing palatial building, at least four storeys high, the size of a small condominium. The architect had opted for grey walls and towering sheets of glass – it reminded Fong of a rich country's embassy. A board on the front gate warned visitors that dogs were on the loose. The corporal pricked up his ears. He thought he could make out the sound of barking. He rang the doorbell nervously, hoping someone would come out to meet him rather than open the gate remotely and expose him to the ire of the dogs.

The woman who came to the gate surprised him. He was primed, after encountering Sarah Thompson and hearing about Maria Thompson, to expect a certain profile from the partners' wives but Joan Thwaites was frumpy and middle-aged. Her wispy hair was greying in patches. She wore an unfashionable blouse with small floral patterns and an unflattering pair of jeans that clung to an over-sized posterior and tapered to narrow ankles. She clutched a small dachshund – some sort of miniature breed, Fong suspected – under her arm like a rugby ball. 'May I help you?' she asked politely.

Fong pulled himself together. He needed to avoid having his pre-conceptions colour his judgement if he was to make any headway as an investigator. 'I'm Corporal Fong of the Singapore Police. I rang. I need to ask you some questions about Mark Thompson.'

'Oh my! That was shocking, wasn't it? Well, do come in and have a cup of tea.'

The dog wagged its tail.

Fong followed Joan Thwaites into the house, noting the marble floors and massive modern art pieces on the walls. Rarely had he seen a woman in such inappropriate surroundings. She led him directly into the kitchen and made him a mug of English Breakfast tea with her own hands despite the maid hovering anxiously in the background.

'So how can I help?' she asked again, when he was comfortably perched on a stool at the small kitchen table.

'Sarah Thompson told us that you were with her on the night of the murder.'

Joan Thwaites nodded her head emphatically. 'Yes, I was.'

Nine

Singh was behind his big desk looking through the bank statements and credit card bills of the various lawyers. He could feel a headache developing at the mere sight of the six-figure bank balances; seven figures in the case of Stephen Thwaites and Reggie Peters.

His mobile rang. 'Yes?'

'It's Fong, sir. I've just been to see Mrs Thwaites. She confirms Sarah Thompson's alibi. They were on some sort of overnight gambling cruise ship.'

'OK – good work.'

He could sense the corporal's pleasure at a kind word. He hoped Fong wasn't going to get cocky, and careless. 'Get back here and write up your report!'

'Yessir,' said Fong, the lilt in his voice still present.

Singh returned to the bank statements. Despite their initial reluctance, the lawyers had apparently turned them in voluntarily – under pressure from David Sheringham, he suspected. If there had been financial hanky-panky at the legal firm, chances were slim that the lawyer in question would have used his or her personal checking account. On the other hand, Mark's murder had been brutal but was unlikely to have been premeditated. There would have been no time for the murderer to think through the consequences of a police investigation and the possible evidentiary trails.

The credit card statements were like a narrative of the lifestyle of the rich and powerful, thought Singh glumly. It was *The Great Gatsby* for the twenty-first century: golf games, expensive wines, hotel rooms, first class flights and, in the case of Ai Leen, an enormous amount of Tiffany jewellery.

Singh turned to Annie's bank statement. She had transferred money on a semi-regular basis to an Indonesian account – her dad's, he supposed. He'd get Fong to check. It seemed that they really were close if she was funding his retirement with such large handouts. Singh shook his great head. He had no children. He and his wife would have to survive on his pension. Fortunately, Mrs Singh was frugal to the point of mean and he himself had no expensive habits except for cigarettes and beer. He shuddered. Perhaps he would have to become teetotal to make ends meet in his twilight years.

There was a timid knock on the door.

'Enter!' snapped Singh.

Sergeant Fuad sidled in nervously and stood just inside the door. The inspector almost smiled. It was really quite amusing the way these junior uniforms were terrified of him.

'What do you want?'

'It's about Mark Thompson's will, sir.'

Singh nodded impatiently.

'All the money goes into a trust fund for his children. His ex-wife received a lump sum payment after the divorce.'

'Maria Thompson gets *nothing*?'

'Nothing under the will, sir. But she's the sole beneficiary of a life insurance policy for one million dollars!'

'Would you call that a good motive, Sergeant?'

'Yes, sir, I think so.'

'Me too!'

So what was he to make of Stephen's testimony that Maria apparently needed cash *plus* this windfall on the death of her husband? Shades of the prison house, indeed.

He nodded a dismissal to the sergeant, held a lighter flame to the cigarette he slipped between his lips and inhaled deeply, watching the end glow red and orange. He was not to be permitted to enjoy his puff – his door was flung open abruptly and Superintendent Chen marched in. Ashes from the cigarette scattered over the front of Singh's shirt, coming to rest gently against his ample stomach. He dusted them off with the back of his hand, leaving grey streaks against the white, put out his cigarette in a coffee mug and looked at the superintendent questioningly.

His boss was doing his best to avert his eyes from the thin wisp of smoke that was making its way gently to the ceiling from the not-quite-stubbed-out cigarette. Singh wondered how long this patience would last. He could see the lines of strain running from the superintendent's jaw down his throat; he was swallowing hard to refrain from delivering another of his "disgrace to the Force" lectures. But right now he needed Singh to solve the case – and that apparently meant cutting him some slack.

'Any progress?' demanded Chen.

'We're proceeding with the interviews, sir. Sarah Thompson has an alibi.'

Chen closed his eyes briefly. Singh supposed that, next to some convenient foreign stranger, a domestic fracas would be his preferred solution to the killing of Mark Thompson. He wondered whether to tell him that Maria Thompson was looking good for the murder and then decided not to offer her as a sacrificial lamb to appease his superior.

'What are those?' The superintendent gestured to the pile of papers in front of Singh.

'Bank statements ...'

'Anything interesting?'

'Not yet.' Singh picked up the bank statement at the top of the pile. It belonged to Quentin Holbrooke. He glanced at it and then sat up a little straighter. He ran a stubby finger down the list.

'What is it?' demanded Superintendent Chen.

'Quentin Holbrooke, unlike his colleagues, seems to have a cash flow problem.'

Chen almost snatched the statement from Singh's fingers. The policeman did not object. He had seen enough.

'He's been withdrawing large amounts of money in cash at regular intervals. What do you think it means?' The superintendent could not keep the excitement out of his voice.

Singh shrugged. 'Anything or nothing. But my first guess would be blackmail.'

In the restaurant at the Raffles, David and Annie couldn't help but stare at the second wife of Mark Thompson. They were not alone. She was the focus of surreptitious glances from the other diners. Whispered comments suggested that she had not gone unrecognised.

'Who are the kids?' asked David.

'Must be hers,' Annie said. 'They're carbon copies of her. I'd heard that she had a couple of children from a previous marriage but I thought they were in the Philippines.' And then, under her breath, 'Damn, she's seen us.'

Maria Thompson looked over at them, debating whether

to ignore them, acknowledge them from a distance or come over to their table. Still holding the children by the hand, she came over.

'Maria, how are you holding up?' asked Annie.

'It is not an easy time for me,' she replied. 'That woman will try to kill me also.'

Feeling unequal to responding to this, Annie said instead, 'Are these your children? They look so much like you.'

Maria nodded and her expression revealed a fierce maternal pride.

'Mrs Thompson, I've been sent out by the London office to try and find out who did this terrible thing. My name is David Sheringham.' He offered her his hand and she brushed it with the tips of her fingers.

Maria sniffed. 'What is there to find out? It was that bitch. I keep telling the fat policeman. But no one listens. Soon I will be dead too.'

Her voice rose to a shout. A few people at the other tables were staring openly now.

David signalled to a waiter and said to Maria, 'Won't you and your children join us?' As Maria visibly hesitated, he continued persuasively, 'You can explain your suspicions to us.'

This was an offer she could not refuse. Behind her back, Annie glared at David. They all maintained a discreet silence as a couple of waiters dragged over a table to adjoin theirs. Maria bent over her children, whispered a few instructions in Tagalog and they both headed to the lavish buffet in gleaming silver serving dishes, the younger one skipping as she went.

'What about you, Mrs Thompson? Won't you have something from the buffet?' asked David.

'No, no! I come for my children to enjoy. I will have a cup

of coffee. I need to keep slim, you understand,' she said, flashing him a look from under her long (and false, I bet, thought Annie) lashes.

David leaned forward. 'Come now, Mrs Thompson, there is no need at all for you to watch your figure. The rest of us will do that.'

Maria simpered. 'You call me Maria, please.'

David poured out her tea, added milk and sugar at her nod, and gave it to her. Maria may have started out as a domestic worker in Singapore but she had got into the habit of being waited on, thought Annie tetchily.

'Now, Maria, tell me what the firm can do to help you. We will do anything in our power.'

Maria snorted her disbelief.

'*You* are Mark's widow,' David insisted.

'Ha! At least you see this. I'm the widow. She is *nothing*.'

Annie felt like pointing out that Sarah had been Mark's wife for thirty years and was the mother of his two children, unlike Maria who had married him for his money six months previously, but she knew that David would not thank her for it.

The children returned to the table with laden plates and started tucking in enthusiastically. David smiled at them and hesitated, unwilling to discuss the subject further in their presence.

'Do not worry about the children. I have explained everything. And anyway their English is not so good.'

'Did Mark ever see Sarah?' David asked.

'Of course not,' Maria said scornfully. 'She is old and ugly. What for he wants to see her?'

'Perhaps to discuss their children? Maybe their studies or money?'

He had touched a raw nerve. 'He would not see her, but if

he did, she would ask for *money*. She is a very greedy woman.'

'And his children?' asked Annie.

'He hasn't seen them since the divorce.'

'That must have been really hard for him,' said Annie. 'Perhaps your children helped to bridge the gap?'

'This is the first time my children come to Singapore.' Maria blinked rapidly a few times – was she holding back tears? 'Mark did not want them.'

'That was very bad of Mark,' said David, leaning towards her sympathetically. 'Why did he feel that way?'

'I don't know,' she said wearily, the strain starting to show. 'Maybe he was jealous?' Maria placed a caressing hand on the head of each of her children. 'I know you all think I kill Mark. But I am not the one, so you must find someone else to blame.'

'Maria, nobody will accuse you of anything you did not do,' said David reassuringly.

Maria was sceptical. 'Why should I believe you? I am a Filipina in Singapore and I do not trust you. Or the police.'

She rose to her feet and picked up her Ferragamo purse, beckoning imperiously to her children, who obediently abandoned their meal.

David got to his feet too. He took Maria's hand in both of his and said, 'Don't worry too much.'

She inclined her head regally at him and swept out of the room, her children trailing after her. A few men turned to watch her go, their expressions more lascivious than curious.

'Well, that's Maria for you; every arrival is an entrance and every departure an exit!' muttered Annie.

'You can see why,' remarked David. 'She really is an exceptionally sexy woman.'

'It was quite clear you thought so . . . all that fawning,' said Annie. She had intended to sound sarcastic but could not

126

help but feel she sounded more aggrieved. Trying to sound objective, she continued, 'I realise that she oozes sex appeal. Presumably that's why Mark married her.'

She noticed to her intense discomfiture that David's grey eyes were twinkling with amusement.

'She doesn't hold a candle to you,' he said, grinning.

Annie scowled and then found she could not maintain the expression. His smile was infectious.

'So where shall we go on our *second* date?' David asked with mock seriousness.

'This wasn't a date,' she insisted and then wondered if she was protesting too much.

'A nice restaurant, a gorgeous woman, good conversation – feels like a date to me!'

Annie knew that she was not beautiful – the cleft chin was too determined, her brown eyes disproportionately large. But she had to admit that it was nice that David Sheringham seemed to think otherwise.

He misunderstood her silence and asked, 'Is it Quentin?' She detected a genuine note of disappointment in his voice.

If David thought there was something between her and Quentin, might the inquisitive inspector have reached the same conclusion? Annie shook her head quickly, denying the relationship. For some reason it was important to her that the man opposite her did not think she was involved with anyone else.

Maria Thompson summoned a hotel limousine with the Raffles "R" emblazoned on its side, bundled the children in and was handed into it by a liveried doorman. She refrained from tipping him – she had worked hard to come by her money and was not going to hand it out to some uniformed car jockey who was doing no more than his job. Besides, she might well be short of ready cash while waiting for the insurance to come through.

Once again, she congratulated herself on persuading Mark to take out the policy. It had not been easy. Her new husband had not wanted to think about his own death or to acknowledge the age gap between them and the inevitability of his pre-deceasing her. She had been forced to tread carefully so as not to confirm his fears that she had married him for his money. Married him for his money? Well, of course she had! Mark had been in relatively good shape for a man of his age with an alcohol habit. He had not been overweight, although his flesh had been flabby, covered in pale, almost translucent, hairless skin with blue veins showing. She shuddered at the recollection. Would that have been her choice? Certainly not. She would have found herself a young, sinewy Filipino man, bronzed by the sun. He would have strong work-roughened hands, not the desk-job softness of Mark's that had felt like a woman's hands on her skin. Well, she could find herself a real man now, she thought with pleasurable anticipation. A new father for her children. One who would teach them to fly a kite and take them fishing. They deserved better than an old man who had refused to meet them or acknowledge their existence. But his money was going to pave the way to a better future for all of them. They owed Mark Thompson something for that.

Still smarting from his run-in with the superintendent, Inspector Singh waited by the main entrance to Mark Thompson's apartment building. He had come to see Maria but she was not at home. The sun was beating down vigorously and his collar was damp and limp. His turban itched around the rim and his singlet was soaked through. The light was shimmering above the road, the air distorted by the intense heat. It was almost time to abandon this pointless vigil, decided Singh. He needed a cold beer – maybe a snack to go with it, something light and savoury like curry puff.

Just as he made up his mind to postpone seeing the widow to another, cooler, day, a limousine from the Raffles Hotel purred down the street. He was immediately certain that this was the sort of vehicle that Maria Thompson would have selected for her transportation. He put up a hand, waved a badge at the driver and rapped on the rear passenger window. He could not see past the dark tinted glass but his instincts had been spot on. The window rolled down slowly and the exquisite features of Mark Thompson's widow looked out at him. Her expression was mildly inquiring, as if she had been pulled up for a minor traffic offence by the waiting policeman, parking on a double yellow line perhaps.

Singh was impressed. This woman was determined not to show fear – although if she read the newspapers she would know that she was the overwhelming favourite to swing for the murder of Mark Thompson.

'I want to talk to you,' he said abruptly. He preferred his suspects on tenterhooks and if an aggressive tone was sufficient to achieve that end, he was happy to employ it. Otherwise he would eventually have to question this woman in the less salubrious surroundings of a holding cell. One thing was for cetain – if he had his way, she would soon stop treating him like a traffic cop.

'I have told you everything I know,' she said as she opened the door and swung her legs out. Two children scrambled out after her.

Singh stared down at them and they edged behind their mother. The children sensed danger. Did their mother? So far, this woman had exuded confidence – but was it a confi-

129

dence born of innocence or a certainty that the crime could not be brought home to her for the lack of evidence? Unlike the lawyers, Maria Thompson did not fear for a few stains on her reputation. The inspector was convinced she was a woman with plenty to hide. Whether that included murder, he was hard-pressed to say.

He fell into step beside her as she walked towards the apartment block, her silver clutch bag gleaming in the sun. Taking small steps, a waddle rather than a walk, he could feel the cloth of his trousers chafe against his inner thighs. He really should try and lose some weight – he didn't want to cross that fine line from physically intimidating to comic.

'What do you want?' she asked aggressively as they got to the apartment door. She stood in front of it, legs slightly apart – a physical barrier to indicate that she had no intention of inviting the policeman indoors.

In contrast to thir effert on David Sheringham earlier, the presence of the children did not inhibit the policeman. 'Mark went looking for you a few months back at a Balestier Road brothel.'

'You are talking nonsense.'

'It's true enough – Stephen Thwaites confirmed the story. Your husband believed that you needed money badly enough to resort to the world's oldest profession.'

He could see from the way she fumbled with the keys that her nerves were finally getting the better of her.

'What for I need money after I marry Mark?' she demanded.

'You tell me.'

'It's a lie!'

'Your husband was starting to doubt you. You had to get rid of him before he divorced you.'

'It is easy to make accusations against me because I am

130

Filipina. But I will complain to the embassy if you keep bothering me.'

One of her arms went around the shoulders of her younger child, the girl. It was an instinctively protective gesture rooted in a maternal instinct as old as time itself. Singh suddenly remembered the photos in her front room when he had visited to break the new of Mark Thompson's death. There had not been a single shot of these beautiful children that she so clearly adored.

'You needed money for your *children*, didn't you?' demanded Singh. 'You said Mark didn't want reminders of your past. He wouldn't give you any money for them.' Singh had spoken instinctively. But from her sudden sharp intake of breath, he knew that his guess had been completely accurate.

The point of his turban was like an accusing finger. 'That's why Mark believed you were moonlighting as a prostitute!'

Ten

Quentin Holbrooke slipped the taxi driver a ten-dollar bill and shook his head at the proffered return. He didn't need a handful of heavy coins to weigh down and distend the pockets of his well-tailored suit. Besides, he would have felt selfish demanding the exact change although, truth be told, he was probably in more financial trouble than the driver. His taxi driver had been middle-aged with a middle-class accent. He suspected that he had been a white-collar worker with a steady job until the recession hit – many of the unemployed took to driving taxis.

He slammed the door of the bright yellow cab and hurried into the building. The cool blast of air, such a contrast from the steamy heat outside, caused a rash of goose bumps to spread across his arms. As he waited impatiently for the elevator, punching the call button over and over again, Quentin felt light-headed. His nose was running and smarting, he had rubbed it raw with a serviette over a long client lunch, a long-winded Chinese buffet featuring a selection of endangered species, from shark's fin soup to sea cucumber.

He had been unable to make small talk, his eyes blinking rapidly and his fingers drumming on the table. Stephen Thwaites had glanced at him once or twice in puzzlement and that was *not* good.

The lift arrived, he hopped in, rode up to the seventeenth floor, fumbled with his keys until he managed to open the door and then flung his briefcase down on an Italian leather sofa that was perspiring almost as much as he was. When he first embarked on flat hunting as a new arrival in Singapore, he had searched for a place furnished in a manner consistent with the hot, damp weather of the island. He had soon realised that prospective landlords were only interested in wealth-emphasising décor – his current apartment had leather furniture, brass fittings and absurd ornate chandeliers that hung so low from the ceiling that he could touch them if he stretched.

Opening a drawer, he grabbed a small clear plastic packet and a CD case and sat down at the dining table. He took a deep breath and pushed his lank mousy hair away from his forehead with an impatient hand. He carefully tipped a thin line of white powder onto the flat surface of the case, took a crisp banknote out of his wallet and rolled it into a slim tube. Then he leaned forward, pointed his makeshift tube at the thin line of white powder and inhaled the raw cocaine like a drowning man thrown a life jacket.

Inspector Singh was sitting at a table close to the entrance of a Chinese coffee shop with his elbows on a faux pine surface pitted with cigarette burns and missing strips that exposed the splintered wood below. His posterior was balanced precariously but expertly on a red plastic stool – the over-hanging layers reminiscent of an overflowing cake tin. Above him, a ceiling fan turned slowly, ineffectual against the steamy evening. In front of him – a much more effective solution to the heat – an ice-cold bottle of beer stood on the table. An empty, clear glass mug squatted expectantly next to it.

This was the way all investigations should be conducted, he decided – with minions to pursue leads, however tenuous, while he did the important cerebral work of piecing together the mosaic of evidence into a picture of the killer.

The spotlight had shifted from the ex-wife to the widow. Sarah Thompson had an alibi and Maria Thompson was the beneficiary under an insurance policy to the tune of a million dollars. If that sort of money wasn't temptation enough to kill an elderly husband, he didn't know what was, especially if that elderly husband had been tightfisted about funds for Maria's children.

He paused to wonder what Mrs Singh's murder threshold was and bared his teeth in an ironic grin – he would certainly watch his back if any human being stood to gain a million dollars from his death. Right now, his wife might get his pension and the few dollars in their savings account. He was still more valuable, albeit annoying, alive. Mark Thompson, on the other hand, had been more valuable dead – and that was precisely how he had ended up.

Singh turned his attention to the lawyers. Quentin Holbrooke's bank statement had revealed a spending pattern that was reminiscent most of all of a blackmail victim. It was just about conceivable that he had killed Mark Thompson because he had been blackmailing him over some not-yet-discovered secret. But that did not square with the partners' meeting the murdered man had called – blackmailers tended not to announce their activities to their colleagues. And Mark's bank accounts did not have any deposits to match the withdrawals from Quentin's. He made a mental note to dig a little deeper. Just because the spotlight was now on Maria Thompson, it did not mean that the lawyers should be allowed to disappear into the surrounding shadows. He remembered his instinct that Jagdesh was hiding something and hoped that he wasn't avoiding any red flags just because the Sikh partner was some sort of distant relative. He had yet to work out the actual family connection and probably never would if it was one of the tenuous but convoluted links that his wife thrived on.

Singh took a gulp of his beer. It was icy cold, just the way he liked it. His wife regularly nagged him about the speed with which he consumed his drink. She did not seem to understand that if he let it sit, the beer would lose its bitter cold edge and become undrinkable. Singh's complaints, when he first became a customer, about the temperature of the beer served at the coffee shop had fallen on deaf ears. But one day the proprietor, a small man with a pock-marked broad face and a grubby off-white vest, had brought him his drink triumphantly, saying, 'Now your beer is vel-ly, *vel-ly* cold, ah!'

Singh had felt at the time that only his tightly-bound turban prevented his head from exploding. The grinning Chinaman had put *ice* – cubes of quickly melting ice – in his beer. His shock must have been visible because the restaurateur had said, 'You no like with ice?'

Singh shook his turbaned head with great emphasis. The beer had been taken away.

Nowadays, they kept a bottle at the back of the fridge, where it was coldest, just for him.

Corporal Fong, the minion, was at his desk at the station. Instead of working, he was looking at a glossy brochure for private health care. Comprehensive services were on offer including round-the-clock care, resident doctors and private apartments. He knew he could not afford any of it, but the problem of what to do with his father was becoming more urgent. He could not bear the state in which he found the old man when he got home now that his mother had almost completely abdicated responsibility for her husband. During Fong's police academy days, his hours had been regular and he had been able to manage but since his assignment to the murder investigation, he was constantly at the beck and call of that black-hearted devil, Inspector Singh. He threw the brochures into the bin with unhappy accuracy. That was not the solution.

Instead, he tried to get his mind around the job at hand. Inspector Singh had gone home – or, more likely, gone for a beer on the way home. It sounded from his interview with Maria as if she had needed money for her children. The exact opposite of the situation he found himself in – he needed money for his parents. However, the terrible weight of responsibility that Maria must have felt was something he could understand all too well. The desperation to find a solution, the constant worry, the willingness to consider more and more extreme remedies – he had experienced all these emotions first hand. If Maria had turned to murder, he, for one, would not be surprised. In fact, he would bet his next pay cheque that she had killed her wealthy husband to solve her financial difficulties. Unfortunately, thought Fong wryly, he wasn't fortunate enough to have a filthy-rich, expendable spouse.

He reached for the phone and rang the Bali number that Annie Nathan had provided. She had not been pleased that the police wanted to speak to her father, insisting that he was an elderly man enjoying his retirement on Bali and she did not want him disturbed.

'We just need to confirm that the monies you've been sending to Indonesia were for him ...' explained Fong.

'I've already told you that! Since when was filial responsibility a crime?'

'It's just procedure, ma'am – we always crosscheck information provided by witnesses.'

There had been silence at the other end. This was not some naïve shopgirl, thought Fong, ready to take a policeman at his word. He could almost hear the wheels turning in her head as she considered her options. Finally, she muttered, 'His name is Colonel R.K. Nathan,' and recited his phone number.

Colonel Nathan picked up the phone on the second ring.

'Sir, this is Corporal Fong of the Singapore Police. I just need to ask you a couple of questions.'

'Is it about Annie? Is everything all right?' The colonel's voice was gravelly with concern.

Fong was immediately reassuring. He had not meant to worry an old man. 'Yes, sir, she's absolutely fine. We understand from her testimony that she sends you money from time to time.'

'What's wrong with that? I've just been a bit unlucky with my investments, that's all.' His words were defensive but his tone was aggressive.

Fong found himself babbling explanations. 'We just need to tie up loose ends, sir. Nothing for you to worry about. It's just a formality.'

'What did Annie say? That I'm always asking for money? It's not true, young man. I've asked for her help once or twice at *most*.'

The corporal remembered that money had been telegraphed electronically to Bali at least three times that year. Colonel Nathan was understandably embarrassed to be seeking handouts from his only child. Fong shrugged. He didn't see how it mattered. He looked after his parents too – he was just unfortunate not to be as well off as Annika Nathan. His contributions were inadequate to the need. Her efforts, although generous, had hardly left her a pauper.

Annie's father was still defiantly explaining his need for funds. 'I was played out by a couple of business partners. It wasn't my fault!'

'Of course, sir. I am sure that Ms Nathan is happy to be of help,' Fong said soothingly.

Colonel Nathan snorted. 'Anyway, I try and assist her too when I can. Sometimes she needs my help as well, you know. It's not all a one-way street!'

Fong shook his head, interrupted the other man with a hurried goodbye and hung up. He thought about his own situation and his inadequately cared-for paternal parent. Did all relationships between fathers and children have to be so fraught with difficulties?

Across town, the police, equipped with the necessary warrants, were searching the Thompson residence. Maria had flounced out hours before, taking her children with her and complaining about harassment until she was out of earshot. The policemen were working painstakingly, leaving nothing to chance. So far they had found nothing. The senior officer at the scene was beginning to suspect that he had been sent on a wild goose chase. However, he had no intention of giving up or reporting failure. The idea of provoking the turbaned man's noisy resentment was too unpleasant. If Inspector Singh believed there were anonymous letters to be found, he and his men would hunt for as long as it took. Besides, he agreed with Singh that the letters, if they really existed, would have been preserved by the late

Mark Thompson. He would have wanted them in reserve to confront his new wife with the accusations contained therein. Hunting through Balestier Road brothels was just the opening salvo.

The policeman took a book from the shelf, a thick volume on his own pet interest, the Pacific War, and rifled through the pages. A sheaf of letters fell out. Curiously, he picked them up and leafed through the first few. 'Only a fool would marry a prostitute' said the first, the words carefully typed and centred on the page. He had hit the jackpot – or found a can of worms. It was a good hiding place – he had to hand it to the dead man – as it was unlikely that his new Filipina wife read very much other than the glossy women's magazines he had seen piled high on the living room coffee table. He beckoned to a uniform and gave him a few brief instructions. The young man, looking daunted, began to take books off the shelf, shaking them out one by one to see if anything else was hidden in the pages.

Singh rose to his feet with difficulty, flexing his toes within his white sneakers. They felt hot and sweaty, bunched together uncomfortably. He wondered whether it was reason enough to hail a taxi but then a mental picture of his doctor's long-suffering expression popped into his head. The man was more effective than a conscience, thought Singh. Perhaps he should walk the two blocks to his home. It might temper the effect of the beer on his health and weight, and reduce the severity of the lecture he would receive at his next medical check-up.

He set out reluctantly, trying to keep within the intermittent shadows along the main road. The evening sun was slanting directly into his eyes and he blinked quickly, wishing that he had a pair of sunglasses. He made way for an

139

Indonesian maid walking two barrel-chested Dobermans. It was typical of wealthy Singaporean dog owners to buy the largest and most expensive breed they could find and then leave it to the domestic help to feed and walk the dogs.

He stepped off the pavement again. This time a Sri Lankan maid was walking the offspring of an expatriate family. She pushed a pram with a sleeping baby while clutching at the hand of a little blond red-faced boy who dragged his heels and whined about the heat.

The diaspora of peoples who sold their possessions and paid middlemen exorbitant fees to come to Singapore looking for a better life mostly ended up slaving away "24/7", as one of those lawyers might say. Singh decided he really couldn't blame Maria Thompson for using any avenue, including sleeping with her employer, to escape the same fate. But had she killed him too?

He glanced at the houses on either side of the street. When he had first moved into the neighbourhood, the area had been forested, with sweeping vistas of hills and valleys. Twenty years on, the horizon was invisible. Monstrous houses, three storeys high with attics and basements, covered car parking, swimming pools and *koi* ponds, all arranged with careful consideration for the *feng shui* elements, loomed large in every direction. Fong had told him about the magisterial residence of the Thwaites. He had seen the Thompson duplex with its tenth-floor private swimming pool and Annie's colonial-era black and white bungalow. It was not difficult to imagine that one of the partners would resort to killing Mark Thompson to preserve such a lifestyle.

Singh wiped his forehead with the back of his shirt sleeve. It came away damp. The humidity was causing his beard to drip perspiration at the point. Why in the world had he decided to walk home?

He continued to puff his way up a hill, abandoning the pavement with its scattered booby traps of dog turds to walk on the road. He could smell the tar as the sun beat down on the tarmac and spotted his home in the distance with relief. There was a flash of blue in the garden. It was Mrs Singh diligently watering the plants. If they were anywhere near as dehydrated as he was, they needed to be hosed down. Gardening was Mrs Singh's second great love, after cooking. The garden was festooned with flowering plants; bougainvilleas that matched her brightest caftans, blood-red hibiscus and drooping crabclaw-shaped heliconias.

He slipped his hand through the gate and shot the rusted bolt with some difficulty. His hand was stained crimson when he took it away. He remembered guiltily that his wife had been nagging him to oil it. Stooping over her precious daisies, Mrs Singh straightened up slowly when she saw her husband.

'You'll have a heart attack if you walk up the hill in the hot sun,' she said, pulling off her knitted gardening gloves and dropping them at her feet.

Singh did not disagree – his chest was hurting. 'Exercise!'

'After beer, I suppose?'

The policeman mumbled a non-committal response. He sat down on the wooden swing, shut his eyes and rocked gently back and forth, trying to manufacture a breath of air to cool down.

'Have you found the murderer yet?' asked his wife, showing somewhat more than her usual level of interest in his work.

Singh opened one eye and shook his head in response to her question.

'Well, perhaps you should stop looking in the bottom of beer glasses. That boy has to go for his sister's wedding next week. He needs his passport back.'

'Eh?'

'Jagdesh has to go for his sister's wedding. He needs his passport!'

He might have guessed that the root of this newfound inquisitiveness about his job would involve a relative. Family matters were the only subjects of any real interest to his wife. 'Not while he's a suspect in a murder investigation,' grunted Singh.

'I don't dare go out of the house – it's so shameful that you are investigating one of *our* people. I don't know where to put my face.'

Singh scowled, his eyebrows almost meeting above his fleshy nose. His wife never seemed to know "where to put her face". He wondered whether he dared suggest a paper bag and decided against it. She was not in a mood to appreciate humour.

'*Everyone* is talking about it,' added Mrs Singh.

Singh knew who "everyone" was – her sisters and a bunch of other nosy Sikh relatives, all determined to do his job for him.

'It would be a lot more embarrassing if I allowed a killer to catch a flight out of Singapore,' he pointed out.

'Jagdesh Singh is *not* a killer!' Her hands were on her hips, the posture one of real indignation.

Singh remembered the way Jagdesh had been unable to meet his eyes when he had mentioned lawyers with secrets. 'That boy is hiding something. Why don't you make yourself useful and find out what that might be instead of trying to get me kicked off the Force?'

Reggie Peters was tucking into a rare steak. It was an expensive hunk of meat, grain-fed and flown into Singapore from Australian pastures. Droplets of blood oozed every time he put pressure on it with his serrated knife or stabbed it with his fork. The blood mixed with the oil on his plate, creating a gory palette of colours. Ai Leen pushed her own plate away. She could not even stomach a salad, not in the company of this man that she despised and now feared as well.

'Not hungry?' he asked, exposing a mouthful of half-chewed meat.

She was forced to admire his calm. They might as well be two colleagues having a casual dinner together, with none of the secrets and lies that underpinned their relationship. She glanced around the restaurant. It was nearly deserted on a mid-week night in the midst of a major recession, which was just as well. She did not think she could force a smile or manage any polite chit-chat with a passing acquaintance.

A flickering candle on each table threw bizarrely-shaped shadows on the walls, as if the creatures of hell were lying in wait. But Ai Leen knew that she was in a purgatory of her own making. She had sacrificed so much, given up so much – had it been worthwhile? She had the official badges of success within Singapore society, the three Cs – car, club and condominium – as well as her hard-won partnership. Was her self-respect too high a price to pay for success? She knew it was too late for regrets – too late to un-make the decisions that had led her to this place. She had to find a way to look to the future. And the first step was to sever the ties that bound her to this man. The very idea terrified her. She did not know what Reggie Peters was capable of doing but she feared the worst.

'I want out,' she said, trying to inject some authority into her voice.

A grin spread over his face. 'I thought you might say that.'

'It's too dangerous!' Despite her best efforts her voice had taken on a plaintive edge. She gritted her teeth. If she sounded like she was begging it would only empower this man. 'We're in the middle of a murder investigation.'

Reggie popped another piece of meat into his mouth and chewed with evident relish. 'Nothing doing,' he said, scraping a sliver of flesh stuck between his two front teeth out with a nail. He smirked at his co-worker. 'A deal is a deal – you should know that. You're a *partner* at a law firm.'

Eleven

Annie tossed and turned all night, sleeping only in snatches. It was a relief to hear the alarm and get out of bed. She set out on her morning bike ride, half an hour round the old abandoned cemetery ten minutes away from the house. The large semi-circular tombs were decorated with floral tiles and carvings, protected by grotesque gargoyles, parodies of frogs and lions. Black and white photos of the dead were glazed onto the headstones, the faces of neat men and prim women. The pictures were of the young but the dates indicated that this was the last vanity of the dead.

Undergrowth lapped the sides of the tombs and the narrow road through the cemetery. Huge trees spread out overhead. A macaque monkey, its tail hanging down in an inverted question mark and its offspring clinging to its belly, chattered to her earnestly. Today her morning ride was especially welcome, a temporary respite from the reality of a murder investigation – and her conflicting feelings over David Sheringham.

She had been determined at first to dislike him and to

keep him at arm's length, probably for no better reason than that he had mistaken her for a secretary on their first encounter. Instead, she had felt a powerful attraction towards him that afternoon at the Raffles. But this was hardly the time – up to her neck in a murder investigation with that fat policeman prying into her life and work – for the distraction of a romantic entanglement.

She drifted back to the subject that was uppermost in her mind, the insider dealing. The law firm knew about it and it seemed Singh did too. They all believed that the culprit was a director from Trans-Malaya. But it was only a matter of time before Tan Sri Ibrahim became impatient and rang back to further expound his theory that the insider dealing at his company emanated from the firm of Hutchinson & Rice. A shudder ran through her slim frame and suddenly this peaceful place that she had grown to love felt shadowy and threatening. There was to be no forgetting, no respite, from the maelstrom of events and emotions triggered by the death of Mark Thompson.

Arriving at the office, Annie's first stop was the pantry. The tea lady had already been in and the coffee mugs piled high in the sink had been washed and put away. The surfaces were gleaming and the place smelt faintly of a lemony disinfectant. She put on the coffee percolator and watched it bubble and boil hypnotically, calmed by its heady aroma. The morning sun was streaming in through the window behind her, highlighting the hint of auburn that she had inherited from her mother.

'I'll have some of that.'

Annie started. Reggie had strutted in. She had not heard the swing doors. He adjusted the length of the tie hanging over his shoulders and commenced tying a knot. It was a thin stripy affair – an old school tie of some sort.

'Good morning, Reggie,' she said, deciding not to be explicit in her dislike of her fellow partner. She took the coffee jug from the percolator and poured a cupful into the proffered mug. 'You're an early bird today.'

'Couldn't sleep,' he confessed.

'Me neither,' she said, feeling almost compassion for him; the murder investigation was taking its toll on all of them.

'What's on the agenda today?' he asked.

'More interviews, I suppose,' replied Annie.

The doors to the pantry swung open, Western style, and Inspector Singh swaggered in as if he was a tough cowboy making an entrance into a small-town saloon. Annie almost expected to see horse troughs and dust devils through the crazily swinging doors. Singh's hands were bunched in his trouser pockets and it caused the cloth to stretch taut across his belly. His zip had baulked at the last centimetre and was not completely done up. Perhaps that was why most fat men wore their trousers under their stomachs rather than over them, thought Annie.

'Good,' said Singh. 'You're here. I checked in your rooms but there was no one to be found. But if you want a lawyer, follow the smell of coffee!' He beamed cheerily at them, apparently pleased with his own deductive reasoning.

Reggie snapped, 'What do you want, Inspector?'

The inspector appeared in no way put out by this rudeness. 'Interviews, interviews ...' he answered. 'The hunt for the truth must proceed.'

'My interview is scheduled for this afternoon,' said Reggie.

'Now then, Mr Peters.' Singh was a parody of an English fictional policeman. 'I'm sure you're the last person to want to delay our progress. Besides, Quentin Holbrooke hasn't

147

come in yet and we wouldn't want Singapore's finest to be twiddling his thumbs, would we?'

Annie could not blame the inspector for the touch of sarcasm in his voice. Reggie had not been a model of co-operation.

'This is unacceptable, Inspector!' Reggie blustered. 'I have meetings this morning, urgent work to do.'

'Nothing you have to do is more important than finding Mr Thompson's murderer,' replied the policeman, a hint of steel in his voice. Reggie looked as if he was going to argue but the inspector carried on, 'I don't want to inconvenience you unnecessarily – you can have ten minutes to rearrange your schedule.'

Unable to think of any convincing excuse and not daring to refuse outright, Reggie turned away so hastily that hot coffee slopped over his hand. He walked out of the pantry, dabbing his hand with a handkerchief and struggling to maintain some dignity.

'Do you think he'll come?' asked Annie, wondering what the policeman thought of his uncooperative witness.

'Oh yes! He'll be exactly five minutes late to demonstrate that he is not pandering to the natives, but he won't dare push it a minute beyond that.'

'And how do you feel about that?'

The inspector gave one of his unexpected belly laughs. 'That's why I gave him ten minutes, and not fifteen.'

Annie watched the policeman stroll out of the pantry and down the corridor. She felt like a puppet on a string.

Fong was already in the interview room, flipping through some papers energetically. He glanced up as Singh came in, leapt to his feet and said, 'Good morning, sir!'

Singh grunted a response and lowered himself carefully

into his own chair, triceps bulging as he tried to prevent gravity taking over.

'What's on the agenda today, sir?' asked Fong, unconsciously echoing Reggie's words from earlier.

'We're having Reggie Peters in first.'

Fong looked at him, his expression puzzled. 'He wasn't next on the list ...'

'In my experience, young man, a self-important bastard like Reggie Peters is best interviewed when his ego has taken a knock! I don't doubt that dancing to my tune is driving him mad – but he knows he has no choice.'

Fong swallowed a retort – dancing to the inspector's tune was driving him mad too but it was probably unwise to say so. Still, the fat man had a point. He was more likely to get information out of a man like Reggie Peters if he was off balance.

'So, what do we know about Reggie Peters?' asked Singh thoughtfully, his attention already focused on his next witness.

His subordinate answered quickly. 'Senior banking partner, wife, three kids – very successful at work but not very popular with his co-workers.'

'Except for the poker-faced Ms Lim Ai Leen!'

'I beg your pardon, sir?'

'We need more information on this apparent chumminess between Reggie and Ai Leen,' explained Singh.

Fong shuffled through his papers until he found the reports from the policemen who had been detailed to tail the suspects. 'They've been spending a lot of time together *since* the murder, sir.'

'What do you mean?'

'They've been spotted dining together a few times, at fairly out-of-the-way places.'

Singh reached for the desk phone, hit the speaker button and dialled Stephen Thwaites' extension.

The other man picked up with a brusque hello, the tone of a successful professional who believed that his time was worth money.

'Singh here. A quick question – were Ai Leen and Reggie Peters on good terms before the murder?'

'I beg your pardon?'

'You heard me,' snapped Singh impatiently. 'Reggie and Ai Leen – chums, buddies, pals?'

Stephen's tone was wary but he answered the question. 'I don't think so – not especially.'

'They've been as thick as thieves since the murder.'

'Really? I had no idea they were close friends.'

'Friends?' snorted the inspector derisively. 'Any relationship that springs up around a murder investigation is very suspicious to me.'

He slammed the phone down without the courtesy of a "goodbye".

There was a tentative knock on the door.

'Come,' growled the inspector.

Reggie walked in reluctantly, dragging his feet like a child in a supermarket.

'I would like to place it on record that you have caused me and this legal firm great inconvenience by re-scheduling our meeting,' he said coldly. He had obviously rehearsed his opening line.

'Fong, you heard the man – record his inconvenience please,' said Singh cheerfully.

Corporal Fong started typing hastily. He was terrified at Reggie's opening gambit, imagining a complaint making its way up the ranks until he had a black mark recorded against him in his personnel file. Inspector Singh didn't seem to care

– probably his file was so thick with complaints already that one more wouldn't make a difference.

Despite the inflammatory beginning, the interview was low key. The inspector was docile and Reggie, his point made, was striving to appear cooperative. He had known Mark Thompson for many years but the collegial relationship had never developed into a real friendship. 'We had nothing in common, really,' explained Reggie Peters. 'Our wives never really hit it off. And once he married Maria – well, that was the end of it …'

When Fong tuned back in, Reggie was discussing his whereabouts during the murder. 'I was at home. The children had gone to bed. My wife was out at a hen night. I didn't actually speak to Mark but I found a message on my answer phone. Ai Leen rang me – she said she'd got a call too, asked me what it was about.'

He looked the inspector directly in the eye. 'I had no idea. I offered her a lift. We were running late so Ai Leen rang the office and had a brief chat with Jagdesh. He didn't mention the murder.'

The inspector, having allowed Reggie Peters to carry on uninterrupted, scratched his nose and asked, 'So who do *you* think did it then?'

Reggie seemed surprised by the question but forbore from making a spontaneous accusation.

'I don't know,' he said, carefully smoothing the remaining strands of hair across his almost bald pate. 'I just can't understand who would want to do such a thing. I mean, it's … *outrageous!*'

'Well, that's one way of putting it,' muttered Inspector Singh.

Fong looked at the inspector curiously. He had expected fireworks, sensing the inspector's antipathy towards this witness. But he supposed Singh had no evidence of wrong-doing on the part of Reggie. His alibi was tenuous but so were most of their alibis. Even Reggie and Ai Leen were not alibis for each other. Either of them could have come into the office, killed Mark and still been in time to meet the other before setting out once more.

'Will that be all?' asked Reggie.

Singh nodded and the lawyer almost strutted out of the room. No doubt he thought that the interview had been so restrained because of his formal complaint at the beginning. Fong wondered if, contrary to what he had thought earlier, the senior policeman had been unsettled by Reggie Peters' threats. He hoped not. He didn't want to think of the infallible Inspector Singh as being susceptible to intimidation.

'Why didn't you ask him about Ai Leen, sir?' asked Fong tentatively.

'Always better to save questions about relationships for the female half,' explained Singh smugly. 'They're the ones who like to talk about their feelings the most – just look at those women's magazines!'

'You've been spending a lot of time with Mr Peters of late.'

Singh's remark was more a statement than a question.

Ai Leen was caught off guard. She straightened her light-blue skirt over her knees, twisted a plain platinum ring on her wedding finger, and asked, 'What do you mean?'

The inspector made a show of fishing around his desk for a piece of paper, found it and looked at it carefully, holding it a couple of feet away from himself. The senior policeman was getting long-sighted, noted Fong. He really needed to get himself a pair of those reading glasses. He hoped it wasn't misplaced vanity that prevented the inspector from correcting his eyesight.

Singh read out in a dry voice all the occasions in the past week when Ai Leen and Reggie had been spotted together. It was a long list and Ai Leen's dismay at the detail the police had of her assignations with Reggie was obvious despite the obscuring quality of a thick layer of make-up. There was fear in her almond-shaped eyes, visible in the expanding pupils, as she listened to the policeman.

Ai Leen swallowed hard but did her best to sound nonchalant. 'What does it matter? We're friends.'

'Quite a new friendship, I understand.'

If looks could kill, Singh would have been prostrate on the floor. Fong had rarely seen such a vicious expression on the face of any individual. Ai Leen was clearly wondering who had told the inspector about her previously distant relationship with Reggie. The corporal sensed that this was a vindictive woman and she would want her revenge against the whistleblower. The senior policeman had now made enemies of his last two suspects. From his expression, Singh wasn't bothered. If anything, there was a smugness radiating from the inspector. Fong guessed, with unexpected perspicuity, that Singh would love to set these lawyers at each other's throats. It was probably his best chance of breaking through their well-constructed defenses.

'Well, Ms Lim? I'm waiting for an explanation.'

'Why do I have to explain anything to you? This is personal – between Reggie and me. It has nothing to do with Mark.'

'*I* will be the judge of that, Ms Lim.' The inspector was at his most cutting.

'We're friends. We support each other in difficult times.'

'How long have you been *supporting* each other?'

'A couple of months. We've been colleagues for a few years but have become closer lately.'

153

'What triggered this?'

'We have a lot in common.'

'Give me an example,' said the inspector disbelievingly, steepling his fingers and peering at Ai Leen over the tips.

Ai Leen glared at him, fear replaced with anger. 'Our work! I'm a banking lawyer too. We're both partners.'

'And is your husband aware of this new-found *friendship*?'

Fong had to admire the lascivious overtone Inspector Singh managed to incorporate into his question.

But Ai Leen was a match for this. 'He's aware that Reggie is a colleague with whom I occasionally have work-related dinners,' she said coldly.

'Quite romantic spots you choose for these "work-related dinners",' Inspector Singh pointed out.

'And why not?' she asked. 'We need privacy to ensure client confidentiality and I personally am fond of good food – as you are, Inspector,' she said, allowing her gaze to drift across his substantial belly.

'You mean this?' the inspector asked cheerfully, patting his ample stomach as fondly as he might have done a favourite mutt. 'This isn't food. It's beer!'

Ai Leen managed to convey her disgust with a slight flaring of the nostrils. 'I really don't see what any of this has to do with the murder. I think you would be doing us all a favour if you tried to solve the crime rather than cast aspersions upon my character.'

'Do you have any thoughts on who might have done this?' asked Singh in a much more conciliatory tone.

'No, I do *not*. I only know it wasn't me. Some stranger killed Mark. He must have snuck past the security guards. In fact, it was probably the security guards who did it.'

This was her final word on the subject because she rose to her feet and, at a nod from the inspector, marched out of the room, powerful calf muscles bunched up above her high pointy heels.

'What do we know about Ai Leen's partnership?' Singh demanded of his sidekick.

'Not a lot, sir.'

'Well, let's find out then.'

Fong found himself hurrying after the inspector as the fat man marched down the corridor. He had a surprising turn of speed for someone of his size. The inspector banged on Annie's door like an irate husband and barged in. Over his superior's shoulder, Fong saw her look up in irritation and then with genuine surprise as she saw who it was.

'Tell me what you know about Ai Leen becoming a partner,' ordered Singh.

Annie's fingernail went to her mouth. Fong had noticed this nervous gesture. He wondered whether it meant anything – that this woman was afraid. The corporal controlled a smile with difficulty. Being intimidated by Inspector Singh was hardly evidence of criminal tendencies.

'I was up for partnership at the same time. One hears stories, of course ...' Annie broke off her sentence mid-way as if reluctant to reveal unsubstantiated rumours.

Fong was unsurprised that Singh did not have the same qualms.

'What sort of rumours?'

'Oh ... the usual stuff. Some partners were very keen to promote the local – you know, Singaporean – staff, others had doubts.'

'How did you feel about it?'

'Well, to be frank, if I'd been turned down, I would have been livid. But I can see why they wanted a Singaporean on the job. It looks better with clients. And she *is* a very good lawyer.'

155

'And Reggie Peters,' asked Singh innocently 'What's his wife like?'

'Reggie's wife?' Annie queried. 'Oh, a long-suffering bottle-blonde. I think she was his secretary once but I could be wrong about that. He does have a habit of hitting on women in the office.'

'How do you know that?'

Annie ducked her head in embarrassment.

The inspector waited impatiently for her response, his sneaker-clad foot beating a silent tattoo on the thick carpet.

She said, 'Well, Reggie's made the odd pass at me at office Christmas parties and such like.'

'What did you do about it?'

'Kept quiet. If I'd kicked up a stink, Reggie would have got a slap on the wrist but I would've been branded a trouble-maker.'

'And the next day?'

'And the next day we both pretend it never happened. At least, I pretend. He may genuinely forget.'

Fong's expression must have conveyed his genuine amazement that sexual harassment of women was possible in an environment of highly paid lawyers.

'It wasn't that bad,' Annie said bracingly. 'Anyway, I'm not really his type. He prefers the Oriental beauty . . . like the second Mrs Thompson.'

Twelve

Singh's knees were stiff from squeezing them under the too-small desk and his lower back ached, a recurrent pain. His head felt musty and crowded, as if someone had stuffed it with old socks. He really would be much happier conducting this murder investigation from his own chair behind his own desk at the police station.

He took a small sheaf of papers out of an A4-sized envelope. These were the anonymous notes that had been found at the Thompson residence, delivered to him at the law offices by a policeman on a motorcycle. There were six notes, almost identical to one another. The messages were on plain white, good-quality paper. He guessed the notes had been done on someone's personal computer, printed with a standard inkjet printer on A4 paper. Gone were the days, thought the inspector longingly, of manual typewriters with their individual idiosyncrasies, bits of newsprint from identifiable newspapers and hidden watermarks leading straight to the desk of the writer.

As for the messages, except that the writer was educated –

the notes were grammatically correct and well punctuated –
there was not much to be gleaned from them. As Mark had
intimated to Stephen, the notes asserted that Maria was still
earning an income from prostitution despite being married
to Mark. "Old habits die hard" as one of the notes pointed
out.

He smoothed his moustache with his thumb and forefinger. It was too long, tickling his upper lip. He looked across
at his sidekick. He was clean-shaven, his jaw so smooth that
Singh was forced to the conclusion that, like so many of his
race, Fong struggled to grow hair on his chin and jaw.

He tossed the packet of letters over to the young man and
the corporal flicked through them with unfeigned enthusiasm. He was the sort of policeman, still wet behind the ears,
thought Singh, who preferred tangible physical evidence to
the testimony of unreliable witnesses. It took a long time for
rookies like Fong to understand that murders nearly always
happened because of personal relationships gone awry, and
they were solved in painstaking conversation with those same
people. Most policemen never got the hang of it – they were
thwarted the moment they were confronted with a killer who
left no physical evidence. Their entire investigative method-
ology revolved around finding a fingerprint, a strand of hair
or some revolting body fluid. Where was the fun in that,
wondered Singh.

'At the end of the day, it doesn't really matter who wrote
these notes or whether the contents were true. What matters
is that Mark Thompson *believed* them to be true,' explained
Singh.

Fong's lips were pinched together like a maiden aunt who
had stumbled over some Internet porn. 'The accusations
aren't very nice!'

'That's why Maria might have killed her husband. It's a

short trip from these notes to divorce and a penniless future.'

Quentin popped his head around the door. 'May I come in?' he asked in a breathless voice.

Singh, looking up from the wad of anonymous letters, nodded curtly.

Once in a chair, Quentin ran a hand through his thin brown hair and leaned forward, his pale blue eyes popping with earnestness. 'Have you made any progress in discovering who did this terrible thing?'

'Who did this terrible thing? You mean who beat your boss to death at his desk?' Inspector Singh did not like euphemisms for murder.

Quentin Holbrooke turned an even whiter shade of pale and nodded uncertainly.

Glaring at him, Singh decided that he disliked insipid men with weak chins who didn't call a spade a spade. He thought of Jagdesh Singh, his young relative. Now there was a man with a jaw to be proud of. He reminded himself, almost regretfully, that a weak chin did not equate with murderous tendencies.

'We really must get to the bottom of this, for Mark's sake and ours,' said Quentin with an air of great seriousness.

Singh did not understand his demeanour or address – Quentin's manner reminded him of one of the prim and proper spinster teachers who had taught him as a young boy. The lawyer was playing a role, but why?

Quentin was still talking. Unprompted, he was recounting finding the body and the events thereafter. He had been pub-hopping when Mark had called. He had prepared a list of the places – he wasn't sure anyone would remember him but it was worth a shot if it got him off a murder rap.

159

He slid a piece of paper across the table to the inspector. 'That's where I was before coming to the office and meeting Annie in the car park.'

'By accident or design?' the inspector asked.

'I beg your pardon?'

'Did you meet Annie by accident or design?'

'Oh! By accident, of course. I do try and meet her from time to time by design, but she's a hard lady to pin down!'

He said this last with a wink at the inspector.

'Has your keycard turned up yet?' asked the policeman tartly, annoyed by Quentin's attempt to forge some sort of masculine bond with him.

Quentin shook his head and the recalcitrant lock of fine hair fell across his forehead again. 'I'm afraid not. I have absolutely no idea where the damned thing has got to!'

'Were you a close friend of Mark Thompson?'

'No, not really. He was too senior at Hutchinson & Rice to hobnob with the likes of me!' He shuddered. 'It was still a shock, finding him like that.'

Singh ignored these professed sensibilities. 'You're working with Annie – Ms Nathan – on a matter in Kuala Lumpur?'

'Yes, the takeover of Trans-Malaya – an interesting deal.'

'Why do you say that?'

'No particular reason. You know, good money-spinner for the law firm, interesting legal issues ...' He trailed off before the policeman's sceptical gaze.

Singh could see that Quentin's fingers were beating an erratic tattoo on the side of the chair. The young lawyer's tone and words were being contradicted by his body language. He was not sufficiently in control, notwithstanding this rehearsed performance, to avoid revealing his nervousness.

'What about the insider trading on the Malaysian file?'

'Oh, you've heard about that? Some dodgy dealing by a local director. Mark wanted to pull Hutchinson & Rice from the deal.'

'And you?'

Quentin shrugged. Bony shoulders were outlined against his fitted pink shirt. 'It's par for the course in Malaysia, isn't it? Doesn't seem much point being too self-righteous – not if it's going to cost the law firm a bundle!'

Singh slid a piece of paper across the table – it was Quentin's bank statement – and remarked nonchalantly, 'I don't know about the firm, but something has been costing *you* a bundle!'

'I have an expensive lifestyle, I guess!' Quentin blinked rapidly a few times and laughed. It sounded tinny and forced to the inspector's ears.

'Cash withdrawals in large sums – you're down to pennies. I need a better explanation than …' he looked pointedly at the small polo pony and rider on Quentin's shirt '… designer clothing!'

'I must have got a bit carried away with the spending. Thanks for the heads-up, I'll try and rein it in.'

Was this young man trying to suggest that Inspector Singh of the Singapore Police Force was providing personal financial advice? It was time to put some pressure on the young fool. 'Do you know what I think?'

The lawyer leaned forward with an air of great interest.

'I think you're being blackmailed.'

Quentin Holbrooke burst into full-throated laughter.

Singh sat back in his chair and scratched his beard under his chin. He was genuinely puzzled. His attempt at pinning Quentin Holbrooke down had resulted in the first bit of real emotion from this amateur thespian – and it was amusement.

161

Quentin spoke in a conspiratorial whisper. 'I'll be frank with you ... I've just had a run of bad luck on the horses.'

Singh squinted at the young man. It was possible, he supposed. Gambling at the Singapore Turf Club in Woodlands was the pastime of serious gamblers as well as part-time punters. It was *possible* – but highly unlikely. Still, his blackmail theory had taken a knock. He would have to find some other explanation for the missing money. Quentin Holbrooke clearly had no intention of coming clean on the subject.

Singh was suddenly sick and tired of prevaricating lawyers. 'That's all!' he said heavily.

Quentin accepted his abrupt dismissal and walked out, swinging his arms with tightly-controlled, feigned nonchalance.

Sergeant Eric Chung was sitting in a clean but nondescript silver-coloured sedan. He remembered that on *NYPD Blue*, his favourite television programme, surveillance vehicles were always rusty old jalopies. That would not work very well on the streets of Singapore where the vast majority of cars were less than ten years old – a by-product of a taxation scheme that rewarded owners for upgrading their cars regularly. Chung was pretty sure that the cops on TV pissed in plastic bottles as well rather than compromise a stakeout. But he and his partner had taken turns to go to the public toilets when nature called. Life really wasn't like television at all, he had come to realise, which made him wonder why he had signed up to be a police officer in the first place. Police work – on the telly – had appeared sexy and dangerous, not mind-numbingly *boring*. Right now, Sergeant Eric, smartly dressed and looking like a computer salesman, was as bored rigid as when he had discovered that he had every season of his favourite cop drama on DVD already.

They had been tailing Quentin Holbrooke for days now. The only thing, thought Chung, that might conceivably be more tiresome than following Quentin Holbrooke was *being* Quentin Holbrooke. All the guy did was come to work every day and stay home in the evenings. He didn't seem to have any friends, let alone a girlfriend. There had been a bit of excitement the previous day when he had walked out of some posh lunch, but all he had done was catch a taxi home. He'd probably gone to bed with a headache while he, Sergeant Chung, had spent the entire afternoon sitting in his car until he was relieved by the night shift.

His partner, a small wiry older Malay man who seemed to have infinite patience, nudged him in the ribs. He looked up and caught a glimpse of Quentin Holbrooke flagging down a taxi in front of Republic Tower.

'Great – another wild goose chase!' exclaimed Chung. 'Just when I need the toilet.'

Sergeant Hassan ignored Chung's griping, slipped the car into gear and eased into a leisurely – the taxi ahead was proceeding at a snail's pace – pursuit.

To Chung's mild surprise, the bright-yellow cab was soon navigating the busy traffic down Geylang Road. The narrow crowded back streets lined with colourfully painted old shophouses and fruit stalls did not seem a likely destination for a city lawyer. The taxi pulled up by the side of the road, oblivious to the double yellow lines, and Quentin clambered out.

Hassan said, 'No place to park – you'd better get out and follow him.'

Sergeant Chung nodded and slipped out of the car, hurrying after the thin figure. He sensed rather than saw Sergeant Hassan continue slowly down the road in his unmarked police vehicle. Chung ignored the gaudy Chinese language signboards, striped awnings and bustling crowds of people as he followed his quarry. He suppressed the desire to grin broadly – now *this* was what he called police work! He almost fell over an old cobbler sitting on the five-foot-way with his worn tools and a pile of old shoes. Quentin Holbrooke came to an abrupt standstill in front of a shuttered karaoke lounge advertising singing personal "hostesses".

A middle-aged Chinese man with a square head resting on square shoulders – he seemed to have dispensed with a neck entirely – slipped out of a narrow doorway. He sauntered over to the lawyer. The man – he looked like a Lego figure, decided the sergeant – glanced up and down the street quickly. Quentin Holbrooke reached into his trouser pocket and pulled out a fat envelope. The other man took it quickly and handed over a small package. The sergeant could not see what it was although he could guess. Quentin Holbrooke shoved the package into his briefcase without a second glance and before Chung could react, he had slipped into another taxi. The two parties to the transaction had not exchanged a single word.

The sergeant looked around anxiously. There was not another taxi in sight and Sergeant Hassan was probably a long way down the road. In any event, Quentin was probably heading back to the office.

There was only one thing to do. He marched up to the Lego man, pulled out his warrant card and said, 'Police – I need to talk to you.'

A brawny arm came up and shoved Chung in the chest. The man took off at top speed. Chung regained his footing and set off in hot pursuit.

*

Mrs Singh was seated on a cane sofa with light-green cushions and decorative white crocheted doilies, flanked on either side by an older sister. She was the youngest of four siblings but the fourth sister had discovered travel post-widowhood and was on a cruise ship on her way around Alaska. Such independent behaviour was frowned upon by her family who believed that travel was something that should be limited to weddings, funerals and children's graduations.

It was just as well, thought Mrs Singh, wedged uncomfortably between the two women, that she had remained skinny – there would have been no room on the sofa for all three of them otherwise. Her two older sisters had succumbed to the Sikh mother-in-law stereotype and grown enormously fat. The baggy trousers of their *salwar khameez* were the size of tents to gird their posteriors. It was a sultry, steamy day without a breath of wind and both women were sweating, armpits damp and wet patches forming under their ample bosoms. The vigorously spinning ceiling fan merely circulated the hot air. One of the two women grasped a magazine in plump be-ringed fingers and fanned herself. The effort required to produce a breeze outweighed the benefits and she flopped back down, patting her forehead with the end of her *dupatta*.

'Too hot nowadays,' she whispered, almost drowned out by the television. Mrs Singh did not consider it necessary or polite to switch off the TV when visitors arrived, especially if it was just family dropping by. Besides, she was waiting for a Punjabi-language film to come on.

'Must be that global warming – my son is learning about it in school,' her other sister remarked. 'He says we must not drive our cars so much.'

'What?' exclaimed the first one, startled into sitting

upright again. 'How to *walk* when the weather is like this?' She began fanning herself once more.

The maid trotted in bearing a tray with mugs of hot sweet Nescafé and a side dish of *paneer pakora*. Both sisters leaned forward, arms outstretched, folds of flab hanging down like heavy drapes. The first one dropped the *pakora* she had seized immediately. 'Still hot,' she explained, licking her finger tips with a pink tongue. The maid handed out side plates and paper serviettes. The sisters were silent for a few minutes as they blew on their snacks to cool the oil and nibbled on them happily.

The oldest sister, a thin layer of perspiration making her flawless skin gleam, asked, 'So – has brother found this *murderer?*'

Mrs Singh scowled and deep lines appeared on her taut skin. 'Not yet. He won't even let that boy go for his sister's wedding in Delhi. He's always so stubborn.'

'He should let him attend, otherwise it looks very bad for the family,' remarked her sister, wafting air towards her cheeks with a plump hand.

Mrs Singh suddenly remembered her husband's instructions. 'Have you heard anything about Jagdesh?' she asked. 'Any secrets? Maybe the mother in India is covering up something about him?'

'Why? What do you know?' There was excitement in her sister's tone at the possibility of some juicy gossip. The other sister swallowed her *pakora* hurriedly and leaned forward to hear the latest.

Mrs Singh shook her head in quick denial at being privy to any untoward information about their relative. 'No, no! I don't know anything. I thought maybe you did.'

There were slumped shoulders and disappointed shakes of the head all round.

She would have to tell her husband that Jagdesh Singh had nothing to hide, decided Mrs Singh. As she had suspected, he was just making unwarranted insinuations against a family member. There was just no way that Jagdesh Singh could have maintained a secret of any importance in the face of the unflagging curiosity of the Sikh community. He was just a nice fellow caught in her unreasonable husband's clutches.

'I'm going to invite that boy here for dinner again,' she said, and her voice was quiet and thoughtful, as if she'd come to a decision of great magnitude.

Thirteen

Annie perched on the edge of her chair like an earnest schoolgirl, wondering how to bring up the subject that occupied her waking moments without revealing more than she needed to – or wanted to – to her colleague.

'What's up?' asked Quentin. He was sitting behind his desk, crescents of sweat visible under his armpits. There were dark smudges under his eyes. He looked as if he had not slept in days, thought Annie. Perhaps he hadn't; she herself was suffering from terrible insomnia. Sleep was a luxury that suspects in a murder investigation could not afford.

'Just dropped in for a chat,' she said casually.

Quentin managed a weak smile. 'Good timing – I just got back in from running a few errands.'

'Have you heard anything from the Tan Sri lately?'

Quentin's expression transformed into one of puzzlement. He smoothed away a lock of mousy hair from his high forehead and asked, 'The Tan Sri? From the Malaysian file? No – why do you ask?'

'Just wondering . . .'

'I don't know how you can think about work right now,' Quentin said, his tone admiring. 'I'm just going around in circles. Have there been any developments on the file I should know about? That fat inspector was asking about the insider dealing – but I can't see how that matters, can you?'

Annie shook her head and changed the subject quickly. 'How was your interview?'

'A bit of a performance. Hopefully they didn't notice.'

She said earnestly, genuinely trying to help a friend, 'You need to stay on the good side of the police. That fat man is dangerous.'

He nodded and Annie smiled at him warmly. She rose to her feet. 'Back to the grind, I guess,' she said, and strolled to the door. She was determined to leave Quentin with the impression that it had been a friendly visit, not a fishing expedition to find out if he had heard anything about the insider dealing.

She literally walked into David who grabbed her by both arms to steady her. It was the first time they had made physical contact since he had grabbed her swinging fist that first morning in Mark's office. She was immediately aware of the strength in his long fingers as she regained her balance. He held on to her, his grip tightening. Then he saw the name on the door from which she had just exited and released her. He did not say a word but she saw that his lips had formed a thin line. She absently rubbed her arm where his grip had almost hurt her. She could not believe that he still suspected that she was in some sort of relationship with Quentin.

She was distracted by the sudden appearance of Singh, ambling down the corridor with Corporal Fong following at his heels like a well-trained dog. He did not seem to notice the tension radiating from Annie and David. He

169

nodded at the two of them in friendly fashion, as if they were acquaintances whose paths had crossed his on an Orchard Road shopping expedition. The policeman peered at the black and gold nameplate for a moment to confirm the room's occupant, raised his hand to knock, changed his mind and twisted the handle. As he marched into Quentin's office without a word of warning, Annie stared at his receding back in surprise, then hurried after him. David was hard on her heels. Their mistrust of each other was put aside for the temporary common purpose of figuring out what the turbaned policeman had up his sleeve.

Quentin looked shocked at the sudden invasion by the police but tried to put a brave face on it. 'Was there something else you wanted to ask me, Inspector?'

Annie and David watched from the door as Singh walked around the desk until he was on the same side as the lawyer. He perched himself on the edge of the teak table and looked carefully at Quentin Holbrooke, his bearded chin no more than a foot away from the lawyer's pale face.

'I really should have guessed,' he muttered under his breath, pink bottom lip thrust out in irritation.

Annie could see that the policeman's steady perusal was having an effect on her colleague. Despite the air conditioning, a sheen of sweat on Quentin's forehead reflected the fluorescent lighting and his hands were curled into tight fists to hide his trembling fingers.

Singh appeared to make up his mind.

'Fong!' he snapped.

'Yessir!'

'Arrest this man ...'

'On what grounds?' demanded David, hurrying forward as if he intended to physically impede Singh in the exercise of his duties.

170

'For the murder?' asked Annie, her voice high-pitched with shock, a contrast to her usual mellow tone.

Fong marched up to Quentin, all professional now, the uniformed action-man ready to carry out his superior's orders to the letter. Only the quick sidelong glance he threw at the inspector suggested to the older man that he was in the dark as to the genesis of this sudden turn of events. Singh was pleased, however, that Fong had not stopped to question his orders – he liked his flunkies to be obedient.

Quentin had gone limp, like a small rodent trying to avoid catching the eye of a bird of prey. His face was drained of colour except for the red inflammation around his nose and the dark circles under his eyes. His pupils were dilated to their maximum. Only a thin ring of his pale blue irises remained – it reminded Singh of an eclipse of the moon.

The young policeman placed a firm hand on Quentin's arm and ushered him – almost dragged him – to a standing position.

As Quentin swayed on his feet like a high-rise building in an earth tremor, Singh wondered for a moment if he was going to collapse. The lawyer's knees did not seem up to the job of keeping him upright.

'What's going on?' demanded David. His voice was firm; he was all attorney now, thought Singh, any misgivings about Quentin suppressed in his desire to protect a colleague.

Singh's eyes crinkled around the edges. His pouting lower lip was stretched thin by his wide smile. He sauntered over to Quentin's brown leather case, resting on the floor by his chair, picked it up and placed it on the table.

'Why don't you tell us what you have in here, young man?' Singh sounded like a school teacher who suspected that a student had a collection of soft porn in his schoolbag.

Quentin was trembling. It was terrifying to see a grown man so reduced by a crude, visceral fear. A major part of the policeman was pleased – such intense dread indicated a guilty conscience. At the same time, Singh could not help feeling a smidgen of sympathy for the young man. He really hoped that he never found himself in a position where he was so publicly emasculated.

The lawyers were all staring at the bag, making wild guesses as to its contents, except for Quentin. In contrast to the engrossed expressions of the rest, his eyes had the blankness of gaze that Singh associated with the blind.

'Well, go on!' barked the inspector.

Quentin reached out an unsteady hand and unclasped the old-fashioned hook. His hands fell to his sides and he shook his head to indicate his inability or unwillingness to carry on.

Singh scowled. 'Have it your way. Fong, tip it out.'

Fong released Quentin's arm and turned the bag over. A few sheets of paper, a couple of pens and a wallet fell out. The junior policeman looked at his boss inquiringly and was rewarded with a rude shake of the head. Fong shook the bag again, this time more vigorously.

A clear plastic bag fell out and landed on the table. It was packed full of a fine white powder just as Sergeants Chung and Hassan had reported.

'Quentin Holbrooke, I hereby arrest you for trafficking approximately forty grams of cocaine!'

Corporal Fong led a dazed Quentin Holbrooke away, leaving the two lawyers and Inspector Singh alone in the room.

'I don't understand,' whispered Annie.

'It's quite straightforward, isn't it?' remarked Singh. His tone was jovial.

'What do you mean?' growled David. Annie thought she had never seen him so enraged.

'Your lawyer friend, Quentin Holbrooke, is a cocaine addict – and he does a bit of trafficking on the side. Mark Thompson found out. Mark Thompson is *dead*.' Inspector Singh enunciated each word carefully as if he was a teacher to young children.

'You have no evidence that Mark knew about Quentin's cocaine habit!' insisted David angrily.

'Did you?' Singh whirled around on the balls of his feet and snapped the question at Annie.

She shook her head. 'I had no idea – none at all.'

'And Quentin and Annie were good friends. That just proves that Mark couldn't possibly have known,' interjected David.

'Mark Thompson was not a naïve young thing ...'

Annie bristled but Singh carried on. 'He might well have spotted the signs of an addiction – it was all there to see, the nerves, the mood swings, the running nose.'

David said, with an air of forced patience, 'If Mark had known about Quentin's addiction to drugs, he would have tried to get him medical help. Not called some sort of big meeting to announce it to the partners! Why would he?'

'I agree with you – *if* Quentin was just an addict. But he might have done some peddling on the side.'

'He *must* have had it for his own use. He wouldn't have been trafficking,' insisted David, his voice as unsteady as Annie's legs.

'There's no way you could know that,' pointed out the inspector. 'Besides, it doesn't matter!'

'What do you mean?'

'Section 17 of the Misuse of Drugs Act – anyone who has an amount of cocaine in excess of three grams "shall be presumed to have had that drug in possession for the purpose

173

of *trafficking* unless it is proved that his possession of that drug was not for that purpose".'

Annie turned pale. What was this tiresome policeman trying to say?

Singh sat down, hesitantly at first and then more quickly as gravity took over. He leaned back in Quentin Holbrooke's chair and folded his arms over his belly. Annie realised that this was a policeman who was confident that he had the evidence and the law on his side.

'Your friend had almost forty grams in that bag. You should know that unauthorised trafficking of more than thirty grams of cocaine means the *mandatory* death sentence. Quentin Holbrooke is going to swing.'

The two lawyers stared at him in open-mouthed horror.

'The only question', he continued, 'is whether he swings for the murder of Mark Thompson as well. It doesn't make a huge amount of difference to me. We can only hang him once.'

Fourteen

Quentin, alone in a holding cell, remembered the first time he had snorted cocaine. He had been pub-hopping along Boat Quay. A friend had suggested a party – one of those expat functions where people brought other people and the champagne cocktails flowed. It was a great place to pick up *sarong party girls*, as the young Singaporean women on the hunt for a rich white husband were colloquially known. The same friend had produced a neatly folded white packet, like a home-made envelope, full of a substance that looked like fine sugar. He had offered Quentin a try and Quentin, flushed with drink and success, had agreed at once. He remembered the burning sensation in his nose and the temporary sense of dislocation which had been followed by a rush of euphoria such as he had never felt before. It wasn't long before he was scoring coke every night. His friend introduced him to a dealer who knew better than to provide his rich young clients with anything except the best – Quentin's little packets were never adulterated with talcum powder or sugar. He lost weight. He had no appetite for

175

anything except the sensation of wellbeing that the cocaine provided. His nose was always raw and runny. He needed more regular fixes so his purchases from the supplier increased and his pay cheque no longer seemed to stretch till the end of the month. He was behind on his rent as well but, the truth was, he felt wonderful.

Quentin lay back on his cot in the single cell. He felt an intense craving for a fix and knew he would not be able to find the solace of sleep. Every muscle in his body was aching for the sense of release and power that a shot of cocaine provided. He could feel his heart fluttering like a small bird trapped in a cage. He rose to his feet and stumbled to the front of the cell. His lips were pulled back from his teeth as he screamed for the guards.

One of them sauntered over. 'What's the problem?'

Quentin rattled the bars furiously. 'I need to get out of here!'

'Not for a long time … if ever,' said the guard to the sound of general laughter from his fellow inmates and the other guards.

'So did Quentin Holbrooke kill Mark Thompson?'

Singh and Fong were back at the police station. Corporal Fong looked at the fat man nervously and the inspector guessed he wasn't sure whether it was a rhetorical question or a genuine request for input. He realised that he wasn't sure himself.

He, Singh, was not happy – not happy at all – with the way this case was progressing. He tried to form a picture in his mind of Mark Thompson, not as he had seen him that one time, slumped forward on his desk, but alive and well. To his annoyance, the mental images that formed were of the black-and-white still photos on the victim's living room mantelpiece. He felt like shouting out loud, 'Will the real Mark Thompson please stand up!' He really needed to understand the dead man's character if he was to find his killer. Which was he: the womaniser who had an affair with his maid, the romantic who believed he had found true love with a Filipina woman, the gregarious senior partner who was useful at kick-off meetings, the ethical partner who wanted to pull out of a transaction because a director was insider dealing, the suspicious husband who tramped around brothels looking for his wife, or the diligent company man who called a meeting late on a Friday night? Singh strongly believed that until he knew the man he would not know his murderer.

He had Quentin Holbrooke in the lock-up – the case against him for drug trafficking was cut and dried. The bag of coke had the lawyer's fingerprints all over it and young Sergeant Chung had distinguished himself by arresting Quentin's supplier after a brief frantic struggle in which the younger man had prevailed. It was now apparent that the large cash outlays from Quentin's bank account had been to purchase the cocaine. He thumbed through the bank statements again – the sums had grown larger and the intervals between purchases smaller. Quentin Holbrooke had followed the lead of countless others before him and progressed quickly from casual user to serious addict. Singh had thought at first that the blueprint indicated blackmail but a drug habit would reveal exactly the same spending pattern.

He cleared his throat – Corporal Fong's attention had wandered as he wrestled with the case in his own mind. 'Quentin Holbrooke has a secret that he *might* have been prepared to kill to preserve. But there is one major flaw in the case!'

177

Fong looked at him inquiringly. Singh noticed for the first time that the corporal's eyes were unusually far apart. He remembered reading somewhere that herbivores had wide-set eyes so they could look out for danger in all directions at once while carnivores had eyes in the front of their heads to spot and stalk prey more effectively. It was typical of his luck, he thought. He needed an aggressive sidekick with a predatory instinct for the truth. Instead, he had this wide-eyed grass eater.

'What is the flaw, sir?'

'Why don't you tell me for a change? This isn't some academy classroom where I can spoon feed you the answers all the time!'

Fong flushed.

'Well?' snapped Singh, knowing he was being unreasonable in taking out his aggravation on the rookie but unwilling to stop. After all, he had to do something to maintain his reputation as an impossible taskmaster.

The young policeman said slowly, 'We don't have any evidence that Mark Thompson knew about the drugs . . .'

'Exactly!' barked Singh. 'Mark Thompson has probably taken that information to his grave.'

'But even if Thompson had found out somehow, do you think he would have called a partners' meeting to tell them about Quentin Holbrooke?' asked Fong, his tone diffident.

'There's the rub,' complained Singh. 'These expats, they don't think much of someone being a drug addict, it's all rehab at swanky medical centres with celebrities. I just can't see Mark Thompson calling a big meeting to reveal a drug addiction to his partners.'

'Was Quentin Holbrooke the one you suspected earlier, sir? You know – based on your analysis of . . . errm . . . human nature?' asked Corporal Fong.

Singh didn't like the way Fong had enunciated the words "human nature" as if the senior policeman had resorted to voodoo investigative methods. The corporal made it sound as if he had brought in a psychic to pluck a murderer's name out of the ether after sensing vibes from the murder weapon. But he had to admit that Fong had a point. Singh shook his head decisively in answer to the young man's question. Quentin Holbrooke hadn't even been a blip on his radar before Sergeants Chung and Hassan had called him with the news of the drugs bust.

'If it wasn't Quentin, than it must have been Maria Thompson, sir. She had a motive – she needed money for her children. Her marriage was on the rocks because of the anonymous letters; you said yourself it doesn't matter if the allegations were true, only that Thompson believed them. Mark Thompson would have had no qualms escorting her to his office ... it *must* have been her, sir!' Fong was uncharacteristically assertive.

Singh rubbed his cheeks with the palms of his hands, giving them a ruddy tinge. This case was not so much going nowhere as going in all directions at once. His superiors wanted a speedy resolution. But Singh felt he was further away from identifying a murderer than when he had first seen the dead man sprawled across his desk. His corporal was still looking at him with a combination of dread and hope, like a stray mutt hoping for scraps but fearing a kick.

'I don't believe it was Maria!' said Singh stubbornly.

He rested his bearded chin in his cupped hands, elbows on the table, and gazed pensively at his neatly turned out colleague. Fong was right, of course. Singh knew full well that Maria Thompson was the most likely culprit, but he wanted to believe that her concern for the future of her children would have prevented her from taking such an extreme step as murder. Unfortunately, he'd just poked holes in his own case against Quentin. The fact remained that an alcoholic philanderer like Mark Thompson was unlikely to have called a meeting of the partnership to discuss a drug habit. Even if he had known about Quentin's addiction, and it was a big "if" unsupported by any tangible evidence, Mark would not have assumed – unlike the law of the land – that Quentin was trafficking. And he, Singh, was still convinced that the partners' meeting was crucial to the murder.

He sat up suddenly and his white shirt stretched taut over his belly. He wagged a finger at his subordinate. 'Drugs – that's the first step. What's next?'

Fong looked blank.

'Money! A drug habit like Quentin Holbrooke's costs *money*, more than he earned even as a fancy-pants lawyer to rich crooks. We know that from his bank statements. Maybe – just maybe – there was some financial hanky-panky going on at the firm of Hutchinson & Rice and Mark Thompson found out about it.'

Annie stood at the door of the Raffles Place police station and felt an almost uncontrollable desire to turn away. If she had not already been terrified of the turbaned policeman, she would be now, after this afternoon's performance, where he had produced the drugs from Quentin's bag like a magician conjuring a rabbit out of a hat. She imagined the fat inspector sitting in a dingy office, files at right angles to each other, rows of pens neatly arranged and him leaning back in his chair with his hands folded over his belly and his eyes closed in thought.

Dismissing her unwillingness to enter the building as a weakness she could ill afford, Annie took a deep breath and marched in. It was a brightly lit foyer, cool compared to the outside, with an inquiry desk at one end and posters on the walls bearing messages from the Singapore police like "Low crime doesn't mean no crime!" Surely, thought Annie, a message like that was possible only in the largely crime-free state of Singapore, the place where Mark Thompson had defied the statistics and been murdered.

'Ms Nathan?' The ubiquitous figure of Corporal Fong materialised at her elbow.

'Inspector Singh sent me down to wait for you,' he explained, 'so that I can take you directly upstairs.'

As they hurried up, she asked him, 'What's happening with Quentin? Have they charged him?'

'Um ... the inspector did not tell me to say anything.'

It was on the tip of her tongue to retort that Fong had not been instructed to breathe either. But she saved the energy for their ascent up another flight of stairs and arrived breathless outside a door with the words "Inspector Singh" in white plastic on black. Corporal Fong knocked and entered with Annie hard on his heels.

Inspector Singh nodded a welcome. 'You wanted to see me?'

'Yes, I have something I need to tell you.'

Annie's long wavy hair was combed away from her face and pinned behind her ears with two plain black clips. Despite her diffident tone, her mouth was set in a stubborn line, underlining her determination to proceed with her chosen course of action.

'Well, what is it?' Singh hoped she had not come all the way to his office to harangue him about Quentin's innocence or the brutality of Singapore's drug laws. He was already dreading the reaction of the international press when they discovered that he had a foreign lawyer behind bars for presumed drug trafficking.

She repeated, 'There's something I need to tell you.'

'Go on.'

There was a further hesitation. Singh straightened up in his chair. Anything that could turn a cocky young lawyer into someone secretive and uncertain was worth hearing. He just wished she would get on with it.

'You remember the Malaysian file?'

'Yup – what about it?'

'I got a call a few days ago from the boss of Trans-Malaya.'

Singh gritted his teeth. She needed to get to the point. He had a murder on his hands. 'So?'

Annie's voice strengthened, as if she was finding a residue of courage. 'He said someone was insider dealing, using information from the takeover process.'

Singh waited for more. This wasn't anything new – Sheringham had already told him about the insider dealing. He'd even asked this woman about it during her interview. Mark's reluctance to continue with a transaction tainted with illegality had given him a belated respect for the dead man, but it hadn't helped him find his killer.

Annie continued, 'Tan Sri Ibrahim is sure that the insider dealing originated in Singapore, with one of the lawyers at Hutchinson & Rice.'

Singh sighed. 'I see.' And he did – the chickens were coming home to roost.

'There's more.'

Singh maintained his silence. He could sense Annie's disinclination to continue her tale but he was not going to prompt her with questions. He wanted to hear what she had to say, in her own words. At the same time, his mind was working furiously, exploring the implications of Annie's information like a chess grandmaster anticipating moves ten steps ahead of the game.

Finally Annie mumbled, 'Mark knew. The Tan Sri called him that Friday, the day he was killed.'

Singh closed his eyes. His dark lids looked like two hollows – as if they were the eyes of the blind. And he had been blind. He had not suspected for a moment that the insider dealing might have originated at the law firm. Like a typical Singaporean, he had been prepared to believe the worst of a Malaysian director. He deserved a solid kick on his ample posterior for falling into such an obvious cultural trap and no doubt Superintendent Chen would be first in line to administer it.

'Who did it? Who was insider dealing?' the inspector asked.

The answer drifted to him, a whisper riding on a sigh. 'Quentin.'

Fifteen

Inspector Singh sat on one of two stainless steel chairs in a small windowless room. Quentin Holbrooke, drug addict, was huddled in the other. Wan, unshaven, uncombed, wearing grubby clothes – he looked to Singh like a shadow of the young, brash, confident lawyer that he must have been before the drugs had taken their toll on his health and long before he found himself in a small holding cell at a Singapore police station.

'How are you holding up?' asked Singh. He felt strangely sorry for this young fool who had turned to insider dealing to fund his drug habit and found himself on an unmapped road to murder.

Quentin did not reply. He buried his face in his hands and his shoulders started to shake. The inspector sat quietly and let the storm of despair wash over his suspect. Finally, when he thought that the young man was more collected, he asked, 'Is there anything you want to tell me?'

Quentin looked up, his pale-blue eyes shining with unshed tears.

'What is there to say? You found the drugs ...'

'Were you trafficking?'

Singh would not have thought it possible but Quentin seemed to grow paler, almost translucent. 'Of course not – I wouldn't do that!'

'That was a big packet we found in your bag. More than sufficient for the death penalty.'

Unlike his colleagues earlier, Quentin did not appear shocked at his words. Singh supposed he must have been acutely aware of the risk he was taking in feeding his cocaine addiction. He was a lawyer, after all – smart enough to know the consequences of his actions but just too dependent on the drug to avoid them.

'It was all for me. I was afraid, with the murder investigation, that I might not get a chance to buy some more for a while.'

Singh nodded. It was plausible. Indeed, it was what he had suspected. 'So that's where all the money went?'

Quentin smiled wanly. 'I'm afraid so. I wish it *had* been horses. Can you believe I'm even behind on my rent?'

Singh felt his respect for the young man grow. He was showing resilience now although it was a bit late in the day. The expression on Singh's face was sympathetic. It was a well-documented, well-travelled road from drug addiction to criminal behaviour. He said, and it was a statement not a question, 'And when the money ran out, you decided to indulge in a bit of insider dealing.'

'What?' There was genuine confusion in Quentin's voice. His tone was shrill and surprised.

Singh felt his first frisson of doubt, but he persevered. 'And Mark Thompson found out – and now Mark is dead.'

'Are you accusing me of *murder*?'

Quentin shook his head from side to side as if trying phys-

185

ically to dislodge the accusation. A thin hand went to his neck as if he could already feel the rough cord of the noose.

'You face a mandatory death sentence for the drugs – what's the point in denying that you killed the boss?' Singh asked the question as if he was the voice of reason itself. He continued, 'Why leave your colleagues and friends with the suspicion of murder hanging over them?'

Quentin dragged himself to his feet and thrust out his hands, a supplicant begging for understanding. 'I didn't do it. The insider dealing, the murder – that wasn't me. None of it was me!'

'This is your chance – maybe your last chance – to do the right thing,' pointed out Singh.

Quentin shook his head. Singh's suggestion that he confess from a sense of altruism had fallen on deaf ears. Instead, the prisoner asked, 'I don't understand, why do you think it was me insider dealing anyway?'

'You needed money!' Singh looked at Quentin Holbrooke thoughtfully. If the young man was not tempted by the noble idea of self-sacrifice, he might prefer revenge. The fat man continued, 'Besides, your colleagues are only too willing to point the finger of blame at you.'

Quentin Holbrooke collapsed back into his chair as if the force of gravity was too much for his weakened body and refused to utter another word.

'I'm not sure he did it.' Singh hated to admit to doubt.

'He must be lying, sir.' Fong was clearly unconvinced by the assertions of a drug addict.

'But he had absolutely *nothing* to lose by confessing to insider dealing – or, for that matter, to the murder. He knows we've got him for the drugs.' The inspector's bottom lip was thrust out so far he looked liked a petulant, albeit hairy, child.

Fong's rosebud mouth was pursed shut, indicating his reluctance to contradict his senior officer. Singh, however, wished he would argue further. He wanted Fong to test his scepticism by disputing it. The inspector desperately wished he could put his finger on what was troubling him. He had been uneasy ever since the interview with Quentin when the young man had denied further criminality in a voice that quavered with shock. It was causing the fat policeman indigestion, a very rare occurrence indeed.

'Any word from the boys in the corporate crimes unit?' he asked.

Fong shook his head. 'Not yet, sir.'

Singh knew he could not expect a response so quickly. He had asked the boffins in the white collar crimes unit for some evidence that Quentin Holbrooke had been insider dealing. They had stared at him owlishly through thick-framed, thick-lensed spectacles. It would be very difficult to find a paper trail, or even an electronic trail – insider dealing was one of the hardest crimes to prove, they explained to Singh. The inspector had refrained from kicking a chair with difficulty. He had merely muttered, 'Well, do your best,' and waddled out of the room.

He would love to have some proof to assuage his hunch that perhaps Quentin Holbrooke was not the murderer after all. It was like an itch in the middle of his back that he couldn't reach to scratch, and it was driving him nuts.

'Maria Thompson?' asked Fong. His tone suggested he was half-heartedly throwing a young virgin into a volcano to appease the gods of law enforcement.

It caused a sudden grin to spread across the senior policeman's swarthy features. The upbeat mood was fleeting as he remembered his doubts over Quentin Holbrooke.

As Fong eyed him nervously, Singh hunkered down in his

chair, the layers of fat on his stomach folded like an accordion. 'All right, let's think this through. What do we believe might have happened?'

'Quentin is a drug addict,' Fong replied. 'He was insider dealing to get money for the cocaine. Mark Thompson found out when the Tan Sri called him. He summoned a partners' meeting. Quentin killed him before he could reveal what he knew.'

'How long has the insider dealing been going on?'

'About six months, according to David Sheringham.'

Singh almost snatched Quentin's bank statement. 'Then can you tell me why Holbrooke was a pauper right up until the murder? He told me he was even behind on his rent! Surely, he would have used some of the funds – even if they were squirrelled away in some Swiss bank account – at least to pay the rent!'

Fong nodded, a reluctant affirmation that the older man had a point.

'We need to take a closer look at this. Who else worked on the Malaysian file?'

'Annie Nathan and Mark Thompson, sir.'

Their conversation was interrupted by the door swinging open with a crash. Singh glanced up in surprise and was confronted with the sight of Superintendent Chen. He didn't need to be a top-notch crime investigator to deduce that his boss was incensed – that was apparent from the clenched jaw and clenched fists.

Superintendent Chen did not mince his words. He pointed a long, bony finger at Inspector Singh. 'What the hell do you think you're doing?'

Singh noticed out of the corner of his eye that Corporal Fong looked as if he was about to wet himself. He didn't blame the boy. Having a superintendent demanding answers

188

was enough to try the courage of even a senior policeman. Not him, of course, he was used to it. Although, looking at his superior from under eyebrows that had flattened into straight lines, he had to admit he had no idea what was bothering his boss.

'What do you mean, sir?' he asked politely.

'Is it true that you've arrested one of the lawyers on a drugs charge?'

Singh nodded his great turbaned head, his pink bottom lip thrust out. 'Yes, sir, we found forty grams of coke in his briefcase. Open and shut case, and a damned good motive for murder.'

'Has he been charged?'

'Not yet.'

'Release him!'

'What?'

'You heard me! Release Quentin Holbrooke.'

Singh pushed on the arms of his chair, stood up and waddled up to his superior. He was so close that his belly was almost pushing the senior man back out of the door. He thrust his bearded chin forward so that chin and turban were a two-pronged attack. Through gritted teeth, he demanded, 'Why in the world should I release him?'

'Can you really be that naïve?' asked the superintendent, taking an involuntary step backwards. 'Don't you think this murder investigation of yours has generated enough bad publicity for Singapore? Now you want to hang some thirty-something *white* yuppie from an international law firm for drug trafficking? You must be out of your mind!'

A slight movement from Corporal Fong caught their attention.

The superintendent barked, 'What is it? What do you want?'

Fong was pale. A lock of jet-black hair had escaped its normal slick neatness and fallen over his forehead. 'We found him with the drugs, sir. He didn't deny it.'

Singh guessed that the senior policeman was pleased to find someone else to vent his anger on, especially when that someone was a rookie who was ashen-faced with fear, his rapidly blinking eyes indicating a profound regret that he had been moved to contradict a senior officer.

Superintendent Chen bit off each word as if it was a piece of sour mango. 'I don't care if you found the drugs in a condom shoved up a body cavity. We are not compounding the economic woes of this country in the middle of a recession by hanging an expat who works in the city – got it?'

Singh found his voice. 'We're just waiting for some proof that he was insider dealing,' he lied fluently. 'What if he killed Mark Thompson?'

'That's another matter entirely. It will show that no killer of an expatriate is immune from prosecution. Justice in Singapore is blind!'

And incapable of irony, thought Singh, but he kept his mouth shut.

The sun was setting over the Singapore Botanic Gardens and the sky was streaked with crimson. There was the merest whisper of wind which swayed the treetops gently. The sounds of crickets chirping and clicking disturbed the stillness and the dusk air was heavy with the scent of white gardenias. Two figures stood under a massive flame of the forest tree, its red blossoms licking the sky like fire. The man and woman were engrossed in each other and had no eyes for the beauty around them. Their bodies were rigid with tension and their conversation took place in heated whispers. Both faces were contorted with such rage that it looked like they were play-acting rather than in earnest.

'That fat policeman suspects something, I tell you! Why else would he have asked if we were close friends?'

'That fool,' said Reggie Peters contemptuously. 'He couldn't find his way out of a room with one door.'

'You're making a mistake, I tell you. We shouldn't under-estimate him. We have to end this once and for all.' Ai Leen was pleading, not bothering to hide her desperation.

He shook his head. 'You're just using this as an excuse to renege on a bargain.'

Ai Leen summoned up a memory of the woman she had been once, the single-minded, ambitious, fearless creature who had let nothing stand in her way. She said, her voice threatening, 'Don't push me too far.'

Reggie leaned forward and grabbed her by the throat, pushing her chin up with his thumbs until she was forced to look at him. For a fleeting second, it appeared possible to Ai Leen that Reggie might kill her, use his superior male strength to throttle the life out of her body. Instead, his body relaxed. He took a step back and then let go. Her hands went to her throat instinctively, protectively, but he made no further move against her.

He said in a menacing whisper, 'Listen very carefully to me, bitch. If I suspect your nerve is going, I'll snap your neck like a twig!'

Fear and defiance fought for mastery over her expression. She might have spoken but no words could navigate the passage of her hurt throat. Reggie turned and walked away. Ai Leen watched him go and then spat violently on the muddy ground where he had stood.

'I know just who to ask to look into this alleged insider dealing!' said Singh brightly.

He seemed already to have forgotten the intrusion by Superintendent Chen and his dubious instructions to release Quentin Holbrooke. Corporal Fong was not quite so resilient. His mouth was dry and his heart was pounding. He wished he had not intervened, it hadn't achieved anything except to provide an easy target for the senior policeman's anger.

Singh continued to muse. 'If we can *prove* Quentin was insider dealing, we'll have a good case against him for the murder. Annie Nathan thinks it was him but the opinions of others aren't evidence. Isn't that right, Fong?'

Fong remembered his earlier fantasies in which he would save the day by nabbing a murderer in the nick of time while his superiors stood around flummoxed. They would have immediately promoted him, bypassing all the standard red tape to reward such an extraordinary addition to the Force. Well, his superiors *were* flummoxed – but so was he. At least Singh was trying to work through the puzzle. He, Fong, was just trying to keep his knees from trembling.

'Are you going to do it, sir?' he asked abruptly.

A sharp vertical line bisected Singh's forehead in two just above the bridge of his nose. 'Do what?' he asked.

'Release Quentin ...'

'Well, you heard the man – let it never be said that Inspector Singh did not follow the instructions of his *superior* officers to the letter!' Singh enunciated the word "superior" with enormous faux respect and then giggled like a schoolboy.

The corporal's face betrayed his confusion. Singh appeared to take pity on his young sidekick because he explained, 'Look, for different reasons entirely, I have no desire to hang Quentin Holbrooke for drug trafficking. That's not my job or my inclination. We'll let him go. He's at the end of his tether. Let's see whether he ties a noose in it again – for the murder this time.'

Fong pulled himself together with a conscious effort. 'Who did you want to ask for help with the insider dealing matter, sir?'

'Inspector Mohammed of the Malaysian police. We worked together on a recent case. A man of great ability, unimpeachable principles and,' he continued almost admiringly, 'an impeccable wardrobe.'

Fong's only encounter with the Malaysian police had been as a boy when his father had been pulled over for speeding on the road to Kuala Lumpur. '*Nak settle, ke?*' the Malaysian cop had asked, pen poised threateningly over the traffic ticket. Fong's father had pulled out a fifty *ringgit* note and slipped it to the policeman. Fong had cowered in the back seat of the car for the rest of the journey, convinced that the long arm of the law would soon yank them off to prison.

Inspector Singh must have had a very different experience with the Malaysian police force if he was prepared to ask them for help.

However, when they got him on the speaker phone, Inspector Mohammed sounded suspicious rather than pleased to hear from his Singaporean colleague. 'Singh, to what do I owe this dubious pleasure?' His expensive education was clearly audible in each syllable he uttered.

The Sikh inspector chuckled. 'Just trying to maintain friendly relations between the police forces of our two countries ...'

It was Mohammed's turn to laugh. 'Yes, I still wake up sweating from your last effort to forge a bond between nations.'

Fong could not help smiling at this. It did not surprise him that Inspector Singh had stepped on a few toes on his

Malaysian case. He had the biggest metaphorical feet of any policeman he had met – perhaps the shiny white sneakers were actually meant as a warning.

Singh cut to the chase. 'I've got a big case on my hands ...'

'I've been reading about it in the papers – some white expat got his head bashed in. Please don't tell me there's a Malaysian angle!'

'Afraid so,' said Singh cheerfully.

Mohammed's sigh was audible despite the crackling line. 'OK, what do you want?'

'One of the suspects might have been illegally trading the shares of a Malaysian company – Trans-Malaya Bhd.'

'Insider dealing?'

'Yup.'

'They'd need a brokerage account here ...'

'Almost certainly not in their own name,' said Singh.

'Money trail?' asked the Malaysian inspector.

'Not a dime. Whoever did it has the cash squirrelled away in some numbered Swiss account.'

'You don't make it easy, do you?' commented Mohammed.

Singh was suddenly serious. 'Neither do the murderers,' he said heavily.

Sixteen

Even thirty years of marriage to this dogmatic, opinionated woman had not prepared him for her latest effort to cause him maximum humiliation, thought Singh bitterly. He was livid and it showed in his drooping jowls and creased forehead. He was sitting at the dining table. A sumptuous spread of food was laid out before him. Almost unthinkably, in the face of such temptation, Inspector Singh had no appetite. This was not because he had taken a sudden dislike to his wife's cooking. It was the identity of his dinner companion that had taken the edge off his desire for food.

Across from him, a suspect in a murder investigation was tucking into his dinner and making polite small talk with his wife. He had asked Mrs Singh to inquire whether Jagdesh Singh was keeping secrets that her nosy relatives might be able to ferret out. Instead, Mrs Singh had invited him home for a meal. He shuddered to think what Superintendent Chen would say if he got wind of this cosy little dinner party.

Mrs Singh was ladling more *dahl* onto Jagdesh Singh's plate. His wife's hair was tied up in a bun, a strand of jasmine flowers threaded through it. The perfume of the flowers could not compete with the spicy scent of home cooking.

'Some more *aloo*?' she asked, almost simpering over the simple question. It was not difficult to deduce that she had been bowled over by her good-looking guest.

Jagdesh nodded, his mouth too full to speak. His plum-coloured lips curved into a smile and Singh was forced to the conclusion that Jagdesh Singh reminded him of a Bollywood film star. Aquiline nose, olive skin, sparkling teeth and warm eyes – hadn't he just seen that combination on the television when his wife had been immersed in one of her innumerable DVDs?

Mrs Singh nodded approvingly at her guest's willingness to have seconds and ladled out a generous helping of the spicy potato and fenugreek dish while Singh pouted at the double standards. He was always being nagged to reduce his food consumption, not invited to have seconds – and no doubt thirds as well.

'I like a boy who has a good appetite,' Mrs Singh said, smiling at the hulking thirty-something lawyer as if he was a skinny ten-year-old who needed feeding up.

Singh's eyebrows almost met over the ridge of flesh that formed a hillock above his nose.

'No, Aunty – my good appetite is my *problem*!' Jagdesh patted his belly fondly.

'Nonsense! You are still young. You need your food.'

If you're lucky, thought Singh snidely, you can eat Indian sweetmeats until you're fifty and then struggle to tie your shoelaces. He didn't utter the thought out loud. He was determined to maintain a sullen silence.

His wife trotted to the kitchen and brought out a dish piled high with fresh chapattis.

'If you marry *Chinese*, you won't get this sort of food,' she said.

She had apparently decided the moment was ripe to go on the attack.

Jagdesh grinned. His incisors were slightly longer than his other teeth and it gave his smile a devilish edge. Singh wondered how he had missed it before.

'I'm sure a willing wife could learn how to cook. Maybe *you* could give her lessons.'

Singh suppressed a smirk. The young lawyer had his wife torn between her horror that he seemed to be confirming the family's suspicion that he had a Chinese girlfriend and her pleasure at the suggestion that her cooking was good enough to teach. His amusement turned to irritation when he noticed that his wife was now positively beaming at the compliment paid by this young scion of the extended family.

'You musn't upset your parents, they have high hopes for you.'

Jagdesh laughed out loud. He said, his tone consoling, 'I'm just joking, Aunty. I don't have a girlfriend. Too busy at work.'

Too busy at work indeed! He would have expected Jagdesh to be fending off the women with a broom, not too absorbed in his job to have a social life. Could anyone be that much of a workaholic? The taciturn policeman frowned. Had Jagdesh's so-called busy schedule included a window to bump off the boss? After all, he was sceptical that Quentin Holbrooke was a murderer, the insider dealing just didn't square with the account statements. He preferred not to believe that Maria Thompson had taken the ultimate step to ensure her financial security. Perhaps it *was* his good-looking young relative who was the culprit. But what possible reason could Jagdesh have had for killing Mark? So far, Singh acknowledged ruefully, his suspicions were based entirely on a gut feeling that the boy was keeping secrets and his exasperation at his wife's fawning behaviour. It was hardly conclusive of guilt. After all, Mark Thompson hadn't been on his case to settle down with a nice Sikh girl.

Unlike his wife, who was not pulling any punches. She said, 'I know some really pretty Sikh girls who are very anxious to meet you. One of them is a doctor!'

It was her trump card, but perhaps played a little too early. Her expression was anxious as she scanned the face of the prospective groom. '*England*-qualified,' she added hurriedly in case he should think that the girl had her medical degree from one of the hundreds of Indian colleges offering dodgy degrees to the offspring of status-conscious Indians from all over the globe.

Jagdesh smiled sweetly at his hostess. 'I would be very happy to meet her, Aunty.'

Despite his earlier determination to maintain an aggressive silence to indicate his disapproval of this enforced tête-à-tête, Singh could not stand the saccharine conversation between his wife – his own *wife* – and this murder suspect.

'What are you afraid of?' he demanded.

Jagdesh looked at him in surprise, his masticating jaw slowing down but not stopping entirely.

He spoke with his mouth still half-full. 'What do you mean, Uncle?'

Singh was distracted by the form of address. '*I'm* the inspector in charge of a murder investigation – and you're a suspect! So let's have less of this "uncle" nonsense.'

Jagdesh swallowed hard and coughed – one large hand covering his mouth. 'I'm sorry, sir. I was just trying to be polite.'

'You shouldn't be so rude to our visitor,' exclaimed Mrs Singh. 'You heard what he said – he's just trying to be polite. Maybe you can learn some manners from him!'

Singh felt a sharp pain between his eyes. His wife was about to trigger a major headache with her wilful blindness to protocol. Not even he, the well-known maverick, could match her efforts to ignore appropriate conduct during a murder investigation.

He tried again. 'What are you afraid of?'

Jagdesh pushed his plate away. Either he was finally full or he had suddenly lost his appetite. 'I'm not afraid of anything, sir. I don't know what you're talking about.'

Singh nodded, as if he was taking his unwanted guest's assertion at face value. But he had been quick to note that Jagdesh's brown eyes had been gazing at the plastic table cloth when he had answered the question.

Mrs Singh was triumphant. 'See – I *told* you he wasn't the murderer!'

Later that night, across town, in a bar in Chinatown, a tall man perched on a red leather barstool polished smooth over the years. The bartender leaned over and tipped the last of a bottle of Chivas Regal into his nearly empty whisky tumbler. He held it up to show the man that the bottle was empty and received a nod of acknowledgement from him. The quiet, brooding sort, thought the barman idly. But he had a big man's capacity for liquor. He had drunk steadily through a whole bottle of whisky. The only telltale signs were a redness around the eyes and a slight unsteadiness when he reached for his glass.

'Can I get you something to eat?' he asked.

The big man shook his head, turning his bleary gaze to the barman. 'No, I've had dinner – thank you.'

The heavy front door of the bar was pushed open and the red lanterns that were strung across the streets were briefly visible. A waft of hot exhaust-laden air accompanied a young Chinese man onto the premises. He stood at the entrance, blinking as his eyes adjusted to the dimness within. He was dressed in black, a body-hugging short-sleeved shirt with oversized shiny ebony buttons all down the front, leather trousers and soft leather ankle boots with silver buckles. He had dressed in black to lend himself an air of sophistication, but his youth shone through. He must have suspected as much, because he nervously ran a hand through his thick spiky hair. After looking around the bar carefully, the corners of which were lost in velvety darkness, he sat down on a stool next to the tall man sipping his Chivas absent-mindedly and put his elbows on the bar. He had tanned, sinewy, hairless arms and his nails were clean and well manicured.

'What'll it be?' the barman asked him.

'Same thing as him,' he said, nodding at the glass of the man perched on the stool next to him. His request drew a bleary glance from his neighbour and the Chinese man smiled at him in a friendly but tentative fashion. On receiving no response, he looked away and sipped his whisky while idly playing with the beer mat in front of him. A large brown hand took hold of his in a gentle but firm clasp. The young man glanced up at Jagdesh Singh and this time his smile was wide and confident.

The mobile by Singh's bed rang. Mrs Singh didn't hear it. She had a pillow over her head to drown out her husband's constant snoring.

For a few semi-conscious seconds, his hand sought his alarm clock. Then the inspector answered the phone grog-

gily, making a silent promise that if the call was not important he would have the badge of the policeman who had
woken him. He hoped it was Corporal Fong. However, after
listening to the caller for a few seconds, he grew alert and
sleep slipped from him like a blanket falling to the floor.

'No! Not yet. Wait for me. I'll be there as soon as I can!'
He was almost shouting. His wife stirred by his side and he
moderated his tone. He really, *really* didn't want to have to
tell her about the latest developments in his case.

The apartment building was concrete, steel and glass. It
towered above the older blocks around it, most of them
empty and slated for destruction. Singh was outside a heavy
door on the tenth floor. He had two uniforms with him, both
of them looking nervous but excited. Singh did not share
their energy or their enthusiasm. He knew he would be much
happier remaining in complete blissful ignorance of what he
suspected lay behind the door.

Sergeant Chung, who clearly thought of himself as some
sort of action man after his altercation with the drug dealer,
said, 'Do you want me to break down the door, sir?'

Singh looked pained. 'Don't be ridiculous.'

'But we suspect the commission of an offence! We can go
in ...'

Singh had never fully understood the expression about
not teaching one's grandmother to suck eggs but he was
damned if he was going to be lectured in the small hours
of the morning by some adrenaline-charged rookie. He
muttered, 'That's why I've asked the security guard for the
spare key.'

Sergeant Chung looked crestfallen. Perhaps, thought
Singh, he should have let the young fool break a leg trying to
smash his way through the heavy door.

201

An elderly man who walked with a limp and was dressed in a uniform festooned in epaulettes and shiny buttons arrived in the elevator. He held a large bunch of keys, one silver key pinched between a sweaty thumb and forefinger. 'I bring you the master keys. But I very worried about what the residents will say. Sure they will be very angry.'

'This is police business,' said Singh brusquely.

The old man, having recorded his disapproval of their conduct, slipped the key into the door and turned it silently. He looked inquiringly at the police. The inspector waved him away.

Sergeant Chung pulled out his gun with a flourish.

'Put that away, you young idiot! What do you think is going on in there exactly?'

'We should be prepared for anything, sir!'

'I'm *not* prepared to get shot in the back by you,' growled Singh.

Chung slipped his gun back into its holster, his mouth slack with disappointment.

The inspector raised a stubby finger to his lips, took a deep breath and opened the door slowly.

The room was empty and in semi-darkness. The dim light came from a single floor lamp. A thin strip of yellow light was visible under a closed door at the other end of the hall. Singh led the way, moving with unexpectedly light feet for such a superficially clumsy figure. He turned the handle and flung the door open.

Two heads popped out from under the crumpled bedclothes. One belonged to a handsome, youthful Chinese man with dishevelled spiky hair whose mouth formed an "o" of surprise. The other man was the inspector's nephew a few times removed, Jagdesh Singh.

Inspector Singh leaned back against the doorpost, hands hanging limply by his sides. His murder investigation had just turned into a gay bedroom farce.

Seventeen

The sun was streaming in the large windows behind him so the lawyer sitting at his desk was a dark featureless silhouette. David could not see the expression on Stephen's face nor deduce why he had been summoned by the senior partner.

Stephen got to the point quickly. 'I just got a call from the police station. Jagdesh has been arrested!'

'Jagdesh has been arrested? What for? You don't mean for the *murder*? What about Quentin?'

'No, *not* for the murder.'

Stephen's voice was calm, but David sensed that the calmness was a thin veneer. The older man stood up and walked around the desk, his eyes stormy and bloodshot. His voice was wheezy, as if he was physically winded by the news he had just received.

'Just tell me!' David hurled his angry request at Stephen. He needed to know. He couldn't understand Stephen's unwillingness to reveal the details after having announced the raw fact of Jagdesh's arrest.

'Buggery!'

David stared at him, genuinely mystified.

'Superintendent Chen called – you know he agreed to keep the firm in the loop – to inform me that Jagdesh Singh was picked up last night. Or in the early hours of this morning, I should say. He was in bed with a young man.'

David was bemused. He ran a thin hand through his short hair so that it stood up like the fur on an angry cat. 'Jagdesh is *gay*? I never knew that.'

'I didn't either. No one did, it would seem!'

'But I don't understand why he's been arrested.'

'As the good policeman reminded me, homosexuality is still illegal in this country,' stated Stephen.

'You must be joking!' exclaimed the lawyer from London.

Stephen shrugged. 'Well, it's not called "unlawful carnal intercourse against the order of nature" in the statutes any more – merely "gross indecency" – but yes, homosexuality is still illegal in Singapore. The law isn't much enforced, which is probably why you weren't aware of it.'

'What's their proof anyway?' demanded David.

'The police tailed him to his flat from a well-known gay bar in Chinatown. And he was caught in bed with a young man by Inspector Singh.'

David shook his head as if he was trying to clear his mind of wayward thoughts. 'I thought you said the law wasn't enforced. So why have they arrested Jagdesh?'

'Superintendent Chen intimated that it might be a motive for murder ...'

'What?'

'You heard me!'

'But I don't understand.'

'Apparently, the thinking is that Mark might have found

out about the homosexuality and Jagdesh killed him to keep his secret safe.'

'That's the most ridiculous thing I've ever heard.' David was speaking through gritted teeth, a white ring of tension around his mouth. 'Aside from the obvious point that there is no evidence that Mark knew, why in the world would Jagdesh kill him over something like that?'

'You're thinking like a lawyer from London,' said Stephen gruffly. 'But Singapore is one of the last bastions of the conservative society. It has an extremely vocal religious crowd – that's why homosexuality is still illegal in the first place. It's sort of like the "red" states in the United States, but without the liberals on the coasts.'

David was snide. 'God, gays and greed?'

Stephen ignored the sarcasm. 'Exactly,' he said heavily.

Annie stopped by the ladies' room on the way to her office. She needed to splash some cold water on her face, try and clear her head of the events of the last couple of days. She had found the courage to tell Inspector Singh about the Tan Sri's call but she was still aghast at what she had done. Quentin thought of her as a friend, a good friend, and she had told the Singapore police that he was insider dealing. She knew it had been the necessary and prudent thing to do. Insider dealing was difficult to prove if the criminal was careful and covered his tracks. But the Tan Sri's allegation would have been sufficient to raise the possibility that she or Quentin might have a motive for murder. Quentin was already in deep trouble over the drugs. There was just no point keeping the Tan Sri's suspicions a secret any more. Not when he was almost certain to call back sooner rather than later and speak to someone other than herself – he might even have gone directly to the police. It was only a matter of time, now that he was back in Kuala Lumpur, before he heard that Mark had come to a violent end. Annie squeezed her eyes shut. She knew she had done the sensible thing in telling Singh. But it didn't make her feel any better about it.

Annie reached the restroom. She flung the door open, stepped in and then stopped abruptly. The door swung shut behind her, clattering into the heels of her sensible shoes. Ai Leen was standing before the tall wall mirror above the spotless sinks. At the sound of Annie's clumsy entrance, she whirled round, hurriedly trying to wind a pretty silk scarf around her neck – but not before Annie had a glimpse of her throat. The butterfly-shaped bruising on her neck had been made by angry hands.

Annie started forward, exclaiming in horror. 'Ai Leen! What happened ... ?'

'Are you all right?'

Jagdesh did not seem all right. He looked as if he had not slept in a while. His usually slick hair was dishevelled. His eyes were bloodshot from exhaustion and worry and he would not meet the inspector's concerned gaze. His jaw, always slightly darker than his skin despite his usual close shave, was covered in a dark layer of overnight growth. He just stood there silently and gazed unseeingly at the floor.

'I'm sorry – I know this is hard for you. But I need to ask you some questions.'

Singh forced himself to ignore Corporal Fong's puzzled expression. He knew his moderate tone was at odds with his usual attitude to suspects and witnesses. But he could not ignore the young man's ravaged face. It must have been bad enough to be caught, to have his homosexuality finally out in the open. But for the man standing outside the closet to be a policeman, and a relative, that was like rubbing salt into an exposed wound.

'Why don't you sit down?' he suggested. Jagdesh was swaying on his feet. He looked exhausted, as if he had dressed in a hurry before being bundled into a waiting police car and driven to the station with sirens blaring – which had indeed been the case – the last bit of fanfare courtesy of Sergeant Chung.

Jagdesh's expression suggested befuddlement, as if the simple request to sit down was too complex for his brain to process. Fong stepped forward and, with unexpected gentleness, ushered him into the chair.

'Are you aware that homosexuality is illegal in this country?'

There was no response from the other man. Singh repeated the question in a more assertive tone. He received a quick nod in reply.

'Are your colleagues and family aware that you're gay?'

Jagdesh leaned forward, elbows on his knees, and buried his face in his hands.

'I'll take that as a "no",' said Singh dryly. He continued, 'Did Mark Thompson know about your sexual preferences?' He hated the line of questioning that he was being forced to adopt but he needed to be sure in his own mind that the young man would not have committed murder to preserve his secret.

'I don't think so – why do you ask me that?' was Jagdesh's confused response.

Inspector Singh's dark eyes were fixed on the young man's face. Was this genuine puzzlement or a clever attempt to act the innocent? It was difficult to imagine that the unkempt young man with the tortured eyes was in a position to maintain any sort of deception. On the other hand, Singh reminded himself, this was a man who had managed to maintain his heterosexual persona in public for a long time, and had done so sufficiently effectively that Singh's own wife was still seeking a suitable bride for him. He remembered dinner at his home – had it only been the previous evening? 'I would like that very much, Aunty,' Jagdesh had said when she suggested introducing him to a few would-be brides. Well, at least he knew now why such an attractive and wealthy young man had seemed peculiarly bereft of female company.

The door opened and Superintendent Chen hurried in, smiling broadly. He stopped when he saw Jagdesh Singh although the young man, lost in his own world, did not appear to notice the interruption.

'Ah ... good! You have the suspect.'

Singh scowled at his superior. This was not the time for the senior man to undermine his carefully laid groundwork. He hoped the boss would leave the questioning of the emotionally fragile young man to him but he was not optimistic. Superintendent Chen was fidgeting like a man who had drunk far too much coffee that morning.

Jagdesh raised his head and looked at Singh, ignoring the other two men in the room. Singh had previously only seen such an expression of desperate pleading on the faces of street children in Jakarta. Then, it had caused him to turn out his pockets. He felt like reaching for loose change now.

Jagdesh asked, 'Does anyone *else* have to know ... you know, about me?'

Singh noticed the superintendent shift uncomfortably but ignored him.

He said gently, 'Not if you tell me everything *I* need to know.'

Jagdesh sat up a little straighter in his crumpled shirt. The inspector noticed that the buttons were done up wrong. The lawyer said, his voice a little firmer than it had been previously, 'All right.'

'Did Mark Thompson know about your homosexuality?'

'I don't think so – he never suggested he did. Why is that important?'

Superintendent Chen could keep quiet no longer. 'Why is that important? Don't try and act the innocent with us! You killed Mark Thompson to hide your dirty little secret. Well – your secret is out. I've already told your bosses that you were arrested for *gross* indecency.'

Singh leapt to his feet in shock. 'Sir, how could you do that?'

Jagdesh looked as if each word had struck him like a cudgel. This was police brutality too, thought Singh, a vicious verbal version of the more common physical abuse.

'Why not?' demanded Chen. 'You're not doing *your* job and asking the tough questions. You're acting like everything is normal just because this – what do you call it? – "queer" is a relative of yours!'

'We have no evidence that Mark knew!'

'Well – find the evidence then ...'

'I will do whatever this job requires without letting misplaced prejudices determine my investigative methods, *sir*,' said Singh stiffly.

Superintendent Chen's eyebrows formed two persuasive semi-circles. 'You must see that this fellow has a motive for killing Mark Thompson?'

Singh nodded hastily to Corporal Fong, who escorted Jagdesh out of the room, a firm hand on his upper arm. If he was going to discuss possible motives with Superintendent Chen, he did not intend to do so in front of a suspect.

'I'm not convinced that Jagdesh would murder someone

210

just because they found out he was gay,' the inspector said adamantly. 'If Mark knew – and it's a big if – at most he would have indulged in a bit of late-night gossip over a glass of wine. There's no reason to assume that *he* was a homophobe!'

Superintendent Chen's words dripped with derision. 'There was so little discrimination and prejudice that he was comfortable telling everyone he was gay? Anyway, he may work for an international law firm, but he's an Indian from Delhi. Not exactly the gay capital of the world.'

There was an uncomfortable silence.

'I understand what you're telling me,' Chen said in a mollifying tone. 'But in this culture, and in his own culture, his sexual orientation might be a motive for murder!'

Singh nodded reluctantly. Superintendent Chen was right – after all, the senior policeman was a living breathing example of the sort of prejudice Jagdesh might have expected to encounter in India and Singapore if his homosexuality had been public knowledge. He didn't want to admit it, but his job was to find a murderer, not to ignore the available evidence because he objected to society's norms.

'I'm prepared to release him from custody for now. We'll decide later whether to charge him for this crime – or any other – once you've done your job and found me some evidence!'

Singh nodded, desperate to get his senior officer out of the room before he was provoked into saying something that cost him his badge. Now more than ever he needed to stay on the job if he was to prevent his relative from being prematurely charged with the murder of Mark Thompson.

'And what about Quentin Holbrooke? Have you released him?'

Singh shot a questioning glance at Fong, who had sidled

211

back into the office. 'Yes, sir, he was released today.'

'Excellent – perhaps one of you policemen might consider finding me some evidence of murder now!' On this parting shot, the superintendent marched out of the room.

Fong said quietly, 'I never suspected Jagdesh was gay.'

'He's gone to great lengths to keep his secret,' agreed Singh reluctantly.

'Do you think he might have done it?'

'Kill Mark? Over this? No, I don't think so. But I must say I'm not sure what to believe.'

The inspector rubbed his eyes tiredly. He had been up all night. He was much too old to be dragged from his comfortable bed for stake-outs and midnight arrests. He snapped. 'Well, let's not worry too much about whether we *believe* Jagdesh killed Mark. This is a murder investigation, not the Oprah Winfrey show. I want evidence that Mark knew about Jagdesh Singh's secret. Without it, we have nothing!'

The two men walked out of the room together.

Jagdesh was sitting on a plastic stool outside the door, a young uniformed policeman next to him.

'Mr Jagdesh Singh,' said Inspector Singh formally. 'I am releasing you for the present. We will decide whether to press charges at a later date. I already have your passport. You are free to go.'

Jagdesh rose to his feet and stumbled towards the stairs. For a brief moment, Singh wondered whether to go after him. He took a small step forward but then changed his mind. Jagdesh needed some time to lick his wounds. Arrested, outed, humiliated and suspected of murder – it was a lot to contend with without a clumsy attempt at kindness from a distant uncle.

212

Eighteen

Inspector Singh was watching videos. Every now and then he would gesture to Corporal Fong who was in charge of the remote controls. The corporal had learnt over the last ten minutes which gesture indicated that he was to pause, rewind or play a particular scene again, so the irritable outbursts that had punctuated the first part of the reel were now over. The film that Inspector Singh was watching was in black and white and of extremely grainy quality. The figures were out of focus and distant. It did not seem to merit his absorption.

The CCTV cameras in Republic Tower were a comprehensive network that covered the lift lobbies as well as every public area. It would have been difficult to enter the building and avoid being caught on film. But the murderer had been lucky and the cameras were out of action. The inspector, however, believed that there was always one lucky break for each side in a case. And now, unexpectedly, Corporal Fong claimed to have found taped evidence, not on the CCTV tapes from Republic Tower, but on the tape from a

213

building half a block away. The corporal had requisitioned all the tapes from a three-block radius as instructed by his tubby boss and watched every single one late into every night. On one of them, spotted by Fong's sharp young eyes but visible even to the rheumy old eyes of the inspector, was Mark Thompson walking in the direction of Republic Tower for his appointment with death. His young Filipina wife teetered alongside on high heels.

Singh sighed. He said, 'Great! More suspects!' He had a surfeit of suspects.

'More suspects is better than no suspects, sir!'

Singh looked at his assistant suspiciously. Was he trying to be funny? It seemed unlikely. He knew very well that his aggravation at Corporal Fong was merely displacement of his much greater annoyance that he was not making better progress with the case. Newspaper editorials were calling for a quick resolution of the murder investigation that was a stain on Singapore's reputation amongst the international community. Superintendent Chen had been the conduit for every complaint about the slow rate of progress from the senior echelons of government and the police force. Singh gritted his teeth. It wasn't as if he wasn't doing his best. He reached for a packet of cigarettes to help him calm down. He thought of Quentin Holbrooke. Was he so different from that miserable young cocaine addict? He too had his drug of choice – tobacco instead of a product of coca leaves. His favourite weed was legal, albeit highly taxed and a regular drain on his resources.

'Fong!' he snapped, extricating a cigarette and slipping it between his thin upper lip and moist pink bottom lip.

The young man was sufficiently inured to the senior policeman's tetchy tones to remain seated but he did turn to look at his boss with a pained expression on his face.

214

Probably thinks I'm going to send him for coffee, thought Singh.

He paused for a moment to light his cigarette, ignoring the corporal's slight grimace as the smell of tobacco-laden smoke reached his overly sensitive nose. 'We have evidence placing Maria Thompson a hundred yards from the scene of the crime. We need to question that young lady again.'

Inspector Singh's and Maria Thompson's positions were almost identical to those they had assumed the night he had gone to break the news of Mark's murder. He sat in the straight-backed chair; she sat across from him on the red velvet sofa. There were changes to the room: subtle, but ripe with meaning. The pictures of her and Mark were gone. In the same frames were recent shots of herself and her children, by the sea, in a garden and in that very room. On the Afghan hand-knotted rug between them, a child had commenced building a train set complete with stations, miniature people and animals. Life now animated the room.

Maria Thompson professed indifference to the anonymous letters, barely glancing at them even when Singh waved them under her nose like an overenthusiastic perfume seller at a department store counter. 'What for do I care what this person says? She does not even dare to put her name on the letters!'

'How do you know the author was a "she"?'

'It was his ex-wife, I tell you!'

Singh shrugged. It was possible. The provenance of the notes was less relevant than their consequences.

'It was because of these letters that Mark went to look for you on Balestier Road.'

'Men are like that sometimes. A wife is not enough. It does not mean anything.'

'He was looking for *you*!'

'Mark would never believe these lies.'

Maria swept her hair up into a knot, exposing the elegant line of her neck. This was a woman, thought Singh, who was instinctively flirtatious – she almost could not help herself.

He had one more card to play. He watched her, a small part of him admiring her porcelain-perfect face, trying to gauge whether the time had come to show his hand. He opened the manila folder he was carrying and slipped a black-and-white photo across the coffee table towards her.

She glanced at it with mild interest and asked, 'What is this?'

He said, 'A photo taken from a CCTV camera two blocks from Republic Tower.'

'What for you show this to me?'

He said evenly, 'It was filmed on the night of the murder.'

She repeated the question. This time her voice had a hard centre, her Filipina accent coming through more strongly.

The inspector stood up and folded his arms, a round figure with an air of menace.

'I am saying that you were near Republic Tower on the night of the murder. You lied to me when you said you were at home.'

She shrank back in her chair and crossed herself furtively, the profound Catholicism of the average Filipina putting in an appearance. Then she pulled herself together. It was a conscious, visible effort. Her back straightened and her hands fell to her sides. She lifted her chin and met his gaze without fear.

'So what?' she asked.

'I discover that you lied to me, that you were at the scene of your husband's murder, a murder for which you have an excellent motive – the best motive of all, *money* – and that is all you have to say to me?'

She did not flinch. She was a woman hardened by experience. She had battled all the adversity that life had dealt her with such a generous hand, using her only weapons – her face and her will. She was not going to snatch defeat from the jaws of victory.

He tried again. 'You were in the area that night. I know it and you know it. Did you *see* anything that would help me find out who did kill him?'

He could see that she was sorely tempted to say something, make something up perhaps. But her innate caution stopped her.

'If I go to the office, maybe I saw something ... but I did not.'

His gambit had failed. The inspector knew that he was no further along than he had been when he rang her doorbell half an hour earlier.

It was time to change strategy. 'All right, yours was the perfect marriage, your husband trusted you completely.' His voice had a hopeful note as he finished his sentence. 'Did Mark ever tell you any secrets – about the lawyers?'

'What do you mean?'

'Did he know something about any of them, something that the other partners *didn't* know?'

Singh held his breath. Was there some small possibility that Mark had confided in her, told her about Jagdesh's homosexuality or Quentin's drug addiction?

Maria was thoughtful, as if trying to decide whether to speak up or keep silent. Finally, she shook her head. 'The lawyers treat me like rubbish. Mark did not talk to me about them.'

Singh's shoulders were round with disappointment.

Maria suddenly laughed out loud. Fissures appeared in the thick cake of make-up on her face. 'Except that the handsome one is a *paminta*!'

'What do you mean?' Singh was not familiar with Filipino street slang.

'You know, the Indian. He's gay. Mark and I spotted him at a bar last month – with a man! I said to Mark, I don't understand. He's good-looking that one, surely he can get a girl.'

Singh winced at the casual dismissal of homosexuality as a predilection of ugly men but persevered. 'What was Mark's reaction?'

She raised her shoulders dismissively. 'Why should he care?'

'Did he tell anyone?'

'I don't think so.'

Singh nodded his great head. 'Here's my card. If you reconsider any of the lies you've told me – give me a ring.'

She took it reluctantly, her hand brushing against his fingers. She looked at him through half-closed eyes before approaching him slowly. She put one slender hand on his chest and he felt his heart beating faster. A shadow of a smile played across her face, like a breath of wind through leaves.

'Can I help you in any other way?' she asked in a low tone, never taking her eyes off his face.

His large hand closed over hers and he stood looking at her, breathing in her delicate scent and admiring the doll-perfect features.

He said distinctly, enunciating each word with full round syllables for maximum impact, 'There is *nothing* you can do for me.'

Annie walked down the corridor with hesitant steps until she was outside Ai Leen's door. She had to confront Ai Leen.

She could not let things stand – not after what she had seen. She took a deep breath, rapped on the door and marched in, not waiting for an invitation. She doubted that Ai Leen would be keen to see her, to speak to her, if her flight from the ladies' room was any evidence. She would have to force the issue.

Ai Leen was standing by a cabinet, rifling through files. Annie noticed immediately that she had the scarf wound carefully around her neck, all evidence of the terrible bruising, the imprint of fingers on her slender neck, obscured by the light silk material.

'What do you want?' snapped Ai Leen, her eyes firmly on the task at hand, refusing, after an initial sidelong glance, even to look at her colleague.

Her fingernail going to her mouth, Annie said awkwardly, 'I just wanted to see if you were all right. You know – your throat ...'

'I'm fine. Now why don't you mind your own business?'

'Ai Leen, please – I just want to help.'

The other woman whirled around on her high heels as she slammed the filing drawer shut. Her cheeks were flushed with anger, slashes of red across her high cheekbones. She marched up to Annie, her gaze penetrating and unblinking.

'You just want to help? Really? Then get out of my room and keep your mouth shut about what you saw. *That's* the only way you can help me.'

She held the door open and Annie retreated hurriedly. She heard rather than saw the door slam shut behind her.

Annie was soon sitting hunched and tense in her own chair. She watched the cursor on her screen flashing repetitively. It was vaguely hypnotic and she enjoyed the sense of respite it gave her. It was all getting too much for her. Her attempt at comforting Ai Leen had been misconstrued and she had no idea what to do next to help her colleague. She supposed it must have been Ai Leen's seemingly unassuming husband who had left those marks and she was too embarrassed to admit it or seek help. Nothing else would explain her rage at Annie's offer of support.

A hesitant knock on the door brought her around. Was it Ai Leen, regretting her earlier outburst? However, when the door opened it was David Sheringham who walked in. She looked at him in surprise. He was pale and the lines around his mouth and eyes were deeply etched, as if he'd received a recent shock.

'What's the matter?' she asked as she stood up and walked around the table so that she was closer to him. She saw that his grey eyes were dark with worry.

'Have there been any developments? Is it Quentin?'

The knowledge of what she had done was like a heavy weight on her shoulders. Had David found out that she had told Singh about the insider dealing? Was he disappointed that she had failed to protect a colleague in trouble?

'It's Jagdesh.'

She hadn't been sure what to expect, although she had feared the worst from David's dour expression. But she hadn't suspected anything to do with Jagdesh.

'What do you mean? What about him?'

'He's been arrested, for "gross indecency". You know – homosexual behaviour.'

'Jagdesh? I never knew he was gay.'

'None of us did . . .'

'But why have the police arrested him?'

'Homosexuality is still illegal in Singapore.'

She unknowingly echoed Stephen's words. 'I know that – but the law's hardly ever enforced.'

'I think they're trying to pin the murder on him.'

'Jesus ... where is he?'

'I just spoke to Singh. They've released him "pending further investigations". I've been trying to get hold of him but he's not responding to my calls or messages. I'm really worried about the poor fellow. I thought you might have more luck contacting him – as his friend.'

Distress was radiating from him like a high fever and Annie put a comforting hand on his arm. David, arrogant and confident, never failed to annoy her. But David admitting to doubt and confusion won her sympathy. He wrapped his arms around her and she felt the strength of his comforting embrace. She looked up at him, needing to see if he was all right. Her eyes met his and a sudden constraint fell between them. Annie became aware that her heart was racing. His cool, grey eyes were warmer than she had ever seen them before, a warmth of affection and admiration that she had suspected he felt – and feared that she reciprocated – and could now read for herself in his expression. His face was too close, his grey eyes were smiling now, and she felt her breath catch in her throat. She tried to take a step back, to escape from this dangerous emotional place, but his grip tightened. He held her gaze and then leaned forward and brushed her mouth gently with his.

The sound of the door opening caused her to start and pull away. David held on for an instant longer, instinctively protesting her decision. And then he let go, a tacit agreement that the moment had been too impulsive, and yet too important, to become part of the public domain. Annie gave him a quick shy smile and turned to face the opening door.

Stephen Thwaites stood in the doorway panting, his face an unhealthy shade of grey. 'Annie, David! Jagdesh is in hospital. He's tried to kill himself!'

Nineteen

Jagdesh lay on a hospital bed in a private room tucked in up to his armpits. He was either unconscious or asleep, his hands lying still and limp on the covers. The solitary sound in the room was the constant beep from the heart rate monitor – its glowing green line forming a hill, then a trough, at regular intervals. As a concession to the exorbitant rates of the private hospital, the curtains were a faded floral print instead of the typical single-tone blue or green. A picture – a print of kittens that appeared to have been cut from a calendar and framed – lent a dismally decorative touch.

Annie asked timidly, 'What happened?' Both she and the senior partner had been too shocked to speak on the way over.

'I don't know the details. I just got a call from the hospital. He took an overdose of sleeping pills. His cleaner found him and called an ambulance.'

'Will he be all right?'

Stephen's rumbling deep voice rendered his answer almost inaudible. 'I don't know.'

'Why do you think he did it – tried to kill himself?'

Stephen gave her a sideways glance.

She interpreted it correctly and said, 'But that's not a good enough reason. I mean, being gay is hardly a crime.'

'On the contrary.'

'I know it's a crime *here*. But I don't think the inspector will press charges. He's just using it as leverage because he thinks Jagdesh might have killed Mark.'

'All I know,' said Stephen heavily, 'is that Jagdesh behaves like a man with an unbearable burden of guilt!'

Annie nodded. The expression in her limpid brown eyes was pensive.

Their brief vigil at his bedside was interrupted by the unforgiving routine of the hospital that slowed for nothing except death. Two nurses in starched white bustled in. One was so thin as to be almost skeletal, with bony elbows and a forbidding expression. The other was younger and sweeter in appearance but went about her business with the same brutal efficiency. They flipped through his charts, swapped his drips, lifted his eyelids, peered into his eyes and checked his machines. Then, acting in concert and with the supreme coordination of synchronised swimmers, they changed the bedding, raising Jagdesh by the shoulders, fluffing up his pillows, replacing the sheets and somehow making his bed with a minimum of fuss despite the presence in it of a comatose man weighing not less than a hundred kilograms. Annie and Stephen shuffled their feet and tried not to get in the way. It seemed, despite Jagdesh's oblivion, to be an invasion of his privacy.

Finally, when it appeared that the nurses were on the verge of leaving the room without having uttered a sound between them, Stephen asked abruptly, 'How is he?'

'No change yet,' said the skinny nurse, her accent indicating that she was one of the Chinese nursing diaspora. 'The doctor will come back to see him in a few hours.'

'But, I mean, how is he now? Will he be OK?'

'Too early to know. They pumped his stomach. But the sleeping tablets were already absorbed into the blood. He's in a coma.' Her normal voice was in stark contrast to Stephen's hushed tone and sounded almost like a shout to Annie's sensitive ears.

The other nurse took pity on him and said, 'If you need more information, you can ask the doctor later.'

Annie was appalled. Jagdesh was in a coma. He might not come out of it. He might not survive. She stared at the still form. Jagdesh already looked as if death held him by the hand and was leading him away. She shuddered to think of what the police would make of this latest development.

On cue, Inspector Singh waddled into the room, Corporal Fong trailing in his wake. He shook his big head when he saw the bulky figure of his young relative lying as still as the dead against the stark white sheets.

'What's the prognosis?' he asked, directing the question at the nurses.

It was Annie who answered. 'He's in a coma. He may not recover.'

'Young fool!' Singh's words were robbed of their import by his drooping jowls. There was genuine sadness here, thought Annie, for all the inspector's superficial callousness.

'You lot should be grateful anyway,' continued the policeman, his gaze still focused on the unmoving man.

'What do you mean?' asked Stephen harshly.

'It will save Hutchinson & Rice the embarrassment of a trial if they have to pull the plug.'

'What trial?' Stephen exclaimed.

'For murdering Mark Thompson,' Inspector Singh replied.

'But why do you think he did it?' asked Annie.

'His lying there looks a bit like a confession, to Superintendent Chen, at least.' Perhaps anticipating their outburst, he continued, 'And so does this!' He took a sheet of paper wrapped in cellophane out of the file he was carrying.

Stephen almost snatched it from his hand and he and Annie stared together at the single sheet of paper torn from a notebook. In black ink, in Jagdesh's unmistakable scrawl, were written the words, "I'm sorry. I'm so ashamed. I cannot carry on."

Mrs Singh was aghast.

'He tried to kill himself?'

The inspector could see that she did not believe him – she probably thought he had his facts wrong or was trying to annoy her with a childish made-up story.

'He's in a coma, unlikely to recover.'

She sat down suddenly, her caftan billowing out and then settling on her bony knees.

'Why? My God! Why? What will his mother say?'

'The family has been notified already.'

'But they haven't called me.' Her surprise was evident in her tone, the voice higher than normal and staccato.

Singh knew that his wife had been in close contact with Jagdesh's family all through the investigation. She had been like a mosquito buzzing in his ear, demanding that he release the young man's passport so that he could return to India for his sister's wedding and insisting that Jagdesh Singh would never have been involved in a murder. She had been a very effective mouthpiece for her faraway relatives on the subject of the guilt or innocence of one of his suspects. As if that was not enough, she had invited him to dinner. Singh profoundly hoped that Superintendent Chen never found out that the

225

boy's last supper before he tried to top himself had been at the Singh residence.

Mrs Singh asked again, 'But why would he try and kill himself? Maybe someone else did it!'

'There was a note,' said Singh crossly.

He didn't need his wife putting it out that Jagdesh Singh had been the victim of attempted murder. He quaked to think of what his superiors would say if such a rumour reached the press.

'What did it say? What did the note say?'

'The usual ...'

'You think he murdered his boss? And that's why he tried to kill himself?'

Singh said bluntly, 'Yes.'

He wasn't sure – he wasn't sure at all. But expressing uncertainty would only provoke his wife to new heights of persistence in her nagging of him. And the fact remained that Jagdesh's closely guarded secret had been in the hands of his dead employer. He had Maria's testimony to that effect. As far as Superintendent Chen was concerned, Jagdesh had an unimpeachable motive for murder. And his own opinion would not count for much if Superintendent Chen had his way.

Singh watched his wife carefully, curious to see if he had shaken her calm faith in the natural order of things. Mrs Singh shook her head energetically from side to side. A few tendrils of hair escaped from her tight bun, a definite sign that she was agitated. 'I can't believe it. He's from such a good family, a well-brought-up boy. You're making a mistake.' She paused for breath and then continued, 'I have no idea why he would try and kill himself. Must have been some girl, probably Chinese. I *knew* I needed to find him a wife. It's all your fault, tying him up in this murder investigation so that he was too busy to meet some nice girls.'

Aggravated by her persistence, the inspector snapped, 'He was found in bed with a Chinese *man*.'

'What?' Her eyebrows leapt up two inches.

It was difficult, decided Singh, to discern whether she was more horrified by the homosexuality or the multi-racial nature of Jagdesh's assignation.

'He's gay – Mark Thompson found out. Jagdesh Singh killed him and then in a fit of remorse, or because his homosexuality is now out in the open, he tried to kill himself.'

'That's why they haven't called me. They must be too embarrassed.'

Singh squinted at his wife and realised she had reverted to talking about Jagdesh's family.

'No wonder he wasn't married! And those people wanted me to find him a wife ... can you believe it?' Mrs Singh was angry now. 'How could I find a wife for a pervert?'

Singh suspected that she felt as if she had somehow been used unfairly, set up to look like a fool, hunting for a wife for a gay man.

'Now are you prepared to believe he's a murderer?' he asked, morbidly curious to see if he was about to witness a moment of rare self-doubt.

He had underestimated his wife. Her mouth puckered in distaste, as if she had added too much lime pickle to a spoonful of rice. 'Of course he did it!' she said adamantly, ignoring her previous diametrically opposite views.

Singh's tufty eyebrows bunched up with annoyance. He thought of his insistence to Superintendent Chen that being gay was unlikely to be a secret worth killing to preserve and the older policeman's relief that the murderer might turn out to be someone whom he viewed as a deviant member of society. He glared at Mrs Singh. It was not difficult to imagine a young gay man going to almost any lengths to avoid the vilification of such intolerant members of society as his worthy wife and his tiresome boss.

Stephen pressed a button and the clear glass walls became opaque. The yellow lighting made the collection of lawyers appear sallow and unhealthy. A tray of untouched sandwiches sat at the centre of the pine table. Mineral water bottles were laid out at regular intervals. The secretaries were ever efficient although the legal firm that employed them was fraying at the seams.

Stephen glanced at the other lawyers. The intervening week had wrought many changes.

This time it was Ai Leen who seemed the most careworn and fragile, her face wan under her make-up, bluish shadows beneath her eyes, a scarf wound unfashionably tight around her neck as if she was trying to ward off a chill. Her united front with Reggie appeared to have faltered. She shrank from him and sought the chair furthest away, avoiding catching his eye.

Reggie, on the other hand, had gained in confidence. He leaned forward and grabbed a ham and cheese sandwich, shovelling it into his mouth and munching with genuine enjoyment. He did not seem to have a care in the world. Stephen felt his stomach turn as he watched him devouring his lunch, tearing away at the sandwich like a half-starved carnivore.

Stephen looked around the room as if to gauge whether they had the strength to absorb further bad news. He said, 'You've probably all heard that Jagdesh is in hospital.' There were a few nods. 'He's in a coma. The doctors are unsure if he'll recover.'

'David said he tried to kill himself. Is that true?' asked Ai Leen.

'I'm afraid so,' answered Stephen grimly.

No one responded. To hear the rumour confirmed was a shock.

Ai Leen broke the silence. 'But why? I don't understand.'

Stephen exchanged a look with David; this was the moment of truth if they were to reveal Jagdesh's carefully maintained secret. He hesitated for a moment before speaking. 'I'm afraid we don't know why he tried to do this.'

Reggie, true to form, was the first to articulate the possibilities. 'Does it have something to do with the murder?'

'There's no reason to think so!' snapped Stephen. He saw Annie look at him in surprise. He knew that this was a contradiction of his earlier position that Jagdesh's behaviour was that of a man with an unbearable burden of guilt. But however strongly he felt that Jagdesh might have killed Mark, he could not bring himself to agree overtly with Reggie.

Reggie pounced on his denial. 'Why else would he have done it, you know, tried to top himself?'

'What are you trying to say, Reggie?' asked Stephen.

A cold voice answered, 'It's quite obvious, isn't it? He's accusing Jagdesh of murder.' The thin, disgusted voice belonged to Annie.

Reggie asked shrewdly, 'What do the police think?'

Stephen said, 'They consider it a possibility.'

Again, there was quiet in the room as everyone took in his words.

'What about Quentin?' asked Reggie.

'I guess they have more than one suspect.' Stephen sounded resigned to the reality that two of his partners were in the frame for the murder of Mark Thompson.

A broad smile broke over Reggie's face. 'Well, *that's* the first good news I've heard in a long while.'

229

His smirk was interrupted by the door opening. They all turned around as one.

Quentin Holbrooke stood at the entrance. He was even thinner than when they had last seen him but his clothes were as tidy as ever and his thin hair was combed neatly away from his forehead. He might have been returning to the office after a couple of days off sick instead of having been incarcerated in a Singapore jail for drug-related offences. Stephen saw that his colleagues were staring at Quentin as if he was the ghost of Hamlet's father. And in a way, he was returning from the dead, thought the senior partner.

Quentin said in a quiet voice, his tone hoarse, 'They released me. Inspector Singh let me go.'

'How come?' asked Reggie.

Quentin raised his skinny shoulders, the bony outlines protruding sharply through his shirt, to indicate that he did not know.

'They're not pressing charges? For the drugs?' It was David who ventured the question, his brows knitted together in puzzlement.

'They've decided not to go ahead. The police said I was to come back to the office and act like nothing had happened. Singh ... Singh said that he "only gave a damn about finding a murderer".'

Jagdesh was still in a coma. That much Singh could see the moment he walked into the room. The stillness of a coma went beyond that of sleep. In sleep, there was the occasional stretching and shifting, murmuring and muttering. For Jagdesh, the only movement was the barely discernible rise and fall of the chest, the only sound the slight whistling exhalation between parted lips, largely drowned out by the machine-generated sounds from the paraphernalia of life support. His passivity was so comprehensive as to be indistinguishable from death.

Singh felt a deep sadness for the young man lying on the bed. Even if he recovered, which seemed unlikely from what the doctors had said, he would still be the same unhappy person who had tried to take his own life in the first place. What was to prevent him trying again? After all, the circumstances that had led to the attempted suicide had not changed. He was still a gay Indian man in Singapore. His country of birth and his country of residence – one a dangerous noisy land teeming with people, the other a highly regulated pristine city state. They did share one thing in common, however – a deep prejudice against homosexuality that was still reflected in the colonial-era laws on the statute books.

Singh scratched his beard. It was itching as usual, reflecting his troubled mind. The primary question for him, bastion of the Singapore police, was whether a man who did not baulk at self-murder might also have committed murder. The case against Jagdesh was far from watertight, but there were plenty of pieces of evidence that added up to an incomplete but suggestive picture. He ticked them off in his mind: a secret that, according to the testimony of Maria Thompson, her husband had known; a gay man who was determined to stay in the closet; an attempted suicide and a note that might constitute a confession. Singh snorted out loud. If Jagdesh was the killer, he wished his epistolary arts had better reflected his chosen profession. If Jagdesh was indeed innocent, that left him with Quentin Holbrooke, an insider dealing coke addict who – no doubt to thwart the investigative efforts of the Singapore police – was skint. Which in turn indicated the beautiful and flirtatious Maria Thompson. She had motive and opportunity. Singh did not doubt that she could have summoned up the will to murder her husband if that seemed the best option for her children. But that left him with a partners' meeting, belatedly summoned, apparently urgent, and yet supposedly irrelevant to Mark Thompson's death.

As for the rest – Stephen, Annie, Reggie and Ai Leen – he had a mild fondness for the first two and a strong dislike of the latter two, but he had nothing evidentially substantive on any of them. Singh scowled. Why did the law firm need so many bloody partners anyway? Presumably they were all just splitting the hairs of angels dancing on the head of a pin – and charging by the hour for their efforts.

The policeman didn't realise he had company until a sudden movement caught his eye. He glanced up in surprise at the youth who stood nervously by the door. If Singh was surprised, the young man was completely taken aback to find someone in the room with Jagdesh. The stranger looked like a rabbit in headlights, trying to find the will to bolt.

Singh bared his teeth in a facsimile of a smile. He asked, 'Are you here to see Jagdesh?'

The youth managed a quick nod in response.

The inspector, wondering why he was so nervous, said, 'Come in.'

The youth started and Singh thought he could not have terrified the young fellow more if he had invited him into a lions' den.

Despite this, he came in, his steps hesitant but committed. He spoke in a gentle voice, barely above a whisper. 'I'm Ahmad. I'm a ... friend of Jagdesh.'

Singh gestured, inviting Ahmad to get closer to the bed and see Jagdesh for himself. Ahmad crept up to the bed and gazed down at the still figure. The policeman was surprised and interested to see a glint of tears in his eyes.

The young man stood by the bed for a while and then turned and asked, 'Will he get better?'

'I don't know. He hasn't got any worse.'

They both gazed at Jagdesh lying prone in the bed, indifferent to his guests.

'Have you known Jagdesh long?' asked Singh, with feigned casualness.

'Not so long, no. We have only met a few times.'

He was a soft-spoken fellow, speaking in the gentle undulating cadences of the Malay. Singh strained to hear him. Growing in confidence, the boy said, 'I read about him in the newspapers, so I came.'

Singh nodded. Jagdesh's attempted suicide had leaked to the press and there had been much speculation as to why he might have done it, the newspapers walking a fine line between titillating their readers and risking a potential libel suit if Jagdesh recovered and was not after all found to be a murderer. The unfolding story surrounding Mark's death was still very much grist to the tabloid mill.

Ahmad muttered a farewell to the inspector and turned to leave, but the policeman took a step backwards, his bulk filling the doorway and obstructing the exit.

He asked, 'Who are you then?'

'I told you! A friend of Jagdesh.'

'I'll bet you are!'

'What do you mean?'

'Just that I know a rent boy when I see one.'

Ahmad stood, quivering. 'Why do you say such a thing?'

'Twenty-five years as a policeman, young man!'

The boy's expression at discovering that Singh was a policeman caused the inspector to burst out laughing, his belly rippling with humour.

'I should throw you in the lock-up,' he said, poking a finger into Ahmad's chest.

Ahmad looked terrified.

'Don't worry. I'm not going to bother. Not now. Only if I find you soliciting.' He continued inquisitively, 'What are you doing here anyway?'

The boy decided that prudence dictated honesty. 'We have met a few times. I thought we were friends.'

'You were a bit of a favourite, were you?'

Ahmad, emboldened by the affable tone, asked, 'Why do the papers say he is a murderer?'

'It's possible that Jagdesh killed Mark Thompson.'

'The *ang moh* who was his boss?' Ahmad asked.

The policeman nodded.

'Jagdesh told me about it.'

The inspector's interest was piqued. 'When did he tell you about it?' he asked.

'That evening. I was with him, you see, but then he had to go to the office. I waited for him at his flat for a long time. When he got back, he told me that his boss had been killed.'

The inspector's eyes almost overlapped as he squinted at Ahmad. 'Listen to me, young man. I am going to ask you a few questions and I want you to tell me the truth. If I find that you've lied to me, you will *never* see the sun again. Do you understand me?'

Ahmad was petrified into a stillness as profound as that of the man in the coma.

Satisfied, the inspector asked, enunciating each word with care, 'Were you with Jagdesh the evening of the murder?'

Ahmad nodded fearfully.

'Both before and after Jagdesh went into the office?'

Again the nod.

'Do you know what time this was?'

'I meet him after work – we have a drink together. After that, we go back to his flat and order some pizza for me. He had to go out for dinner with some relatives. But he got a call. He said it is the boss – this Mark Thompson who was killed. It was about seven-thirty.'

Inspector Singh interrupted him. 'How do you know what time it was?'

'The pizza arrive when Jagdesh was on the phone. I check the time because if they come late, they give you a discount. After an hour, Jagdesh went out. He said he would be about one hour but he did not come back till midnight.'

'You were with Jagdesh until about eight-thirty in the evening?'

'Ya.' Ahmad appeared puzzled by his emphasis.

'And in that time, you did not go to his place of work?'

'Of course not! For sure Jagdesh would not want to be seen with me near his office.'

This rang poignantly true to the policeman. Jagdesh had not kept his sexual preferences a secret only to flaunt a delicate-looking rent boy in the vicinity of his workplace. The inspector took out his big white handkerchief and patted his brow.

Jagdesh Singh had an alibi. He was not the cold-blooded killer who had bludgeoned Mark Thompson to death at his own desk. And his apparent innocence meant that there was still a murderer at large. This was a zero sum game. The exoneration of one person meant only that the killer was another of the lawyers, or the widow. Singh grasped the metal rod at the bottom of the bed frame with both hands. He couldn't believe that the young fool lying in the bed in front of him had preferred to brazen out a suspicion of murder rather than produce an alibi that would have revealed his homosexuality.

'Well – back to square one,' muttered Singh to no one in particular.

But a big part of him was genuinely relieved that his foolish young relative was not, after all, a murderer.

235

Twenty

Stephen knew that the life that he had worn like a comfortable suit of old clothes would never be the same again. Replaying the memory of relief that had played over the faces of his colleagues when he had told them that the police suspected Jagdesh – or perhaps Quentin – of the murder, he had longed to get away. Not even Quentin's release could temper his disgust. He grabbed his briefcase, then put it down again, walking out of the room empty-handed.

Now he sat in semi-darkness, slumped in the leather armchair in his study, wondering how he had let his wife and the interior decorator turn his private room into this pastiche of commercial masculinity with its dark wood, red leather, heavy curtains and, unbelievably, hunting prints and a ship in a bottle.

Joan, his wife, came into the room. He had thought that she had gone out for the day with Sarah Thompson, that friendship still blooming despite the pressures of recent events. She had not seen him, sitting in a corner, lost in his own thoughts. He thought about drawing her attention to his presence and then changed his mind. He wanted solitude, even from his wife. Instead, he watched her as she sat down at his desktop computer and switched it on, remembering the girl he had fallen in love with and comparing her to this middle-aged, frumpy woman for whom he had a tepid affection based on a shared history and a commonality of mundane purpose.

He noticed with mild surprise that she was printing something. He would not have thought that she knew how to switch the machine on, let alone print documents. Stephen felt awkward. His desire to be undisturbed had left him in a position where he felt that he was spying on his wife. He saw with relief that she had finished what she was doing, gathering up the sheaf of papers and making for the door.

The sound of his phone ringing stopped Joan in her tracks. She started with fright and dropped the papers, staring at her husband as if she had seen a ghost.

Stephen fumbled for his phone. 'Sorry, love. Came home early.'

Galvanised into action, she started picking up the papers hurriedly. Stephen came over, but as he stooped to pick up a sheet she snatched it from his fingers, trying to shield the papers from his view. He had seen quite enough.

Stephen sat across from his wife in the family room. It was a comfortable place, the only part of the house that was not a monument to an excessive interior design budget. The sofas were of good quality but well worn. The coffee-table books were not the usual untouched hardcovers on architecture and spa resorts, but were well-thumbed travel guides and photo albums. Pictures of family covered one wall, grandchildren, graduations and holidays. It was a room that suggested that the domestic situation of the family living there was a funda-

237

mentally happy one. Stephen remembered that he had felt nothing but a mild affection for his wife of thirty-plus years when he had seen her in the study. He realised now that she was of utmost importance to him; he had merely lost the habit of acknowledging it to himself, let alone telling her so.

'Joan, what were you thinking?'

She sat across from him, knees drawn primly together, hands folded in her lap, hair shot with grey and tied back from an expressionless face.

She shrugged helplessly. 'It wasn't my idea, it was Sarah's ... I thought it might help her get the anger out. You know, a sort of therapy.'

Stephen exploded. 'Therapy?'

He averted his eyes from the papers on the coffee table – the anonymous letters that had sent Mark Thompson to a Balestier Road brothel hunting for his new bride.

'I'm so sorry,' muttered Joan.

Stephen rested his head in his hands wearily and clutched at the thinning hair. His deep eyes, sunken in a lugubrious face, looked up and met those of his wife. 'Maybe you should tell me exactly what you did.'

'When Mark left her for that woman, Sarah was beside herself ...'

Stephen remembered that Sarah had spent a lot of time closeted with Joan after the break-up of her marriage to Mark. He had maintained a prudent distance, with all the reluctance of the male of the species for getting involved in a domestic fracas.

He nodded his understanding and she continued: 'She was convinced that Maria was no better than a prostitute, after his money. She tried telling him but he was besotted with Maria. She wanted *me* to tell him. Of course, I refused. Then she hit on this idea of sending him anonymous letters.'

Stephen asked, picking up one of the letters gingerly, 'This stuff about moonlighting as a prostitute … was it true?'

Joan shook her head. 'I don't know. I don't think Sarah did either. She just put in the worst things she could imagine.'

'But I don't see why you got involved …'

'Sarah knew she would be suspected of writing the letters. So she asked me to send them with a local postmark while she went back to England.'

Stephen was puzzled. 'But what were you doing today?'

'Sarah was worried that there might be something incriminating in the letters. She asked me to print out copies and take them to her so she could have a look.' She trailed off uncertainly, barely able to meet her husband's eyes.

They stared at the letters lying between them.

Joan broke the silence. 'I'm afraid there's more.'

Her husband looked at her questioningly, almost fearfully.

'I lied. I *wasn't* with Sarah Thompson that evening. You know, the evening of the murder.'

'What?' Stephen's heavy jowls dragged his thin lips down until his expression was one of pure shock.

She held up her hands, a gesture of apology. She spoke quickly, the words falling over each other in her rush to get them out. 'She begged me – she said she'd be the prime suspect for Mark's murder if I didn't make up an alibi for her.'

'For bloody good reason!' was Stephen's angry response.

'What are you going to do?'

Stephen took a deep breath, doing his best to calm himself down. He leaned over and grasped his wife's hand. He said gently, 'We have no choice, we have to tell Inspector Singh.'

*

239

The flashing cursor marked each second that Ai Leen sat at her desk, staring at the computer screen and the letter she had just drafted. Her hand stole to her neck, still wrapped in a gossamer scarf. She no longer felt any pain from the bruising but the gesture had become a nervous habit. She made up her mind and clicked on the print command, getting up to hurry to the printer room. It was imperative that she retrieve the letter before anyone else set eyes on it in that public place. She wrested the door open and found Reggie standing there.

She took an inadvertent step back and he seized the advantage to put a foot in the door. She considered pushing past him, but the interested glance of her secretary, her attention drawn by the frozen silent tableau, stopped her. Reggie propelled Ai Leen back into the room by the simple expedient of stepping forward. She was forced to retreat. He shut the door behind them. Her eyes were drawn to the computer where the letter was still on the screen. Reggie looked her over, his gaze personal and insulting. He reached out and touched her cheek with one finger. It might have been a caress but for her reaction.

She slapped his hand away and shrank from him, hissing, 'Don't touch me!'

Reggie enjoyed her fear; there was a hint of a smile on his face. He gloated, 'That's a change of heart!'

Ai Leen slipped behind her desk, creating a barrier between them. She said, unable to hide the tremor in her voice, 'I mean it – don't touch me.'

Reggie came around the desk and perched on the corner. He put his hands up in a conciliatory gesture and said, 'I came in here to see whether we could make a deal.'

She did not reply and refused to meet his eyes.

He said sardonically, 'After all, we made a bargain before and I kept my end of it.'

Ai Leen closed her eyes against the greed and ambition that had led her to this point.

Reggie waited a moment and said, 'Jagdesh killed Mark. End of story.'

'There's no evidence that it was Jagdesh!'

'All right, Quentin then – I don't care. The point is that our dear colleagues are lining up to put their heads in a noose. And as long as the police are focused on them, *we* have nothing to worry about.'

His audience of one looked unconvinced. She said, 'They've already let Quentin go . . .'

'For now!' He continued, 'Look, we have nothing to worry about. You and I can put this behind us. But I need your guarantee that you'll keep your mouth shut.'

It was only through a singular effort of will that Ai Leen refrained from looking at the screen. Instead, she nodded just once.

Reggie said, 'I want to hear you say it.'

Hatred burned in her eyes.

He took a step in her direction and she whispered, 'I won't say anything.' Her hand went to her throat.

He did not miss the fearful gesture. The tension went out of his body.

'Good,' he said cheerfully and turned away from her. At the door, he stopped and glanced over his shoulder. His parting words were, 'It's been fun!'

Ai Leen watched him go, her palms clammy with perspiration. She remembered the letter and hurried to the printer room. To her almost light-headed relief, the room was deserted and the letter was still there, obscured in a pile of other printed material. She glanced over it and was satisfied with what she saw. Then she walked over to the shredder, a fixture in any legal office, and fed the letter through, watching the remnants rain into the waiting bin like wedding confetti.

*

Reggie Peters walked down the road to a phone booth. It was empty, spotless and in perfect working condition. He smiled to himself at the contrast to the red kiosks in London where he had first started practising as a lawyer almost thirty years previously. There, chewing gum was, more often than not, stuck into every crevice including the coin slot and little cards offered sexual services by women whose pictures suggested that nature had contributed only partly to their robust physiques. Reggie much preferred living in Singapore. He grinned suddenly – the women were more to his taste as well.

He fished a piece of paper out of his trouser pocket and dialled the number that his secretary had been obliging enough to procure for him. On the third ring, a brusque voice answered.

Reggie said in a low voice, 'I have some information for you.'

'Who is this?'

'That's not important ...'

'What's it about? I don't have time to waste, you know.'

'The Mark Thompson murder,' said Reggie. He could almost sense the journalist at the other end sit straighter in his chair. He had not doubted for a moment that this impatient press man would be all ears when he dropped Mark's name into the conversation.

'Well, go on.' The tone was still hasty but this time it reflected the reporter's interest in getting to the bottom of the story.

'Quentin Holbrooke was arrested.'

'For the murder? We haven't had any information like that from the newswires.'

'He was arrested for drug trafficking – a large bag of

cocaine, enough for the death sentence was found on him,' explained Reggie.

'Well, go on!'

'They let him go without charging him. He's back at work.'

'Why would they do that?' asked the newspaper man.

'Too embarrassing for the authorities to hang an expat so soon after one is murdered at his desk.'

'I see,' muttered the journalist. 'Typical double standards.'

'Exactly,' agreed Reggie. He knew that what he was doing was unconscionable. But he needed the police, especially the ubiquitous Inspector Singh, to focus their attention on his colleagues – he didn't care which ones as long as it wasn't Ai Leen or himself. And after all, he rationalised quickly, Quentin was only getting what was coming to him. It was not as if he, Reggie, had planted the bag of cocaine on him or anything like that.

The voice at the other end of the line was suddenly suspicious. 'What has this got to do with you anyway? Why are you telling me this?'

'Oh! I just want to see justice done,' said Reggie Peters in a voice of genuine good cheer.

Ching, Annie's secretary, came into the room. She usually drifted in, bearing messages or documents, tidying shelves or putting away files. Today she paused, equidistant between Annie and the exit, as if she wanted to consider her options again before passing the point of no return. Annie felt a surge of impatience.

'What do you want?' It came out more harshly than Annie had intended. She asked, in a more reasonable tone, 'Is anything the matter?'

The woman made up her mind and took another step

towards Annie. This generated unexpected momentum, and she rushed forward saying breathlessly, 'I didn't realise it was personal or I wouldn't have read it!'

'What are you talking about?'

'I thought it might be important.'

Annie said through gritted teeth, 'Ching, just tell me what this is about.'

'I was in the printer room, hunting for something of yours. I was going through a stack of papers ...'

Annie knew that all the secretaries rifled through the printed documents – their curiosity about their wealthy bosses was insatiable. She played along. 'All right, you *accidentally* read something private but important in the printer room. What has it to do with me?'

Ching looked uncomfortable. 'I didn't know who else to tell!'

Annie gave up any hope of getting to the root of the matter without invading the privacy of the author of this mysterious note.

'What did it say?'

Her secretary took a piece of paper from the file she was carrying.

'You took it?' exclaimed Annie.

'Photocopy!'

Annie held out her hand and her secretary handed her the single sheet of paper and then stepped away from the desk hurriedly, as if the document was a ticking time bomb.

'I will leave it with you,' she muttered and almost ran from the room.

Annie looked down at the letter and began to read.

Corporal Fong hurried through the fluorescent-lit hospital corridors, trying to ignore the antiseptic smells that assailed him. He overtook an old woman being wheeled gently through the corridors by three generations of family. Her husband kept pace next to her with the help of a three-pronged cane, a daughter-in-law did the actual pushing, and her grandchildren skipped ahead, indifferent to the pall of mortality that hung over the place.

As he approached Jagdesh's ward, he continued to guess at the reason for his urgent summons. He found Inspector Singh waiting for him at the nurses' station, one elbow on the desk, dark eyes staring off into the distance.

'What is it, sir?'

He had to repeat himself to attract the attention of the Sikh inspector but when he did, Inspector Singh didn't mince his words. 'Jagdesh is dead,' he said.

Fong gasped, he felt winded. He had known, of course, that the young man was in a coma – nearer death than most human beings could imagine. And yet, there had been something semi-permanent about the figure lying, immobile and silent, on the bed. The even features, the vicissitudes of his recent experiences smoothed from his face, had reminded Fong of a bronze sculpture.

The boss beckoned him into the room that had been Jagdesh's until so recently. Of Jagdesh, there was no trace. The bed was empty, stripped of its bedding. The flowers that had been wilting in two vases on his bedside table were no longer there. Corporal Fong felt a wave of compassion for the loss of the confused, unhappy young man.

'Such a waste, sir,' he said to the inspector. He did not expect a reply. The inspector would probably be quite tetchy that he was wasting words on emotions rather than facts but he felt that he owed it to Jagdesh to acknowledge his passing before being taken up in the details of death rather than the life that had gone before. Still the inspector

245

remained silent. Fong sensed that this was not his typical impassivity. There was turbulence within the senior police-man that was discernible in the deep hollows of his eyes.

'What is it, sir? What's the matter?'

The inspector gave a small sigh. 'It might have been *murder.*'

A short while later, Inspector Singh, Corporal Fong and the doctor who had been in charge of Jagdesh's care were sitting in the hospital canteen drinking coffee.

The doctor was young and diffident, expressing himself with frequent throat clearings, a bobbing Adam's apple and much hesitation, but his underlying competence carried a weight of conviction. 'You see, although the patient's central nervous system activity had been depressed to the extent that he had lost all cognitive function, possibly permanently, and there was some liver and kidney damage, we did not believe he was at immediate risk of death.'

Singh pondered this information. Jagdesh had not been in any immediate danger of death although there had also been very little hope of a complete recovery. Exactly like his murder investigation, thought Singh irritably, Jagdesh too had been trapped in limbo.

'Fine, Jagdesh was going to live forever except for being out for the count – then why is he *dead*?'

The doctor's eyes blinked rapidly behind his thick glasses. Perhaps he did not understand boxing metaphors, thought Singh. 'Well?' he demanded.

'Well, you see—' Singh suppressed an urge to yell that he did not *see* anything '—a preliminary investigation into cause of death ... it bears all the hallmarks of asphyxia.'

'Suffocation?' asked Singh in a querulous tone.

'Well, to be precise there were clear signs of petechial

246

haemorrhage on the conjunctiva.' In response to the bewildered expression on Corporal Fong's face, he explained, 'Tiny pinpoints of blood on the whites of the eyes from ruptured capillaries.' He continued, 'And further examination of the deceased led to the finding of a few strands of white fluff about Jagdesh's nostrils that matched the fabric of the white cotton hospital pillow covers.' The young doctor seemed capable of speaking in full sentences only when he sounded like a medical text or an autopsy report.

'So you're saying that someone killed Jagdesh Singh by holding a pillow over his face?'

'Yes,' said the doctor baldly. And then perhaps regretting his certainty, he muttered, 'The preliminary findings will have to be confirmed by a post-mortem, of course.'

Singh leaned his chin on interlocking fingers. A person or persons unknown, as the coroner would undoubtedly say, had murdered Jagdesh Singh. In a coma, Jagdesh would not have known, understood or struggled against what was happening. He had simply crossed the border between dreamless sleep and easeful death. Perhaps he had made the journey without pain or fear or doubt, but Singh was damned if the murderer would have it so easy. The killing of an innocent, defenceless man on his watch had hit the policeman hard.

The doctor rose to his feet, nodded his goodbyes and hurried away, white coat flapping on his bony frame.

'Well, call the station and find out whether any of those coppers trailing the lawyers ended up at this hospital in the last twenty-four hours. That should give us a clear indication of guilt!'

Fong turned pale, almost waxy.

'What's the matter?'

'Didn't you know, sir? Superintendent Chen pulled them off the job. I thought you must have agreed!'

'But why?'

Fong was clearly quoting verbatim: '"We have the murderer – that gay foreigner. We don't want the rest of the expats to think that Singapore is a police state."'

The irony was almost too much to bear, thought Singh. He took a deep breath – he would spell out his thoughts on unwarranted interference to Superintendent Chen later. Right now, he had a double murder on his hands.

'Perhaps the two murders are unrelated,' the inspector suggested tentatively.

Fong shook his head and Singh sighed gustily. His side-kick was right – the murders had to be linked, which meant that his failure to find the killer of Mark Thompson had probably cost Jagdesh Singh his life.

'It really wasn't your fault, you know,' said Corporal Fong.

'Only to the extent that I didn't hold the pillow over his face.'

Fong was silent – unable or unwilling to provide his superior further absolution.

Finally, Singh said, 'Ok, how about this for a hypothesis? Whoever killed Mark thinks that we all suspect Jagdesh. It's all over the newspapers. Superintendent Chen has been dropping hints at every press conference. The murderer knows that there is only one real danger – that Jagdesh wakes up and insists he is innocent. No one would guess that Jagdesh would hide a perfectly good alibi.'

'So he, or she, killed Jagdesh?' suggested Corporal Fong. 'And now Jagdesh can't wake up and plead not guilty.'

'*Only* the murderer would think that the measure of doubt left by Jagdesh's death was better than the certainty of being found out,' Singh added reflectively.

They nodded in unison. It was guesswork but it fitted neatly with the facts at their disposal.

'Unfortunately,' said Singh with a pensive sigh, 'we're no closer to knowing who killed Mark, and now Jagdesh.'

Twenty-One

Singh was in the staff canteen drinking sweetened water-melon juice through a striped bendy straw. He pondered the fact that there were people in the world who devoted their time to the betterment of straws. Did they feel a frisson of pleasure every time they saw a state-of-the-art straw, like he did when he was able to write "case closed" on a file? He ignored his corporal who sat patiently across from him waiting for instructions, insights, abuse ... he had no idea what the young fellow was seeking from his superior officer.

Out of the corner of his eye, he saw Superintendent Chen enter the cafeteria, a pile of papers under one arm. Chen's head swivelled in a semi-circle as he scanned the room care-fully. Singh paused to regret that his turban would always single him out in a crowd. The superintendent spotted him and made a beeline for his reluctant inspector. As he got closer, his mottled face and bloodshot eyes reminded Singh of the symptoms of death by suffocation as described by the doctor earlier in the day. His boss wouldn't appreciate it but he looked more like Jagdesh Singh dead than when the handsome young lawyer had been alive.

Chen arrived at the table and dropped the pile of papers – the afternoon tabloid was on top, noticed Singh – in a heap on the table. He yelled, oblivious to the stares of the other diners, 'Now see what you've done!'

The inspector glanced at the headlines. 'POLICE RELEASE DRUG TRAFFICKER WITHOUT CHARGE.' He turned the front page over and scanned the article quickly. It was all there: Quentin Holbrooke's arrest and subsequent release without charge. The newspapers had maintained a factual approach to the case. The blogosphere – Superintendent Chen had printed out some choice articles – had been less restrained. Various writers had gone to town on the apparent double standards in law enforcement. 'One law for Singaporeans, another for so-called foreign talent?' thundered "Angry Singaporean" in one piece.

'Did you leak this to the press?' demanded Chen.

Singh was genuinely confounded by the accusation. 'Me, sir? Of course not. I was quite happy to see Quentin Holbrooke walk.'

The superintendent pointed an accusing finger at Fong who shook his head mutely, too shocked to speak.

Singh ignored the literal and metaphorical finger pointing and asked, 'What are you going to do, sir?'

'What choice do I have? We're probably going to have to hang him after all. My God, this has made us look like fools.'

Singh nodded his vigorous agreement and received an angry glare for his conciliatory gesture.

'Are you going to re-arrest him?' asked Singh.

'Not yet. We can't look like we're reacting in a panic to the press reports. I've put out a statement saying that investigations are still ongoing into the matter.'

Singh nodded.

'You'd better find the murderer pronto, Singh. We need a breakthrough to restore our reputation,' growled Superintendent Chen before storming out of the canteen.

'Who do you think did it, sir?' asked Fong.

'Leaked this?' Singh gestured at the papers between them and then shook his great head. 'I'm not sure. Someone who wanted our attention on Quentin Holbrooke?'

The inspector sucked in the last of the juice – his efforts were accompanied by a snorting, gurgling sound as he moved the straw around the base of the glass like a vacuum cleaner. A pip made its way up the tube and provoked a hoarse coughing fit. 'All I can say is that we have enough bloody red herrings to fill an aquarium.'

'Maybe Quentin Holbrooke *is* the murderer, sir?'

Singh glared at his colleague.

'The case against him is watertight!' insisted Fong.

'A couple of days ago you told me that the widow was definitely the murderer,' pointed out Singh.

Fong flushed, his pale face suffused with a shade of pink that Singh had previously assumed only appeared in nineteenth-century novels, but he stuck to his guns. Ticking off his points on thin fingers, the corporal said, 'Quentin needed money badly, he was insider dealing, Mark Thompson found out about it, Mark Thompson was murdered!'

'We still haven't been able to find hard evidence that he was insider dealing ... Inspector Mohammed hasn't called back. And besides, I just can't believe that Quentin killed Jagdesh.'

The older man massaged his fingers. Clutching the cold drink had provoked an arthritic ache in each knuckle. He remembered the gaping wound in Mark Thompson's head. He found it easy to imagine that Quentin Holbrooke had clubbed Mark to death in a drug-induced frenzy. But he had a second corpse on his hands now. Singh paused for a moment and scratched the crease between neck and chin. He thought of the smiling young Sikh tucking into his wife's home-cooked dinner with relish. He was struck by the belated realisation that Jagdesh Singh had been a decent young man in an impossible situation.

'Can you really imagine a weak-jawed young man like Quentin Holbrooke committing a cynical cold-blooded murder in order to pin the blame on someone else?'

'Maybe *his* murder has nothing to do with the law firm. It could be an old boyfriend ... or something like that, you know ... who killed Jagdesh.'

Singh could feel his head beginning to throb. 'You're right – that's possible ... but unlikely.'

The young policeman was determined to press home his point about Quentin. 'Who else could it be?'

'Jagdesh had an alibi. Stephen Thwaites and Annie have no motive – but what about the rest? You said yourself that Maria had a great motive and she was with Mark just before he was killed. A woman like that would not hesitate to kill a defenceless man if it suited her purposes. When it comes to those children, her maternal instinct is almost feral.'

Fong nodded.

'We need more on Reggie and Ai Leen as well. They're the two most unpleasant people in the office. Surely we can find something on them?' said Singh grouchily.

He could see that the rookie was biting back sharp words. He supposed it was ridiculous to try and pin the murder on someone just because he disliked them. Still, nothing else had worked so far – he had followed the evidence diligently and it had led him up the garden path.

Back in Singh's office, Fong asked, 'What now, sir?'

'Get Holbrooke on the phone. We'd better warn him that the vultures are circling.'

Quentin Holbrooke, when they reached him at the office, had already seen the newspapers. His voice was barely audible as he asked, 'What does this mean?'

'It's not good,' said Singh brusquely. 'The big shots don't like egg on their faces. There's a real possibility that they'll charge you with the drug trafficking after all.'

He didn't need to see the thin lawyer to imagine his drawn, frightened face. To have offered Quentin his freedom and then, at the last moment, to lasso him with a noose, that surely constituted cruel and unusual punishment. Singh said, trying to sound reassuring, knowing that he was not being honest, 'It might not come to that. Once we track down the murderer, the press will have other stories to run. And the bosses will be too busy resting on their laurels to remember you.'

There was a half-hearted chuckle at the other end. The inspector supposed that the idea that Quentin's best hope was his solving the murder was almost amusing. There had been no evidence so far that he would be able to do so. The bodies were piling up, the suspects were thick on the ground but the murderer was tiresomely elusive.

'Did you talk to anyone? How did the story get out?'

Quentin's answer radiated puzzlement. 'I have no idea. It certainly wasn't me!'

'It must have been one of your colleagues then – they're the only ones who knew about the original arrest.' In addition to Fong, the superintendent and himself, he could have added, but didn't. He was quite sure that the leak hadn't emanated from the police department.

'But ... but why?' stammered Quentin. The knowledge of betrayal had been a body blow. Singh was not surprised. It was always an ugly moment, the discovery that there were people, so-called friends, family, colleagues, who were willing to do one harm to protect their own interests. Quentin no longer knew whom to trust. The sense of isolation, of paranoia, would be terrifying to a weak-willed young man who was a cocaine addict to boot.

He answered the question. 'I'm guessing to keep the police busy, keep the spotlight on you.'

Quentin found his voice. 'You mentioned earlier that one of my colleagues said I was the one insider dealing as well . . .'

Singh grunted his acknowledgement of the truth of the statement. He had let that piece of information slip to see if it provoked Quentin into any reciprocal accusations but it had not worked at the time.

'One of them must really hate me,' muttered Quentin.

'No reason to assume it was one and the same person,' pointed out Singh.

'I suppose you're right.' Quentin's doubts were audible in his voice.

What was that expression, wondered Singh – even paranoid people have enemies. It was hard for Quentin to fathom that there might be more than one person who was willing to throw him to the wolves. Singh said sharply, 'Watch your back, keep your head down and your nose out of trouble!'

There was silence at the other end. Quentin Holbrooke was lost in his own thoughts.

Singh snapped the phone shut with a heavy hand. He needed a breakthrough, a stroke of luck, anything really that would give this investigation impetus. He felt as if he was swimming to a distant and yet visible shore against a very strong current.

Corporal Fong's mobile phone rang. He listened silently for a moment and then handed the device to Singh without explanation.

It was Stephen Thwaites, sounding unusually tentative. He said, 'Inspector Singh? I'm afraid I have a confession to make.'

Singh remained silent. Was it possible that he had been wrong and Stephen Thwaites had killed a man in order to step into his shoes? He couldn't believe it. He had taken a liking to the gruff lawyer with the bushy eyebrows who was prepared to accompany Mark Thompson around Singapore brothels rather than abandon him.

'Sarah Thompson wrote the anonymous letters.'

Singh suppressed a sigh of relief. It was not a confession of murder. He had half-suspected that the ex-wife was the letter writer – she had been sufficiently determined that the new marriage should fail. But the letters had been post-marked in Singapore and she had fled to England.

'How do you know?' he asked curiously.

'She emailed them to my wife who posted them for her in Singapore.'

'I see,' remarked Singh. So much for the evidence of Singapore postmarks. He would not have expected anyone to be naïve enough to lend the ex-wife a helping hand in her pursuit of revenge.

'How come there was nothing on Sarah Thompson's hard drive?' he asked.

'They used anonymous PCs at internet cafés, apparently.'

Singh scratched his temple. He blamed the movies for this working knowledge that even the most unlikely culprits had on how to cover their electronic tracks.

Still, although the contents of the letters might amount to criminal libel, he personally didn't give a damn. His job was to hunt murderers, not to protect the fragile reputations of second wives. And the first wife had an alibi so notwith-standing her letter-writing skills, she had not taken the ultimate step to ruin her ex-husband's marriage.

'There's more,' said Stephen quietly. 'She lied – my wife lied. She *wasn't* with Sarah Thompson that evening.'

'So what the *hell* did you think you were doing?'

Singh's voice ratcheted up several keys as he scowled at the two women sitting across from him. He had not bothered to ask Fong to bring in chairs as he had done the first time he interviewed Sarah Thompson. He was quite content this time to glare at her across his expansive desk while she sat sheepishly on an uncomfortable red plastic chair, her alibi-providing, falsehood-propagating friend next to her. Perhaps if he had been more authoritative, authoritarian even, these women would not have dared lie to him and Corporal Fong in the first place.

Neither of the women had responded to his question. He supposed there had been a rhetorical flourish about it. The policeman discovered that he was actually grinding his teeth with irritation and forced himself to stop. His visits to the doctor were both regular and unpleasant – he didn't want a dentist on his case as well.

'I'm sorry,' said Sarah Thompson finally, her tone barely above a whisper. 'It was my fault. I persuaded Joan to say I was with her.'

'Any reason?' asked Singh bitingly.

'I was afraid you would think I had murdered Mark ...'

Singh's jaw ached. He was sure that he had read some- where that it was a sign of an impending heart attack. The policeman hoped that these women were not going to be the death of him. He had always assumed that his beloved wife – or her excellent cooking – would play that role. Massaging his chest with the heel of his palm, he asked tiredly, 'So did you kill him?'

There was a brief shake of the head from Sarah

Thompson – it was almost as if she did not expect to be believed. And why should she, pondered Singh angrily. After all, this was the person with the most personal animosity towards the dead man.

'Where were you?'

'Joan asked me to come with her on this casino ship ...' Singh noted Stephen's wife stir uncomfortably in her seat at the first mention of her name ' ... to forget about Mark for a while. I went on board, but I just couldn't carry on. I had to talk to Mark, convince him that he had made a mistake. I know it's pathetic but I was prepared to take him back ...'

She twisted a small handkerchief in her lap and the inspector noticed that the former Mrs Thompson had strong, masculine hands. Hands that could have bludgeoned her ex-husband to death?

Her voice grew fainter and fainter as she continued her story. 'I called the house. The maid told me that Mark was at the office. I knew I couldn't get in there. I decided to wait for him outside his apartment block so that I could waylay him on the way home and he would have no choice but to let me say my piece. I waited for hours, just sitting on the pavement.'

Sarah Thompson's eyes were filled with tears. 'He never came back,' she said simply, a wealth of grief in her voice.

Annie arrived home and sat in her car in the driveway. Everything appeared so normal. The house gleamed gold in the evening sun, the windows picked out in black paint. The cat was asleep on the veranda table, so relaxed he seemed like a furry black-and-white rug. She looked at the briefcase next to her and the dangerous secret it contained, then glanced at her watch. She would mix herself a very stiff drink and wait for David. She had called him and he had agreed to come over at once. He had wanted to know what it was about but she had refused to reveal anything over the phone, merely insisting it was urgent. Annie knew that Inspector Singh should have been her first port of call but she had turned to Sheringham instinctively. Annie acknowledged that it was the first time in her adult life that she had felt such a strong attraction to anyone. Prior to this, she had always been too immersed in her career, in the accumulation of a protective layer of wealth, to have had the time or patience for a serious relationship. From David's tone, she was confident that her sentiments were reciprocated. She knew that, in the midst of a murder investigation, with all their senses sharpened with anxiety, both of them were probably feeling the mutual appeal more strongly than might have been the case if they had met in more normal circumstances. But a growing part of her believed that the prematurely grey man with the broken nose and appealing smile had an important part to play in her future.

Getting out of the BMW, Annie headed into the kitchen and was mixing herself a drink when she heard the grinding of gears that heralded the arrival of a taxi. David was early. She smirked like a schoolgirl. Well, she would mix a drink for both of them.

Carrying two gin and tonics outside, Annie was astonished to see Quentin standing on the veranda. She exclaimed and spilt some of the liquid over her hand.

She glared at him, setting down the crystal glasses and licking her fingers. 'Jesus, Quentin! What are you doing here?'

He would not meet her eyes but instead settled on a careful perusal of the middle distance. She noticed how worn and pale he looked. He was not in a position to get any more drugs – not now that the police knew his history.

'Now is really *not* a good time, Quentin.'

'I must talk to you!' His tone was determined despite his frail appearance.

Any sympathy that she felt receded into the darkness and was replaced with annoyance. 'I'm expecting someone.'

'I know you are,' said her colleague evenly. 'I asked your secretary where you were and she told me that you'd gone home to meet David Sheringham.'

Annie made a mental note to fire Ching at the first opportunity. 'Well, if you knew that, I've no idea what you're doing here.'

Quentin seemed to have a change of heart, or at least a change of approach.

'Annie, I just need fifteen minutes ... please!'

She glanced at her watch and decided the quickest way to get rid of her unwanted visitor was to hear him out. 'OK, you can have ten minutes. Let's go for a walk.'

They set out together, drinks left untouched. Annie, from habit, set a purposeful pace and headed in the direction of the cemetery.

As they entered through the massive wrought-iron rusty gates, Annie, trying to keep the impatience out of her voice, asked, 'What did you want to say?'

Quentin picked his way through the overgrown paths and sat down on a squat gargoyle, covered in lichen and moss and guarding an ornate, tiled semi-circular grave. The monument glowed orange and green in the half-light. Annie remained standing, glaring down at him, her arms folded. A stone statue of a young goddess stared up at her with a matching expression.

He muttered, 'About the insider dealing ...' and stopped.

Annie's wary gaze was fixed on her colleague. She sat down on a moss-covered tombstone.

'I didn't believe the inspector at first – that it was someone from Singapore. But he said there was no mistake; they had spoken to you and cross-checked the story with Tan Sri Ibrahim.'

Annie's response penetrated the dusk like a searchlight. 'The Tan Sri called me a few days before you were arrested.'

'That's why they thought I might have had a motive to kill Mark.'

Annie nodded her understanding. 'It's because the Tan Sri told Mark about his suspicions the day he died.'

Quentin's face was lost in the lengthening shadows. He said quietly, 'That fat policeman told me that someone in the office had fingered me.'

She folded her arms tight across her chest.

'At first I thought it must have been Stephen, or perhaps Reggie. But I've been thinking and thinking – and I've realised it had to be you who told him.' Quentin's voice was thin and echo-less.

He continued, 'You're the only one who knows enough about the file – the only one that Singh would have believed.'

She nodded briefly.

He sighed and walked over to the gravestone. The inscriptions were brief and to the point. Gold flaking paint gave the names and dates of birth of the patriarch and his two wives.

'But Annie,' he said, 'I didn't do it. The insider dealing, I mean – it wasn't me.'

Twenty-Two

Singh dropped his briefcase by the door and collapsed into his favourite armchair. He leaned back, trying to find some comfort in its familiar contours, but his upper back was too stiff with tension. He pushed against the heel of one trainer with the toe of the other, hoping to kick it off.

He still could not believe that Joan Thwaites had lied about Sarah Thompson's alibi. Stephen had been horrified by his wife's behaviour – and with good reason, thought Singh grimly. He had a good mind to charge her with obstructing the police in the course of their investigations. Idiotic woman with messy hair in her ill-fitting jeans – what had she been thinking? Undoubtedly, she had been bullied into doing it by the stronger personality, but did that make Sarah Thompson a murderer?

His wife walked in with a cup of hot tea. He accepted it gratefully and mumbled his thanks. Strong sweet tea was the only thing that stood between him and a blinding headache. He closed his eyes and pictured Sarah Thompson, her skin pulled surgically taut over her face but wrinkled around her neck like a lizard with neck flaps, platinum blonde hair with dark roots showing, high heels and a short skirt. What was that expression? Mutton dressed as lamb. He opened one heavy lid and looked at his wife – thank goodness she did not aspire to an inappropriately youthful appearance. He vaguely recalled that his own mother had worn caftans like his wife did now.

He remembered the tears in Sarah Thompson's eyes as she had described waiting for her ex-husband to come back to the home they had shared during their marriage but which now housed his nubile young widow. Those tears had been genuine.

Besides, notwithstanding the collapse of her alibi, it was highly improbable that the ex-wife would have been escorted to the office by her former husband. And as someone who believed at the time that she had a watertight – albeit-fake – alibi, there would have been no need for Sarah Thompson to risk killing Jagdesh. He slammed his fist into his palm, suddenly angry. Mark Thompson had left a trail of destruction that had culminated in his murder. But that had not been the end. Jagdesh Singh had been a victim too.

Singh heard a sudden sizzling sound – batter in hot oil. A rich scent of fried *cempedak* emanated from the kitchen and he felt a simple gratitude towards his wife.

'Fried *cempedak*?' he asked hopefully.

'Yes – just ripe today.'

The inspector nodded his pleasure. He threw her a bone – she deserved it, this skinny wife of his who had guessed that only his favourite teatime snack could restore him on such a truly frustrating day. 'You were right – Jagdesh was innocent.'

'Actually, once you told me he was a homosexual type, I said he did it.'

'Well, *before* that then ...'

263

'How do you know?'

'He had an alibi – a young man was with him.'

'I don't know what's happening to the world that one of our boys can be like *that* but at least he's not a murderer.'

'Poor fellow,' said Singh. 'He didn't deserve the way things turned out.'

Both of them paused and looked towards the dining table, picturing the young lawyer tucking into his dinner and agreeing that he would like to meet a nice Sikh girl and settle down.

'The mother collapsed, you know – only son,' explained Mrs Singh briefly.

Singh nodded. His failure to find the killer of Mark Thompson had resulted in a young man's death at the hands of some unknown killer. And far away in Delhi, a family had been destroyed.

Mrs Singh went into the kitchen and returned with a plate of the fried fruit in golden batter. 'He really enjoyed my cooking, you know,' she said sadly.

Singh took one of her hands in his and gave it an affectionate squeeze. 'He really did.'

Quentin took both Annie's hands in his, bringing them up to the level of his chest. He looked into her eyes, the brown pools turned almost black as her pupils widened to catch the last light of the day.

'And that's not all, is it? It wasn't enough to tell Singh that I was insider dealing. You told the newspapers that I'd been let off ...'

'Of course not!' She tried to free her hands but his grip tightened.

'I don't believe you. My God, Annie – I thought you were my friend.'

'Let me go, you're hurting me.'

His pale eyes glistened in the encroaching darkness. His hands were sweating from the contact of skin on skin in the humidity.

Again, she tried to wrest her hands free.

Quentin's head was pounding, twin hammers on his temples. There were sharp pains behind his eyes. He blinked rapidly. It felt as if he was looking into a hot bright light even though the two of them were shrouded in gloom. He could feel a damp layer of cold sweat on his face and neck. A breath of wind passed through the trees and he shivered.

'How could you do this to me? I trusted you!' he said and his voice ascended until it was a shrill animal scream.

Bats, quick black shadows, flitted back and forth chasing unseen insects. Something brushed against his cheek, a rush of velvet. He started and saw that it was an early owl.

He was weak, almost lightheaded. He needed to go home and inhale a line of coke – it was the only thing that made him feel good, strong, powerful. But there wasn't any. The police had his stash. His dealer had been arrested. He had no money and the police had told him – he remembered Singh's beard thrust aggressively into his face, he had smelt of curry and cologne – that if he crossed the line again there would be no second chances. He felt the first flames of rage and it was almost a relief to feel his self-control waver.

He wrapped two hands around Annie's neck. It was a fragile stalk, smooth and warm to the touch. He felt he could snap it, just like that. And she deserved it, this woman who had lied to the police about him, a so-called friend who had betrayed him. And he had nothing to lose in gaining his revenge – after all, he already faced the death penalty.

'Let me go!' she screamed.

His concentration wavered for a moment as a wave of

dizziness swept over him. She wrenched free and turned to run. His arm went round her neck, yanking her head painfully back. Her back was to him, her body pressed up against him. She screamed and he stifled further sound with a hand pressed against her mouth. Annie stamped on his foot with all her might, and as his grip loosened in shock, she bit the hand over her mouth as hard as she could. He released her mouth, exclaiming in pain and shock, but the arm round her neck tightened. Annie screamed at the top of her lungs. Quentin struggled to muzzle her again. He tried to control a rising tide of panic, reminding himself that the cemetery was deserted. She fought him furiously. He could feel that each effort to pull free was further asphyxiating her against the arm around her soft throat. He was starting to feel giddy, praying that she would falter first. She was stronger than he had anticipated – he was not sure how long he could hang on.

Suddenly, unexpectedly, he felt a hand on his collar and he was yanked backwards with enormous force. Annie fell to her knees, choking and retching, dragging painful gasps of air into her lungs. Quentin felt as if he was fighting a creature composed more of shadow than of substance. He desperately lunged out, swinging wildly with both fists. It seemed impossible to make anything except chance contact, while his opponent's blows were landing with precision – dull thuds that landed on his face and chest with the regularity of a pile-driver. For one highly-strung moment he wondered whether his opponent was a figment of his imagination, a drug-induced hallucination. There was a lull. Quentin stood swaying on his feet. David Sheringham hit him hard, fist to jaw, and Quentin crumpled in a heap.

Inspector Singh's jaw dropped. 'What happened?'

His shock was understandable, thought Annie. They had not briefed him on the phone – just asked him to hurry over. Now he stared at the three of them in astonishment. Both Quentin and David were muddy and dishevelled. Quentin was by far the worst for wear – one of his eyes was almost shut, his bottom lip was split, there were cuts and bruises on his face and arms and he stood heavily on one leg, unable to put weight on the other. His defeated expression, eyes half shut, lips turned down, shoulders bowed, emphasised his physical state. David's shirt was torn and blood trickled down his cheek from a cut above his eye. Annie did not know it but she presented the most telling evidence of an altercation. Her knees were muddied, she had a glorious bruise on one cheek and her eyes were enormous pools of shock and fright in a face from which all the blood had drained.

David put an arm around her shoulders. 'Quentin attacked Annie,' he said matter-of-factly.

There was no response from the man who stood accused. His silence rang like a confession. The inspector, a round figure but light on his feet like a dancer, moved to whip out the handcuffs attached to his belt and deftly encircled Quentin's wrists.

He said to Corporal Fong, 'Get him cleaned up. Make certain the police doctor sees him. Put him in a cell and then wait for me. I'll decide what we're charging him with – assault or something more – later.'

They all watched Quentin being led away. He got into the back seat of the car, Corporal Fong slipped in next to him and they sped away.

Singh made his bewilderment plain. 'I don't understand.'

David put up a hand to stop him. 'All explanations in a minute. Let us get cleaned up and then we'll talk.'

Fifteen minutes later, Singh was waiting for them in the

living room, looking relaxed in a comfy chair with a drink clutched in one hand. David appeared, wearing a T-shirt from Annie's drawer that was several sizes too small for him. Annie handed him a beer. He took it gratefully and waved away the first aid box, making it clear that he thought the medicinal properties of alcohol were superior to any external ointment. Annie curled up on the sofa next to him.

'Why don't you tell me what happened here, seeing as I have a man in custody?' asked the inspector, taking charge of proceedings.

'I came home from work, having arranged to meet David. Quentin turned up a short while later.'

David cut in to say, 'I'm sorry I was late. I couldn't get a taxi.'

Annie nodded her understanding. 'You were just in the nick of time!'

She paused, knowing that there was going to be frustration and disbelief from David that she had kept quiet about the insider dealing for so long. 'I should tell you – I've already briefed the inspector – I had a call from a client in Malaysia a few days ago, accusing someone at Hutchinson & Rice of insider dealing.'

She sensed David stiffen by her side.

'Tan Sri Ibrahim told me that he spoke to Mark the evening he died.'

David almost yelled at her, 'Mark knew? But that could have been why he called the meeting!'

'I thought of that. I knew that you would all suspect Quentin, and perhaps me, of the murder ... so I didn't say anything at first.'

Singh asked, 'You were afraid of being accused of murder?'

'I was protecting Quentin,' she said, her chin sticking out

defiantly. 'Later, when Quentin was arrested, I realised that he must have needed money for his drug habit. I didn't feel I could keep the truth from the police any more ...'

She stopped, a fingernail going into her mouth. 'Quentin turned up here ... I wasn't sure what he wanted.'

David leaned over to give her a quick hug.

Annie smiled at him and said, 'We went for a walk to the old cemetery at the back.' She gestured in its general direction. 'Quentin was furious that I'd told the inspector about his insider dealing. He seemed to think that I'd informed the papers that he'd been let off on the drugs charge as well.'

She shook her head. 'He attacked me.'

Singh exhaled gustily and swallowed some gin as if the drink might make the news more palatable.

Annie took up her tale again. 'David turned up just as things were getting nasty.'

'How did David know where you'd gone?' asked Singh.

'I was running late. I finally got a taxi ... we were coming up the road here when I saw Quentin and Annie. I got out and followed them. It was getting dark and the cemetery is overgrown, full of trees and shadows. I wasn't sure what to do. I was just turning back when I heard Annie scream.'

The lines on his face deepened.

Annie was still puzzled. 'But why did you follow us?'

David's face flushed. He cleared his throat and took a deep breath. 'I thought that there was something between you and Quentin. I decided to follow you and see for myself.'

Singh looked at his red face, mortified at having to confess to such juvenile behaviour, and started to chuckle. David glared at him but was forced to concede that the story had its funny side. He began to laugh too.

Annie said resolutely, 'I don't want you to charge Quentin with attacking me. He's in enough trouble already.'

Singh took a healthy swig of his drink. 'Are you sure?'

David echoed the question, a worried expression on his face. 'What if he tries again?'

'He won't. He's just really fragile right now because of the drugs. And he has a right to be angry – I *did* tell the inspector about the insider dealing.'

'Insider dealing to get cash to feed his drug habit, attacking you,' muttered Singh, his thick brows forming into an angry line. 'I can almost believe *he* killed Mark.'

'What do you mean? Jagdesh killed Mark,' interrupted Annie hurriedly.

'Jagdesh had an alibi,' explained Singh, leaning back in his armchair tiredly.

'What?' Annie hardly recognised her own voice, high-pitched, shocked, slurring from her swollen lip.

'Yes, a young man was with him that evening,' the inspector said calmly, reminding everyone in the room that he was a police officer. 'He preferred to lie about it to keep his homosexuality under wraps.'

Looking around, Annie could see that she was not the only one who had not known about the alibi. David looked stunned.

The policeman's tone was deliberate. 'I decided to keep Jagdesh's innocence a secret – to see what the murderer would do if he believed he was off the hook. And now we know ...'

'I don't understand,' muttered Annie in a barely audible voice.

'The murderer decided that his purpose was best served by Jagdesh taking the secret of his own innocence to his grave.'

'You mean ... ?'

'I mean Jagdesh Singh was *murdered*.'

Annie stammered, 'But ... how?'

'Pillow over the face,' said Singh succinctly, holding a pudgy hand against his mouth and nostrils to indicate the crude but effective method that had dispatched Jagdesh.

'I need another drink,' whispered David.

Annie rose to her feet dutifully, her face a ghostly mask. She put the coffee machine on, trying to occupy her trembling hands – the inspector's words were a body blow greater than anything Quentin had inflicted on her. As she walked slowly back into the living room, she caught sight of her briefcase. Her exclamation of shock interrupted proceedings.

'What is it?' snapped the inspector.

Annie could not believe she had forgotten the letter. There had been so much going on, so much unpleasantness to divulge and digest, it had gone clean out of her mind. With trembling fingers, she reached for the bag, opened the clasp and slipped the photocopy out.

Singh stretched out an impatient hand. 'What is it, for God's sake?'

Annie handed the paper to the inspector without a word. Singh held it a couple of feet away – his long-sightedness affecting his ability to read and his patience. It was headed "Resignation Letter" and addressed to "The Partners, Singapore Office". He read it out loud, taking in every word:

I hereby tender my resignation from the partnership of Hutchinson & Rice with immediate effect. Before I go, I would like to inform the remaining partners of an episode of which I am deeply ashamed. Approximately six months ago, my elevation to the partnership was under consideration. I had understood from office rumours that Reggie Peters was the fiercest opponent of my promotion. I decided to confront him.

271

He told me that he did not feel I was a lawyer of sufficient quality to join the partnership.

He said it was within my power to change his mind. He made it clear that he would support my partnership application in exchange for sexual favours. I agreed to his terms and we commenced a sexual relationship. In due course, I was elevated to the partnership with his support. I tried to end the relationship thereafter but he refused, saying that he would reveal what had happened if I did. He insisted that I would come out of it with my reputation severely damaged but that he was senior enough and rich enough to weather the storm.

Subsequently Mark was killed and I wondered whether Mark had somehow found out about us and Reggie had killed him to keep our secret. I was also concerned that the same motive applied to me. It seems that Jagdesh Singh murdered Mark. I no longer fear being accused of murder. I find that my reputation and career mean less to me now than when I agreed to Reggie Peters' terms. I believe it is important that he be prevented from abusing his position again, if indeed this is the first time.

Yours Sincerely,
Lim Ai Leen

The inspector nodded his head. Many things were clearer now: the inexplicable friendship between Reggie and Ai Leen; their attempts to put up a united front; the recent distance between them where Ai Leen's body language – as she cringed from Reggie and flinched when he spoke – suggested genuine dread.

David said, 'I don't believe it,' but his tone suggested he believed it all too well.

Singh demanded, 'Where did you get this?'

Annie answered in a small voice, 'My secretary found it at

the printer. She made a copy and gave it to me.' She looked at their shocked faces and said, 'I asked David to meet me here to tell him. But so much happened that ... I forgot I had it!'

'It's addressed to the partners. Why hasn't she delivered it?' Singh demanded.

David shrugged. 'Perhaps she changed her mind. It's an inflammatory piece of work.'

Annie added, 'She won't know we have a copy. My secretary put the original back as she found it.'

Inspector Singh smiled approvingly at this cunning. This unknown secretary was a smart cookie. He asked, 'Do these allegations sound plausible?' He didn't doubt the contents of the letter for a moment – it was a piece of the puzzle that fitted very neatly into one of the holes in the case – but he was curious to see if the others were of the same mind.

Annie's affirmation was immediate.

David nodded too. He said, running a hand through his short hair so that the grey strands stood on end – 'What a sorry mess!'

'Jagdesh has an alibi. Does that make Reggie the killer?' It was Annie with the query.

Singh looked at her quizzically. It was curious that she was the first to point out the possibilities, the one most willing to accuse a fellow partner of murder. He remembered her reluctance in the early days of the investigation to make any accusations, her reticence so much in contrast to the other lawyers. He wondered what was at the root of the change of attitude.

David demanded impatiently, 'Well, does it?'

The inspector squinted at them thoughtfully. 'There are loose ends. How would Mark Thompson have found out about the two of them?'

David waved away the question with an impatient hand. 'He could have seen them together, overheard them ... we might never know exactly. My money's on Reggie.' He added quickly, 'I certainly don't believe it was Quentin – he wouldn't commit a premeditated murder.'

Inspector Singh looked at him penetratingly. It was interesting that David was willing to exonerate the man who had just attacked a woman that he clearly cared about. Either he was a man of such profound integrity that he could separate his personal feelings from his assessment of the case, or he knew something he wasn't telling the police. Singh had taken a strong liking to the young man from London, but he doubted that he was capable of such a selfless analysis of the facts. This case was like a *kueh lapis* – layer upon layer of secrets and lies.

Annie's frustrated exclamation dragged him back to the matter at hand. She said, 'But there isn't any proof!'

The lawyers turned to the inspector, the final arbiter on whether it was possible to arrest Reggie.

Singh shook his head. 'No, there is motive ... but nothing to place him at the scene – either scene! I don't have enough for an arrest, let alone a prosecution.'

Twenty-Three

Maria Thompson looked at the accumulating bills on her dead husband's rosewood desk. She opened a smoothly sliding drawer and brushed them all in with a sweep of her arm. Unfortunately, out of sight was not out of mind. She had maintained the lifestyle she had shared with Mark when money had been no object. Her children deserved it – they had waited long enough in a Filipino village in the care of her ageing crone of a mother while she fought for a better life for them. But now money was short. The insurance people still refused to pay up on Mark's policy. Her acrylic talons dug into the palms of her hands. They were dragging their feet on the grounds that the murder was still unsolved.

She would have to sue the insurance company, involve more lawyers in her affairs, even though she was sick to death of the whole tribe. Her knee was bouncing up and down furiously as she thought about the time, effort and – most importantly – money a legal battle would cost. She had seen the blood-sucking attitude of these legal types up close. After all, her husband had been the senior partner at just such a firm of parasites. She'd be lucky if there were even a few Philippine *pesos* left after a court wrangle to get hold of the insurance money.

Well, perhaps the time had come to cash in one of her other chips, carefully preserved for just such a financial emergency as this.

Reggie Peters walked out of the meeting he had been chairing at the client's offices. It had lasted for hours and achieved nothing but he didn't really care, not while he charged by the hour anyway. He switched on his mobile and it beeped urgently, indicating missed calls. There were three, all from the same number, one that he did not recognise. He was on the verge of returning the calls and then thought better of it. It could wait till he was back at the office. He stepped out of the building. Immediately beads of sweat popped out along his upper lip like a translucent moustache. He dabbed a handkerchief on his brow and squinted at the sun. It was almost lunchtime and he was only a couple of blocks away from Republic Tower. He decided to walk. He had not gone five hundred yards before he regretted his decision. Reggie was not a fit man and he was starting to turn a mottled pink, the colour of cooked lobster. His fine sandy hair was damp against his scalp, the creeping baldness more noticeable. He had worn a suit to the meeting and although he had loosened his tie and was carrying the jacket, the scratchy wool made his legs and crotch itch.

Reggie wondered whether to duck into a nearby Starbucks for some respite. His ringing phone pre-empted the decision. Reggie hurried into the air-conditioned lobby of the nearest building and recovered his phone from the inside pocket of his jacket. He saw at a glance that it was the same person who had been trying to reach him earlier.

276

Ai Leen was at home alone. She lay back in bed and stared at the ceiling, unknowingly adopting Quentin's posture in a jail cell across town. She felt trapped, unable to decide what to do. Intimidated by Reggie the previous day, she had temporarily given up her plan of sending her resignation letter to the partnership. But she knew she would come about; she was just not sure how. She gripped the bedclothes tightly and repeated the last thought to herself. She dragged herself out of bed, showered, dressed and curled up in the sitting room armchair to watch a re-run of a chat show on daytime television. She realised once again, as if she needed reminding, that to work was as essential to her as breathing. She could not conceive of a life where she did not have an office to go to and work to lose herself in. It was just as well she had not committed herself to leaving Hutchinson & Rice by delivering that resignation letter. There would be other solutions.

A loud frantic knocking on the front door interrupted her train of thought. Ai Leen hurried to the entrance wondering who was making such a racket. Probably a meter reader, she thought with annoyance. Opening the heavy door a fraction, she saw that it was Reggie. She tried to slam it shut again, but he was too quick. A broad foot wedged the door open and, despite her putting her weight against it, he managed to get his shoulder and then his body into the apartment. She fell back, her hand instinctively groping for something to fend him off with. Her hand closed round a bunch of keys.

She screamed, 'What do you want? Get out, get out, I tell you!'

Reggie was breathing heavily and his eyes were bloodshot. He put a hand on the door to support himself. She could smell him, dried sweat and the musky scent of fear.

She repeated, 'What do you want?'

He said, 'I got a call ... from Maria.' He looked at her almost pleadingly.

Ai Leen's body was rigid with tension but she said in a puzzled tone, 'Maria? What does she want?'

'She says she saw me that night.'

'What night?'

'The night of the murder. She says she saw me at the office!'

'I don't understand.'

The only sound was Reggie's wheezing, rasping breath.

Reggie said again, enunciating his words, 'She wants money, or she will go to the police.' He continued, almost pleading for understanding, 'But I wasn't there!'

Ai Leen ignored this latter part as irrelevant and said, 'It's not my problem.'

Reggie put a hand over his eyes. He said, 'She knows about *us*.'

There was a silence as Ai Leen absorbed the implications of what he had said. She asked in an unnaturally calm voice, absent-mindedly replacing the keys on the table, 'How much does she want?'

'A million US dollars.'

'Well, where is he?'

Sometimes he felt like the babysitter of a bad-tempered child, not the sidekick of the most successful murder investigator on the force, thought Corporal Fong. He answered patiently, adopting the firm but kind voice of a nursery school teacher, 'He left the office for a meeting a couple of hours ago – he hasn't returned yet.'

'I finally have enough evidence to lean on that smug bastard and you can't find him?'

Corporal Fong wondered whether to be leaned on by Inspector Singh would constitute the sort of enhanced interrogation techniques so beloved of the intelligence services of so-called civilised nations. He said smartly, a young man in control of events, 'Sergeant Chung is waiting at the office and Sergeant Hassan is parked outside his home, sir! We'll find Reggie Peters soon enough.'

'What about Quentin Holbrooke?'

'I released him.' Fong did not sound pleased at the outcome but he supposed that they had no choice. Annie had been adamant that she would not testify against Quentin about the attack and David Sheringham had agreed with her. The lawyers were protecting one of their own. Still, it was only a matter of time before the superintendent had Holbrooke re-arrested and charged with drug trafficking.

He added, remembering the exhausted regretful young man whom he had put in a taxi that morning, 'I don't think he'll go looking for trouble again.'

'That fellow doesn't have to look, trouble follows him around like a pet dog.'

Fong refrained from commenting on this flight of fancy.

'All right,' said Singh grumpily. 'Let's go round and have a chat with Maria Thompson in the meantime.'

Maria opened the front door herself. She was, as always, perfectly turned out, dressed in a pair of designer jeans, a silk shirt and open-toed stilettos. The toenails peeping out from her shoes, her fingernails and her lipstick were an identical shade of crimson. Ai Leen had to admire the woman's confidence. She had used her looks to trap herself a wealthy husband. And when that well had run dry, Maria had turned to another source of income with the sort of dogged single-mindedness that she, Ai Leen, had shown in pursuing her own goals.

Ai Leen walked confidently into the room, following hard on the heels of Maria. She was calm and collected, a well-dressed woman paying a social visit to an acquaintance. She gave no outward sign that the nature of their errand was unusual in any way. Her footsteps in low-heeled court shoes were muffled in the thick carpeting. Except for the hum of the air conditioning, the place was silent and oppressive.

Reggie stumbled in after them. He was perspiring heavily. His stentorian breathing was audible to Ai Leen even though they were a few metres apart. Ai Leen shut her eyes briefly. She felt nauseous at the sudden memory of their hasty couplings, his clumsy hands on her body. She did not know, could not understand, how she had ever allowed such a thing to come to pass but she was determined that, after this day, Reggie Peters would never dare to approach her again.

He glanced at her, his hangdog expression pleading with her to take the lead in their discussion with Maria. She threw him a contemptuous look, noting with disgust that perspiration had caused his remaining strands of hair to stick to his scalp like congealed noodles at the bottom of an unwashed bowl.

Maria indicated with a gesture that they were to sit down and they both did, sinking into the sofa until their knees were slightly higher than their waists. Reggie put the briefcase he was carrying down by his feet but Ai Leen kept her capacious handbag on her lap.

'I don't understand why you bring her,' said Maria, nodding scornfully at Ai Leen, her remarks directed at Reggie.

Ai Leen showed no sign that she had heard the contempt in Maria's voice. Her face was the frigid mask she reserved for clients and colleagues although her grip on her bag tightened convulsively and the knuckles showed white with tension.

Reggie cleared his throat – he was struggling to get words out. 'I need to talk to you.'

Maria said rudely, her natural assertiveness putting in an appearance, 'I have nothing to say to you. I have said it all. Now I want the cash – all of it!'

'Look, Maria, we brought the money.' Reggie gestured to the briefcase at his feet and then wiped his sweaty palms on his trousers.

'Then you can go. I do not want to see your ugly face any more.'

Reggie said, his voice guttural with trepidation, 'But I need to talk to you. I just don't understand. Why are you saying you saw me at the office? I wasn't there. I didn't kill Mark!'

'Of course you killed him – both of you – to keep your *dirty* little secret.' Maria spat the words at them in disgust.

A woman who had prostituted herself for advancement was capable of deriding others for using the same tactic, thought Ai Leen. She said conversationally, 'Actually, Reggie is right. He didn't kill Mark.'

'How do you know? Was it you?' demanded Maria.

Ai Leen wondered whether the woman standing across from her was really stupid enough or greedy enough to blackmail someone she believed capable of murder. How could Maria imagine that she, Ai Leen, would ever allow herself to be the victim of such a ploy? Well, it was time to bring this charade to an end. She had no intention of falling into the clutches of Maria Thompson. She knew full well that if they succumbed to her attempt to extricate funds from them, it would never end. Women like Maria, once they had sunk their red-painted acrylic talons into you, never let go.

'We're not going to pay you, Maria. Neither of us was near the office and neither of us killed Mark.'

Maria spat on the ground at their feet and they all watched, as if hypnotised, as the white froth sank into the plush carpet, leaving a small dark stain. She said, 'Of course you will pay. Otherwise, I will tell everyone, the partners, the police, the newspapers, about your little arrangement.'

Ai Leen rose to her feet with difficulty, reached into her bag and almost casually pulled out a serviceable looking handgun. Her tone was even – she might have been extracting a legal document from the bag. 'Even if I have to kill you, Maria, we are *not* going to pay.'

'My God, Ai Leen. What are you doing?'

Reggie's voice was a hoarse wheeze and she could hear the breath rattling in his chest. The shock had brought on his asthma. Perhaps he would do them all a favour and die of natural causes.

Her lips twisted, more spasm than smile. 'Saving us some money,' she answered.

Maria had remained silent. She was staring at the dark circle of the gun barrel, her mouth opening and closing like a goldfish. Now, she took an instinctive step backwards.

Ai Leen's gun arm was outstretched. The weapon was heavier than she had realised and she gripped it a little tighter to keep it steady. The handle was cool to the touch. Her index finger, curled around the trigger, was rigid with tension.

'What are you saying?' demanded Reggie. Spittle had gathered in the corners of his dry mouth. 'We brought the money. We should just pay and get out of here.'

Ai Leen rounded on Maria, her voice showing the strain

now. 'How did you find out about Reggie and me? Did Mark tell you? How did *he* know?'

'He overheard you talking on the phone to Reggie,' whispered Maria.

Ai Leen shrugged and brought up the other arm so that the gun was held between her two hands. 'It was bad enough to be unable to escape from this bastard. I certainly don't plan to let *you* milk me for the rest of my life.'

Reggie said feebly, 'We shouldn't kill anyone ... there's no need.'

Contempt dripped from his colleague's voice. 'Look at you, you pathetic creature! You make me sick.'

'What are you going to do?' whispered Maria, staring at the weapon with a fascinated gaze, like a creature mesmerised on a highway by the bright glare of headlights.

'Kill you, of course. And I don't suppose Reggie here will be that keen on his assignations at the Fullerton after I do that!' Ai Leen was pleased that her voice had remained steady throughout. From the expression on the faces of the others, she had been completely convincing. She had no intention of telling them that she had stolen the gun from her husband's gun cupboard and that leaving a bullet in Maria would be the equivalent of writing her name in blood on the large gilt-edged mirror above the mantelpiece.

As she pointed the gun squarely at Maria's chest, Reggie stepped forward. He put a hand up pleadingly. He said, 'Please don't do this!'

Ai Leen swivelled around quickly until the weapon was pointing at her erstwhile partner in crime. She didn't need him to interfere with her plan. Maria had to believe that she would gun her down in cold blood rather than pay a penny of the blackmail sum. And she wanted, needed, Reggie to fear her as well – to be so terrified that he would never come near her again. Then, and only then, was she prepared to lower her weapon, agree to give them both one last chance to leave her alone.

Maria, seizing her opportunity when the gun was trained on Reggie, leapt forward. Ai Leen didn't see her coming, didn't know quite how convincing she had been. Maria reached for the gun hand, her fingers claw-like in desperation. The weapon shook in Ai Leen's grip, her finger tightened spasmodically and the gun went off. Reggie fell to his knees and then keeled over clutching his chest. Neither woman spared him a glance.

The battle for survival was in earnest now. Maria knocked the weapon out of Ai Leen's hand. The gun slithered under the couch and Ai Leen made a dive to retrieve it. Maria saw the danger and launched herself at Ai Leen, knocking her away from her target. But Ai Leen was now fighting like a madwoman. She lashed out with her foot, catching Maria sharply on the elbow. Maria clutched her arm and screeched in pain, the high sound of an animal caught in a sharp-toothed trap. Ai Leen tore into her, scratching and screaming. No one noticed a pounding on the front door. Maria, on the ground now, crawled painfully towards the gun. Ai Leen flung herself at her but a well-timed kick by the prone woman knocked her back. Maria grabbed the gun and scrambled to her feet.

Suddenly, a shot rang through the air and both women froze. Heavy footsteps pounded down the corridor and Inspector Singh burst into the room.

Twenty-Four

'Drop your weapon!' shouted Singh, his breath coming in loud painful pants.

Maria kept the gun trained on Ai Leen. Her hand was shaking and Singh was terrified that she would pull the trigger. Even from where he was standing it was obvious that a key suspect, Reggie, was dead. His eyes were open and staring, watching unfolding events with unseeing eyes. His careful comb-over had fallen away from his scalp, leaving it shiny and bare. The front of his shirt was a bloody mess. He had taken a bullet to the chest. It must have severed an artery to judge from the volume of blood pooling around his corpse.

Singh's own chest hurt. He could feel his pulse pounding in his ears. He felt like holstering his Taurus standard issue revolver and rubbing the spot directly over his heart. He wasn't some sort of gallant figure, able to stumble upon a scene like this and save the day with panache. He had no idea what was going on. He had just wanted to question Maria Thompson again while waiting for one of his team to pick Reggie Peters up. He'd heard screams and then a shotgun fired. As he had shot out the front door lock and raced through the apartment, he had not been sure what to expect: a robbery in progress; a lovers' tiff that had got out of hand; a suicide attempt ... He certainly had not anticipated coming upon one key suspect holding a gun over the corpse of another. Singh felt a trickle of cold sweat escape the brim of his turban. It traced a course down his forehead via the grooves above his nose and trickled into his eyes. They began to smart and he blinked a few times to clear his vision.

He spoke calmly, trying to keep from breathing so hard. He didn't want Maria to think that the only other person in the room with a gun was about to keel over from a heart attack. There were quite enough bodies associated with this case already. He didn't want to personally add to their number.

The policeman was first and foremost a practical man. He might rue the circumstances, but he had to deal with the situation as he found it, not long for alternatives in a universe of infinite outcomes. He barked, injecting a note of belated authority into his voice, 'Put down your gun.'

He noted that her weapon was a small-calibre revolver. He might even survive a bullet, assuming that – unlike Reggie Peters – he was lucky enough not to be hit in a vital spot. Still, he certainly hoped that he wouldn't have to play the hero and try and take the gun off Maria forcibly. When Maria did not respond, he spoke again, louder and more aggressive this time, 'It's over!' The steadiness of his gun hand was in marked contrast to the wavering weapon Maria had trained on Ai Leen.

Singh's words seemed to penetrate Maria's stupor because her eyes swivelled around to stare at him. The whites of her eyes were predominant. It was the same look he had seen in stray dogs cornered by dog catchers.

Singh said more gently, speaking directly to the Filipina woman, looking into her taut, panicky face, 'It's over.' He realised he was working from the standard hostage rescue texts – establish authority and then seek a relationship with the hostage taker. He needed Maria to trust him if more bloodshed was to be avoided. She stared at him and then turned to look at the body on the floor. He said, 'Maria, don't do anything foolish. Remember, your children need you.'

He had found the magic words. He might have guessed that the only way to get through to this woman was to use her children as the chisel to chip away at her hard exterior. She dropped her gun hand and let the weapon fall. It hit the ground with a muffled thud.

There was an audible sigh of relief in the room. Singh realised belatedly that it had emanated from him. He felt much better now that he was the only person in the room holding a gun. He intoned formally, 'Maria Thompson, you are under arrest for the murder of . . . err, Reggie Peters.' And then he added in a puzzled tone, 'Why in the world did you kill Reggie?'

Maria's pupils dilated with shock. 'What are you talking about?' she whispered.

He snapped, 'What do you mean?'

'She want to kill me!' Maria's tone grew stronger as she gesticulated angrily at Ai Leen. 'When he – Reggie – tried to stop her, she shoot him.'

Singh shifted the point of his gun carefully so that it pointed at Ai Leen, not Maria. He wrinkled his nose. The strangely sweet cloying smell of fresh blood was overwhelming. He decided, looking at Ai Leen, that he had never

287

previously been subjected to such a venomous stare.

He said, 'Ms Lim Ai Leen, I arrest you for the murder of,' he paused for a moment, 'Reggie Peters.'

Ai Leen spat on the ground, an angry, defiant gesture. 'You have *nothing* on me! I tried to protect myself from a blackmailer, that's all. Reggie Peters—' her voice was like the slow progress of a glacier '—Reggie Peters was just unlucky.'

'Blackmail?' Singh raised an eyebrow at Maria Thompson.

She pursed her lips tightly shut. He noticed that there were cuts and scratches on her forearms where she had tried to fend off the enraged attack of the other woman. 'I don't know what she's talking about.'

Inspector Singh looked at the carnage around him. 'You're going to have to do better than that.'

Singh sat on the end of a hospital bed. The mattress sagged under his weight and the white cotton starched covers creased around his posterior. His feet, in spotless white sneakers, hung over the side just above the ground. The policeman bounced up and down as if testing the springs.

Maria Thompson was lying on the other single bed in the twin room. She wore a pair of faded blue drawstring hospital pyjamas. Her cuts and bruises had been treated despite her protests that she was fine and only wanted to go home.

'You must be feeling terrible,' remarked Singh. Her face was scrubbed clean of make-up and an older-looking, care-worn woman glared at him. Despite this, thought Singh, she was more attractive now. In the absence of her customary paint job, the delicacy of her features and the character in her face were more clearly visible. She reminded him of Chelsea Liew, the ageing supermodel in his last major case.

Maria propped herself up on an elbow and said angrily, 'I just want to go home to my children.'

'That would be nice, wouldn't it? Unfortunately, you're going to be sent to prison for a long time. Blackmail just isn't very popular with sentencing judges.'

Maria collapsed back down onto her pillow. Singh remembered that Jagdesh Singh's life had been snuffed out no more than a hundred yards down the corridor in this same hospital. He knew he was being cruel to threaten this woman with separation from her children. But he had to find out what had happened in that apartment. Besides, if he didn't get to the root of things pretty soon, Superintendent Chen would kick him off the case and this woman would have a far less sympathetic audience.

He continued, watching her face carefully, 'In fact, I believe the prosecution services are looking at charging you with Reggie's killing too.'

'Ai Leen shot him!'

'*Only* because you were trying to blackmail them. A charge of "culpable homicide not amounting to murder" might stick.'

Her eyes were closed and he noticed that her lids were bluish with fatigue.

'I guess you're used to being away from the children.'

There was still no response from the woman in the bed.

Singh's tone was almost pleading. 'Look, Maria. I need to find out what happened. If you tell me, I'll do my best to protect you. I can't promise you anything. There's nothing my superiors would like better than to pin the murder of Mark Thompson on you or put you on the first plane out of the country. I don't believe you killed him. I don't think you'd have taken the risk of being put away for murder – you love your kids too much. But I need to know the truth.'

For a long moment, there was absolute silence in the room except for the wheezing of the air conditioning. Singh held his breath, hoping that Maria Thompson would see that he was her last hope to avoid jail, and perhaps even the death sentence, if a jury found the circumstantial evidence against her for the death of her husband compelling.

'I needed money,' she said quietly. 'The insurance people – they say they cannot pay me yet.'

Singh nodded his big head but did not interrupt her.

'Ai Leen is a slut. She sleep with Reggie so that they make her a partner. I call him and ask for money or I tell the whole world what they do.'

'How did you know about it?' asked Singh.

She looked surprised at his lack of reaction to her incendiary information. 'Mark told me – I think he hear them talking about it.'

'Was that what the meeting was about? You know, the partners' meeting just before he was killed?'

Maria was sitting up in bed now, the blankets tucked up to her waist. She shook her head, her brow creased with puzzlement. 'I don't know, I don't think so. Mark said he was going to ask them both to resign quietly because he did not want to spoil the law firm's reputation.'

Singh scowled – that was actually plausible. Mark might well have preferred to keep a lid on the bedroom shenanigans of two of his partners while quietly turfing them out.

Maria looked sheepish. 'I also told Reggie I saw him at the office the night of the murder.'

'Did you?'

She shook her head. 'I just wanted to frighten him.'

'Do you think Reggie or Ai Leen – or both of them – killed Mark?'

He watched her eyes. He could see the internal debate raging as she weighed her options, trying to decide where her interests lay.

At last, she said, meeting his eyes, her voice regretful but determined – and, Singh thought, honest, 'Ai Leen said that she not kill Mark. Reggie also said the same thing.'

'And you believed them?'

'She was going to shoot me – what for they lie?'

What for they lie indeed, wondered Singh.

'Reggie Peters was such a close friend of yours – and you put a bullet through him. It must be devastating for you.' There was a heavy thread of sarcasm in Singh's voice.

She turned her head away and stared at the white walls of the interview room at the police station, refusing to look at the Sikh inspector. 'It was an accident.'

'A very convenient "accident"!'

'What's that supposed to mean?' Her tone was wary.

'We know about you and Reggie,' said Singh cheerfully.

'You've already made your unwarranted insinuations about our relationship. I've told you that we are – we were – just friends.'

'Then how do you explain this?' Singh pulled a photocopy of Ai Leen's resignation letter out of his pocket with the flourish of a magician producing a rabbit out of a hat. He grinned at her broadly, as if he expected admiring applause.

She practically snatched the document from his hands. She held it between her thumb and forefinger as if she was handling something unclean – and in a sense she was, thought Singh. It was evidence of such thoroughly reprehensible behaviour that it had shocked even a jaded old policeman like himself.

'Where did you get this?'

'What does it matter?'

'It's a fake ...'

Singh had to admire this woman. She was as hard as the

nails gripping the handle of her handbag. He would get nothing from her that he did not prise loose.

'Our technical staff have already found the original on the hard drive of your desktop computer.' Corporal Fong did have his uses, thought Singh. That was the sort of evidence he might have missed.

She decided to brazen it out. 'So? I made a mistake. I'll probably lose my job over it. What does it have to do with the police?'

'A man with whom you were having an illicit relationship dies by your hand – I think the police have every right to be interested.'

She sighed. 'It really was an accident.'

'You actually intended to kill Maria?'

Her head snapped up – she was not going to be trapped that easily. 'Of course not, I just wanted to scare her, so that she would abandon the blackmail attempt.'

'How did Maria know about your plan to sleep your way to the top?'

She grimaced but did not bother to argue with his characterisation of her behaviour. 'Mark told her, apparently he overheard a conversation between Reggie and me.'

'That's not really important, is it? The key point is that he knew. And you, or Reggie, killed him to protect your reputations and your jobs.'

She looked at him through hooded eyes. 'There's no way you're going to pin Mark's murder on me.'

Singh's phone rang. 'Saved by the bell,' he remarked and stepped out of the room.

The number had the prefix that indicated the call was from Kuala Lumpur.

'Singh here,' he answered curtly.

'As good-tempered as ever, I see.'

Singh grinned. 'Inspector Mohammed, what can I do for you?'

'Have you been kicked off the Force yet?'

'Not yet ...'

'Well, I'm not sure it's in the best interests of our two countries but I might be able to keep you in gainful employment for a little while longer!'

Twenty-Five

Annie's hair was tied away from her face. She was wearing jeans and a T-shirt. She looked much younger than Singh had ever noticed before, shorn of the uniform, make-up and manner of a corporate lawyer. Stephen had told him, when he had gone to the office looking for her, that Annie had resigned from Hutchinson & Rice – apparently unwilling to be associated with the tainted reputation of the law offices any more. He had finally tracked her down at home, having coffee on the verandah with David Sheringham, their sunny mood dampened by the unexpected presence of the fat policeman. Annie sat across from Singh and clutched David's hand possessively. The contrast between her brown hand – a product of her parentage – and his tanned one was less a matter of colour than of tone, Singh noted with interest.

She said, after she had served them all steaming cappuccinos, 'I heard that you arrested Ai Leen for Mark's murder!'

He nodded. 'I'm guessing it was some sort of conspiracy between the two of them – Ai Leen and Reggie – when they realised Mark knew their secret. She's denying it, of course.'

Annie gazed at the inspector with friendly brown eyes. 'She'd be bound to do that,' she pointed out. 'It doesn't mean anything.'

Frown lines appeared in neat parallels on David's forehead as if someone had drawn them in with a dark felt pen. 'Are you sure it was them?'

'I agree with Annie,' said Singh comfortably. 'Ai Leen will still be protesting her innocence to the gallows. She's not the sort to give up or give in.' He tapped his forehead with his forefinger. 'After all, who else could it be?'

'Quentin?' asked Annie doubtfully. Her wrinkled nose lent her the air of someone reluctantly pointing out an alternative.

'No *motive*,' explained Singh.

'What do you mean?' demanded Annie. 'What about the insider dealing to fund his drug habit?'

'That wasn't him,' said Singh cheerfully, the curve of his lip matching the curve of his belly.

Annie asked, and her voice was as calm as a windless day, 'It was someone from Trans-Malaya then?'

The girl had courage, thought Singh. She was trying to brazen it out – only a sudden rigidity in her body suggested that she was afraid.

He said, 'No – it was *you*.'

Annie's bruises from her altercation with Quentin were fading but they were thrown into stark relief by her sudden pallor. David's hand tightened around Annie's convulsively but Singh noted with interest that he did not look surprised.

She faced the inspector with her jaw thrust out. 'How dare you accuse me of such a thing?'

'The Malaysian police tracked down a brokerage account in the name of one Colonel Nathan – your father,' he added

295

unnecessarily. 'And it seems that he was very lucky, very clever or well furnished with inside information when it came to trading shares in Trans-Malaya.'

Her head was bowed.

Singh waited patiently for her next gambit. He had the greatest admiration for this woman's ability to finesse the truth.

'I had nothing to do with it. My father must have based his trades on our conversations. My God – I trusted him!'

'Curiously, that's exactly what he said. He tried very hard to protect you, you know.'

She looked up at this, eyes wide. Her father's willingness to sacrifice himself for her had caught her by surprise.

'But there is no way that any supposed casual conversations would have contained the detailed information needed for the insider dealing,' pointed out Singh. 'You have, very carefully and very systematically, been using your inside knowledge to instruct your father to carry out various trades in the shares of Trans-Malaya for personal, illegal profit.'

Annie's head had dropped, a curtain of hair obscuring her features.

The policeman added, 'I won't charge you with *that* crime. It's not my remit. I just want to know for my own peace of mind.' He sighed – a fat man with troubles. 'You know how I hate loose ends.'

Annie relaxed on hearing this and her hunched shoulders straightened slightly. But she still did not respond to the accusation.

Inspector Singh asked, turning his attention to David, 'How did *you* know?' His voice had a petulant edge, as if they were schoolboy friends and one of them was keeping secrets.

David held his gaze for a moment and then his eyes dropped. It was not an unexpected response. Singh had seen many a decent man discover that they could not – when push finally came to shove – lie to the authorities. At most, they could maintain an unhappy silence while regretting the chain of events that had led them to a place where extemporising or evasion were their only viable alternatives. Singh's back curved like a bow. Extra folds emerged between his chest and stomach. It never ceased to amaze him what an honest man was prepared to do for a woman. And in the end, they were the only ones who got hurt.

David addressed his answer, when he could finally find the words, to Annie. 'I heard the end of your conversation with Quentin that night he attacked you ... and if it wasn't him insider dealing, it had to be you.'

'Why didn't you say anything?' Singh guessed that she knew the answer but wanted to hear it directly from David.

David held up his hand so that they could both see their interlocking fingers. He smiled at her a little sadly. 'I wanted to protect you.'

'There's more, isn't there?' Singh asked the question gently, his tone that of a kindly, elderly relative.

Annie's face was impassive, but Singh knew it was a mask so fragile that any hint of pressure would crack it like an eggshell – if he could find the right pressure point.

She asked, 'What do you mean?'

'*Murder!*'

David sat up, his movements wooden with distress. 'What are you trying to say?' he demanded.

'That your girlfriend here killed Mark Thompson, and Jagdesh Singh.'

Annie's voice, however, was as close to normal as Singh had ever heard from a suspect accused of murder. 'Don't be ridiculous!' she snapped.

David spoke, and his voice was the embodiment of fear. Fear for Annie? Fear of the truth? Singh was not sure. 'But Annie wouldn't *kill* anyone! That's just nonsense.'

If Singh noticed that the denials were being issued by David, not the woman who stood accused, he did not point it out.

Instead he turned to Annie. 'Tell us what happened,' he said quietly.

'I have no idea what you're talking about.'

Singh sighed. It was a gentle sound tinged with genuine regret. He felt truly sorry that it was this girl; he would so much rather it had turned out to be one of the others. He knew he was being sentimental because Annie was female and young and beautiful and had her whole life ahead of her. But Singh was not about to shirk his duty. He understood what had led Annie to such terrible deeds but he could not excuse it.

He said, 'I can appreciate why you killed Mark – you were in a complete panic that the insider dealing had been found out. Mark insisted that the partnership had to know. It must have seemed, in that instant, that murder was the only solution. But I can't forgive you for holding a pillow over Jagdesh Singh's face. That was a cold-blooded, pre-meditated, *cruel* murder.' He spat out the adjectives like an angry English teacher.

She shook her head, unable to form words.

'He was defenceless! In a coma.'

The memory of the big man lying as still as the dead was crystal clear in his mind's eye. Singh knew he would carry the burden of Jagdesh's death for a long, long time.

David removed his hand from Annie's. Perhaps he too was remembering the young homosexual lawyer who had died to keep a secret. It was a small gesture of rejection that

298

Singh suspected would be the final straw to break this young woman's defiance. Annie did not seek his hand again. She tucked a tendril of hair behind her ear. Her forefinger went to her mouth and she began to nibble on a nail. Singh recognised the gesture – he had seen it so many times over the last couple of weeks.

He said evenly, 'It hasn't been that hard to find evidence, once we knew what we were looking for. Corporal Fong has been busy since we found out about the insider dealing. It seems you rang for a taxi from the phone box down the road from your home to take you to the office. You took another cab back, the driver has been traced – apparently you were agitated and wouldn't respond to his overtures of conversation. I'm not surprised, you had just killed a man. But then you pulled yourself together, had a shower, drove your car into the office and sent Quentin Holbrooke ahead to discover your dirty work.'

There was no response from either Annie or David.

'I suspected you at the beginning, you know. It was just that so many of your colleagues were determined to draw my attention to their own shortcomings, I started to doubt my own mind.' Singh could not keep the complacent note out of his voice at his own genuine, albeit ignored, foresight.

'What do you mean? How did you know?' David was trying to create reasonable doubt. But his voice was too hesitant, it revealed his own reservations.

'The log of Mark's phone calls from the office the evening he was killed . . .'

'What about them?' demanded Annie, finally finding her voice.

'Mark called you *last*.'

'So?'

'It's human nature to put off to the last the most unpleasant thing we have to do. When I saw the list of calls, I *knew* you must have murdered Mark. But there didn't seem to be any motive. Your colleagues were competing for my attention – determined, it seemed, to prove themselves capable of murder. I wish I had arrested you then, not doubted my own conclusions. It would have saved Jagdesh Singh's life.'

Annie didn't need to be an expert on human nature to know that David Sheringham believed she was a murderer. Singh had been convincing. The unlikely rotund self-proclaimed expert on human nature had persuaded a man she was beginning to care for deeply that she was a killer. He was sitting back in the chair, staring at her, the worry lines on his face underlining his dismay.

He asked, and his voice was a whisper – as if he had to force the words out, did not really want an answer to his question – 'You killed Jagdesh? My God! Annie, why?'

She remembered how he had held her in his arms the afternoon of Jagdesh's attempted suicide. She had known at that moment that she could not risk losing him, that she needed the murder investigation to be resolved quickly.

'I really didn't want to hurt Jagdesh,' she whispered. 'He was my friend.'

David blanched white at the unlikely words – an assertion of friendship by a murderer for her victim.

Annie continued, 'Jagdesh was so close to death anyway. And if he was dead, I thought Inspector Singh would stop poking his nose into our business. Life would get back to normal.' She smiled at David. 'I was hoping that there might be something worthwhile between us . . . if only we could put the murder investigation behind us.'

David flinched. Annie knew that the thought that he might have formed a part of her motive was too much for him to bear. She continued, desperately seeking a hint of understanding, 'I didn't know that he had an alibi. I just thought it would make the whole thing go away.'

She reached out and touched David gently on the face. She said, 'I'm really sorry about the way things turned out.' Annie turned to the inspector with a crooked grin that failed to conceal her wretchedness. 'What now?' she asked.

Singh said, 'You're under arrest for the murder of Mark Thompson and Jagdesh Singh ...'

Epilogue

The presiding judge did not hesitate to impose the death penalty for the double murder. He ordered, in the language of statute and precedent, that the accused "be hanged from the neck until dead". Annie had refused to appeal despite David Sheringham's urgent pleas. Once she was on death row – in her thirty-square-foot cell with the sleeping mat and toilet – she had refused to see him, even after she was notified four days before of the Friday – it was always Friday – on which she would walk to her death.

Singh, a reluctant emissary on behalf of David, was told by the guards while the prisoner was being escorted to the meeting room that she had also refused television privileges, special meals and to see her father. But she had asked to donate her organs, hoping, he guessed, to make amends for the lives she had taken.

Now, they sat on chairs on either side of a clear glass window. Prisoners on death row were not allowed physical contact with anyone, not their families, friends, and certainly not arresting policemen.

'David really wants to see you,' explained Singh.

She refused with a small shake of the head and the policeman noticed for the first time that her glossy hair had been cut short.

Her manner was calm and there was a small smile on her lips. 'There's no point,' she said. 'It will only upset him.'

Singh recalled the distraught young man who had begged him to visit Annie and could find no sensible response to this belated concern for David's emotional state. They sat across from each other now, neither of them speaking. It was a friendly silence, a strange sensation in that small closed space. Singh guessed that, in many ways, Annie was relieved that her ordeal was almost over. The murder of Mark Thompson had not been pre-meditated. Everything else that had taken place had assumed a nightmarish quality of inevitability until she found herself holding a pillow to the face of an unhappy young man.

'What's happening with Quentin?' she asked, and he was surprised that she had the energy to think of others.

'After your arrest, I ordered that passports be returned to the other lawyers as they were no longer suspects. Quentin caught the first flight out of Singapore. I understand from David that he's in rehab in London.' He continued with a slow wink of his heavy eyelid, 'I had *forgotten*, you see, that Quentin was wanted on drugs charges.'

The woman across from him smiled with genuine heartfelt relief. 'Good work,' she said quietly.

The inspector nodded. There had been hell to pay. Superintendent Chen had been apoplectic. But it had been worth it. There had been enough death already and Singh was not prepared to facilitate another.

He changed the subject abruptly. 'Why did you do it?' he asked.

She did not misunderstand the question. He was not asking about the murders. He wanted to know why a wealthy successful young woman would have used her own father to trade shares illegally for money.

'It's hard to explain. When we were growing up, we were always short of money. My dad, he was a risk-taker, always looking out for the next business opportunity, always willing to gamble everything on "making it big"!'

Singh tried to remember his own father, a civil servant with the British administration who had worn a massive turban and starched trousers that would stand upright without him. The old man had always kept a careful record of the family's every expenditure in a small notebook to ensure they did not exceed his income.

'We were constantly in debt, there were bailiffs at the door and sometimes gangsters if Dad borrowed money through more informal channels ...' She looked at the policeman, meeting his eyes, seeking his understanding. 'We were always afraid.'

Singh nodded. Despite her elucidation, he struggled to fathom her motives. But he wanted to hear more.

'One day, when I was about eleven, three men came to the house. My father owed them money. He was away – he was always away when things got unpleasant. They insisted we pay them. My mother gave them the cash we had in the house but it was a derisory amount, not enough to persuade them to leave. One of them grabbed Mum's hand and yanked the wedding ring off her finger.'

She was re-living the moment, he could tell from her hoarse, fear-laden voice. 'I heard the bone in her finger crack, Mum screamed, I was crying, begging them to go away.'

There were tears in her eyes now. 'She had a gold chain around her neck – she always wore it. It was the one thing she never let my dad pawn. She would smile at me and say it was for a rainy day. One of the men grabbed the chain and yanked. At first, it didn't snap. Mum's hands were around her throat and I was afraid that she was going to choke. He twisted the chain and it broke. Mum fell backwards and hit her head on the corner of a table.'

She fell silent. This time around it was a silence fraught with unshed tears and unfinished tales.

'I tried to raise her up but she was too heavy for me. And then I saw that there was blood on my hands. The men, when they realised that Mum was injured, they ran away. By the time the ambulance arrived, Mum was dead.'

She looked up, meeting his eyes. 'It's not an excuse. There's no excuse for what I did. But I swore that day that I would never be short of money, never allow myself to be in such a position again.'

Singh sighed deeply. 'It's not an excuse but I think it is, at least, an explanation.'

She nodded her thanks. Perhaps, he thought, there was solace in a story told to a sympathetic listener.

'May I tell David?' he asked carefully.

She nodded once, rose slowly to her feet and walked out of the room.

The execution was scheduled to take place just before dawn – at six a.m. exactly. The executioner had visited Annie the previous day and taken her weight, in order to be sure to use the appropriate length of rope. Singapore used the "long drop" method of hanging, which causes a cervical fracture in the neck and almost instantaneous paralysis and unconsciousness. Singh knew that it was argued by proponents to be the most humane method of judicial execution. The inspector also knew that an inexperienced hangman could leave the victim asphyxiating in slow agony or decapitated.

The hangman was an old acquaintance though, a seventy-year-old prison guard in knee-length shorts and a T-shirt, wearing long socks with trainers, who had carried out hundreds of executions, first for the British and then for the Singaporean government. Singh whispered to him to be extra careful and received a nod and a smile in return. When Annie arrived she was already hooded and Singh was glad – and ashamed of himself for being glad – that he would not have to look into her soft brown eyes once more.

He had decided to attend the hanging, something he rarely did, to provide some comfort to David Sheringham, the young lawyer who had become his friend. He wanted to be able to tell him that someone she knew had been with the woman he cared about at the moment of her death. If Annie found some reassurance in his presence, he did not mind that either. It was cold comfort to him that she had earned her place on the platform by killing two people. Corporal Fong, clutching his letter of promotion in a firm grip, had offered to come along but Singh had refused the company. This was something he preferred to do alone.

He watched as the chief hangman escorted Annie over the trapdoor. She went willingly and quietly. There was no struggle, no protest. The coroner and prison superintendent stood by him, both silent. They had all witnessed many executions in their time, but even to these hardened men there was something pitiful about this slim hooded figure.

Annie Nathan stood very straight and very still as the noose was placed gently around her neck.

8/13 - H
2/130
8/14 W
8/15 C
2/16 H